I0642592

Hey,

There's no better time than now. The world is yours!

~Kiameshia B.

Please enjoy this glimpse into my imagination. Thank you for giving me a chance.

Don't forget to leave a review on Amazon.

If These Eyes Could Talk

Contents

Chapter 1 Best Friend

I don't remember much exciting happening before I turned 14. Back then I hadn't had my first kiss, job, or boyfriend yet. I guess you could even say what's going on with me today is directly related to what started that year of my life. I'd like to persuade you from making some of the same mistakes I've made in the past, so I will start by telling a story about the biggest mistake I've ever made. It all started in the Summer of 99. It was hot as fish grease, and the best gel in the world couldn't hold my hair together for more than 2 minutes once the outside humidity set in. There was a fingertip rule in school for girl's skirts, and every day I pushed it. I kept an extra shirt and a stick of deodorant in my bag for added protection. It was always hot during the summer, but that summer there was a heatwave.

I was born and raised in Atlanta. I grew up in Summerhill, smack dab in the middle of the city. If you ask me, I would tell you I was your average teenager. Like many young teens, I was just starting to come out of my shell. I had been a straight-A student my whole life, my mom was a hard ass, and I was ready to rebel. That same summer, I met someone who would eventually become my best friend.

I was walking home from the bus stop after school one day. I was in my zone, listening to Ghost Town DJs, "My Boo." My groove was interrupted when I approached this group of girls on the corner of my block fighting. One was at the bottom of the pile and was getting dog walked. I didn't know her personally, but I knew she was from my neighborhood. It wasn't any of my business, but I put myself in it. I ran over and pushed one of the 4 girls on top of her off. Next, I swung on the girl that was kicking her. "Back the hell up!" I demanded. "And who the hell are you?" One of the girls asked.

4

"You're about to find out!" I bucked at her. I reached into my bag while quickly walking towards her. Having no clue what I was going to pull out, I bluffed her. One of the girls got spooked and shouted, "She got a gun!" Then they all took off. The beat-up girl groaned in pain as she started to get up off the ground. I reached for her, but she pushed my hand away.

"I don't need your help!" she snapped.

"You're right. You need some bandages, some wraps, and ice *fa ya eye*." I still helped her up despite her rude attitude. She seemed pissed off that I jumped in. I usually didn't mess with any girls from the neighborhood, and I should've kept it that way.

"You want to tell me what that was about?" I asked.

"No, not really. It's over now." she said, casually dusting herself off.

"OK, I get it. When I see them jumping on you tomorrow, I'm just gonna mind my business like I should've done today." I warned her.

"And when they do try and jump me, I'm gonna stand here like I did today and fight them back." she boasted.

"Girl, you were fighting the bottom of some sneakers." I corrected her.

"Whatever, I was holding my own." She tried to sound convincing, but I thought she was more delusional than anything.

"If holding your own means getting stomped out, then you held your own shawty." I turned to walk away and leave her be. Someone with her attitude probably had it coming anyway.

5

"Wait." she called out. "I'm LaBresha, but everyone calls me Bre. Thanks for having my back." She tried to shake my hand, but I was over it. I left her hanging on the handshake but met her halfway on the introduction.

"I'm Katrina. You must be thanking me in French because it damn sure ain't English." I told her.

"I guess I deserved that, but it's cool because my sister will be coming up the street in just a minute." Bre said confidently. Right then, I saw a girl come running up the block.

"What are you standing around for?" She grabbed Bre's hand and tried to pull her away. "Where are they at? Let's go find them!" The girl demanded. She was out of breath and running on pure adrenaline. She looked just like Bre, but a slightly taller, more slender version. They both were deep chocolate-complected, eyes slanted like foxy brown, with perfect teeth. Bre's hair was long and straight down her back while Britney had her hair in micro braids.

"Chill Brit! We have to be strategic because it's more of them than us." Bre said while motioning her hand in a circle. Her sister and I looked at each other confused. "Who is we?" Her and I asked.

"Britney, this girl just saved my ass. Crystal, Tee, and those 2 high school girls they hang with tried to jump me again. Katrina came and backed all of them up. Katrina, this is my sister Britney. Britney, this is Katrina." Bre put her arms around us as if we were one big happy family and we both pulled away. "Aren't you in my art class?" Britney asked me.

"Yeah, I'm in your art class." I said, completing the dap she initiated.

"Preciate what you did for my sister. That's cool, but why are you involving yourself in her beef tho?" Britney asked, not cracking a smile.

"I'm not a fan of people getting dragged in the street, and your sister was getting dragged." I told her.

"Oh please! I wasn't getting dragged." Bre jumped in.

"Girl bye! You were getting dragged, whether you want to admit it or not, and after seeing your attitude I can see why." I'm sure I wasn't the first person in life who told her that.

"Look, I said sorry!" Bre grabbed my hand attempting to show sincerity.

"Sorry for what?" Britney asked, lost while Bre and I went back and forth.

"Sorry for acting like she ain't care that I saved her ass earlier." I said, bringing Britney up to speed.

Britney looked over at Bre. "What is she talking about LaBresha?"

"Well, I ain't ask her to jump in it, she chose to." Bre said snidely. Britney smacked her teeth at her sister. "That's your problem now Bre. You don't appreciate anything. She could've left you in the street getting jumped on. You need to be thankful somebody for once was on your side and didn't stand by watching you get your ass whipped!"

Britney chided her sister, and I was there for every minute of it. She didn't automatically take Bre's side, and I appreciated her level head. I still felt at the very least Bre owed me an explanation. Although she didn't ask, I did put myself in danger, and I wanted to know was the fight worth it.

"So, why were those girls jumping you?" I asked again.

7

"She was at a party playing truth or dare and things got a little crazy." Britney interjected.

"Yea, it wasn't nothing, but clearly those girls were tripping about it." Bre said nonchalantly. I could tell neither of them were telling the complete truth. "It's cool." Bre stunted boldly standing there with a busted lip. Instead of probing further, I told them both I was out of it and gonna head home. Britney could sense her sister's sudden anxiousness.

"So, you helped her out, and now you're done with it?" Britney asked me.

"Yep, it's not my fight. Bre was getting beat down, and I only jumped in so she could get back on her feet. Now that it's two of you, y'all should be ok." I regretted involving myself in the first place.

"We're still outnumbered though." Bre added.

"It's more than what you started with when you were out there by yourself." I reminded her.

"Leave then! We don't need you anyway. I got my sister's back. Come on Bre." Britney snatched Bre by the hand and walked away. I turned to head home. I looked back once, and Britney did at the same time. I could tell she and Bre were talking about me, but I ain't care to know what they were saying. "Katrina, wait up." Bre yelled.

"What do you want Bre?" I answered, but I didn't bother to stop walking.

"Please just hear me out. My sister is stubborn so she ain't gon say it, but we need your help. I don't know if you know how Crystal and her friends roll but you are in this now rather you want to be or not. If we don't settle this beef today, you gon have to watch your back when you're walking home tomorrow too." she warned me.

Bre had a point. I didn't even think about what could happen to me for jumping in her mess, and after knowing her for 5 minutes, I could see why she wasn't liked. She seemed like the type that did what she wanted and never thought about the consequences. Britney and I had stopped walking, but we didn't approach each other.

"Come on Brit. We need her." Bre pleaded with her sister to come over.

Reluctantly, Britney came back. "Look, I'm not gonna beg someone to help me in a fight but let me just say this. You made it worse for Bre by jumping in the fight, and now you just want to leave like that. I think it's suspect, and maybe you ain't as tough as you out here acting." Britney started to size me up like I was the target. She was trying me, and I was ready to give her all the chimney smoke she wanted.

"Oh, I'm not tough because I don't wanna save your sister twice? First her, now you? Y'all both got some nerve. If you're so tough, why does it matter if I'm there or not? Can't you two handle your own beef?" I asked.

"See Bre, I'm not about to do this. You can talk to this heffa if you want to!" Britney walked off again.

"Well bye! Y'all scary-ass need me, not the other way around." I shouted.

Britney stopped in her tracks. She turned around full speed ahead. "What did you just call me?" she asked.

"You heard what I said, scary."

 Bre jumped in between us. "Y'all trippin. This ain't about us fighting each other. We're supposed to be fighting the girls that started this. Katrina, I appreciate what you did for me. You probably don't care, but trust me if it were you out there, I know my sister would've done the same. Y'all acting just like each other right now. Britney, you know good and damn well we need her, so just chill, let's link up. Your Taurus horns are showing." Bre turned to face me. "I wouldn't doubt you're a Taurus too." she said, trying to lighten the mood.

Britney and I were having a stare down contest so I couldn't break focus, but I heard what Bre said. She was right, but I wasn't anxious to admit someone who I had imagined was soon to become an enemy of mine shared my astrological sign. I stood there quiet, and now that Bre mentioned it, Britney was acting like a stubborn bull. I didn't break my gaze, but I answered Bre's question. "I actually am a Taurus." I said.

"You ain't no Taurus! When is your birthday?" Britney asked aggressively as if I would lie.

"April 27!" I declared like I was reppin my set.

"Girl, I'm the 28th!" Britney relaxed once she realized we had something in common. Maybe we were too much alike.

I wasn't thrilled but it was quite a coincidence. Imagine going to war with someone who reminded you of yourself. I had always believed people were true to their signs, and Britney was no different.

"Listen, you're right. I probably did make this worse for y'all by jumping in, but I don't want to be caught up in beef that ain't mine." I admitted.

"I get it, and you don't owe us anything. I just wanted for once to have a chance at beating them. They always pick on my sister, and even though Bre is a handful, it's my job to protect her no matter what." Britney had honor, and I could only respect it.

"You wanna come over to our house for a minute? Maybe we could reset and start fresh." Bre asked.

I agreed because one, I didn't have anything better to do, furthermore, I was open to making some girlfriends in the neighborhood. The three of us made the two-block walk, and they both welcomed me inside a modest but well-kept home. Their room was way in the back of the house, and there was a twin bed on each side. I sat on Britney's bed, and we ended up talking mess for hours. Britney was cool, and besides us getting off to a bad start, I could tell she and I were going to be good peeps. I liked her way more than I liked her sister. Bre went into her mom's liquor cabinet and poured herself some wine. She offered me a glass, but I declined. Britney looked at her disappointed. You could tell of the two of them, Bre was the troublemaker and Britney was the one getting them out of it. Bre hyped us up to go looking for the girls. "Y'all ready? Let's go settle this once and for all." She couldn't even keep her balance long enough to put on sweatpants. Britney went over to the mirror to put her hair in a ponytail. Britney saw Bre struggling to change clothes and demanded she stay home. "You ain't gon do nothing but get beat up again, so stay your ass home!" Britney insisted.

"I'm not sitting on the side for this. They drew blood from my mouth. I'm not staying home." Bre pushed back, slurring her words obviously tipsy. Britney walked over to her and stood nose to nose, intimidating her little sister. With that, Bre flopped down on the bed.

I was down to find the girls that beat Bre up because I figured if I didn't deal with it that day, I'd have to the next day. Even though the odds were still stacked against us, Britney and I had a better shot without Bre. I already seen what she could do and it wasn't much.

We left Britney's house and walked up the block until we saw the 4 girls sitting on the corner with a group of guys. "There they go." Britney said, exposing a menacing grin. I was so nervous because Britney and I were still outnumbered. Before I could ask if she was going right or left, she ran up and started dragging one of the girls. Without a second thought, I swung on the one closest to me which just so happened to be the same girl I had words with earlier. The guys crowded around and started cheering. There was no way to tell whose side they were on, but they didn't do anything to stop either of us. I caught a glimpse of Britney while I was throwing my own punches and could see that she was quick on her feet, handling the much bigger girl with ease. Another girl sat there shouting, "This is stupid, stop fighting." The 4th jumped in and tried to defend her friend from my blows, but I was able to pull her down by her hair and easily keep her pinned while her friend and I swapped it out. When Britney was done boxing her opponent, she jumped in my melee. We had the upper hand, and it was about to get embarrassing for the girls.

In the nick of time, the bus pulled up. Must've been one of the girls' moms who hopped off. She started swinging on everyone within arm's reach with her purse, making us all scatter. She cursed all the boys for allowing it to happen and encouraging our bad behavior. Britney and I ran across the street laughing. My adrenaline was rushing, and I couldn't feel a thing. It wasn't until Britney asked where the blood was coming from that I realized I was bleeding. I looked down and could see blood coming through my jeans. I rolled my pant leg up to see that I had a very small stab womb. I never felt anything, but one of the girls must've stabbed me with something.

"That looks pretty bad." Britney said.

"Nah, it doesn't hurt or anything. I think it'll be fine." I pressed on the womb and blood started gushing out.

"We should go to Grady right quick to make sure." Britney suggested. Another #55 bus was coming up the street, so we hopped on it and went to the hospital.

 We waited forever to be seen, but it was a good thing we waited. The doctor ended up pulling a 1-inch broken piece of pencil lead out of my leg. He stitched me up, prescribed some antibiotics, and sent me on my way.

On the ride back to the neighborhood, Britney broke down crying.

"What's wrong with you girl?" I asked.

"I can't believe you rode for me like that. I've never had someone be on my side and defend me, not even Bre. I'm always the one bailing her out."

I told her it wasn't a big deal, and just keep one in the chamber for me, meaning if I ever needed her, she needed to have my back as well. Britney and I were inseparable after that, and I have a permanent scar on my leg that links us for life.

   There were only a few weeks left in school and summer break was around the corner. I loved going over to Britney and Bre's house because their mom was never home, and we pretty much did whatever we wanted. I had even convinced my mama to let me spend the night over there on more than a few occasions. Britney and I would sneak out of the house and go to the juke joint up the street. Deon, one of the neighborhood boys' dad, owned the spot and made him work the door. Deon would let me and Britney in because he had a major crush on her. Britney never paid him no mind, but I always thought Deon was cool. Britney and I never would bring Bre at first because she was always in some shit. Anything Britney and I tried to do on the low, Bre would blow it up. When we finally did allow her to come to the

Juke Joint with us, she got into a fight and got us all put out. Deon got in trouble for sneaking us in and stopped speaking to us after that. I could tell it wore on Britney how much she had to look after Bre. Everything one did was attached to the other. Bre was very flamboyant and extra. People assumed because they were sisters, they both were. Ultimately, Britney was not an angel, but she was nowhere near as bad as Bre. It didn't help that Britney and Bre's mom was always out of town for work. Bre thought that was a free ticket to have boys over. Britney and I did what we could to keep her under control, but anytime Bre was let out of our sight she managed to do something shady that had people looking at us all sideways. From messing around with girl's boyfriends, to stealing out of the mall, down to fighting everywhere we go, Bre was just attracted to drama. Because Britney was my best friend, I inherited the role of her sister's keeper as well.

After school, Britney and I would go to The Spot, a teen hangout near our school. It was a house, but the owner Evelyn had turned the front into one big open room with a couch on each wall. She charged kids $2 to get in and sold snacks, shots, cigarettes, weed, and whatever else your money could buy. So much went down there. Evelyn had one rule, no parents, and if your parents did show up looking for you, you were banned. Most kids took their first sip and smoke in The Spot. Girls and boys would hook up and get into all types of trouble. I loved going to watch how the older opposite sexes interacted. I would be going to high school soon and wanted to know what to expect. Britney and I were among the younger crowd and did our best to play it off and blend in. Guys would hit on Britney sometimes, but not me so much. I would end up playing wingman so I wouldn't be obviously awkward, but I did wonder what it was about me that didn't peak guy's interest. Britney said it was because I was too uptight, but I wasn't for everybody, and I wanted that to be clear.

Everyone pretty much stayed in their own clique at The Spot. High school girls would mean mug us and try sizing us up because they knew we were still in middle school. Britney was always down to get with any of them because she wanted our reputation to precede us when we started 9th grade next year. I wanted to keep the peace because I didn't want a whole lotta enemies when I started high school, but of course I always had my friends back. Like the time we were there, and she saw this girl that had been hassling Bre. Britney wanted to run down, but I told her it was a bad idea because I couldn't tell of the girls in the crowd who was who. Britney didn't listen and per usual, she fired off. She walked up to the girl and straight-up asked, "What's your problem with my sister?" The girl was an upperclassman and wasn't going to let Bre's 8th-grade ass approach her with that type of energy, so she stepped up. I didn't have a choice but to defend my friend. We got jumped by like 8 girls. We made it out, but not without a few scrapes and bruises. My friend was a hot head, and just like she felt she had to defend Bre, I felt I had to defend her.

We went to Southside High School. It was called "South" for short or even "*Souf*" depending on how country you is. I was a 14-year-old, wide-eyed freshman, and for the most part, I only talked to Britney. School hadn't been in long. I was still peeping who's who and checking out my peers. One day during the fourth period in the gym, I was sitting in the bleachers talking smack with Britney. We were talking about boys and last night's episode of Living Single, my favorite show. I always wanted to be like Khadijah James growing up, and Britney wanted to be like Maxine. We were so much like their characters on the show in real life. I was cool, collected, and artistic; Britney was witty, charismatic, and straightforward.

During gym period to kill time, Britney and I would play a secret game where we would rank all the boys in order of most attractive to just plain ole' ugly. Other freshmen girls spent gym period creating twerk routines that would get them noticed by the opposite sex. It's not like I wasn't into boys, I just didn't want to get their attention that way.

Some guys were playing a game of 2 on 2 on the basketball court. One of them threw a pass, and it flew right at my head. I ducked, then this big kid came crashing into me. I fell back into the bleachers, and I immediately jumped up in attack mode. I spazzed on him, "Watch where the hell you going! It's basketball, not dodgeball!" The boy stood there speechless. There I was this teeny girl talking to one of the most popular seniors at the school like he was a lame. His boys were standing around, and they all had stopped playing the game to see how their friend would respond to the 5'2 freshman calling him out. Another girl who I assumed at the time was his girlfriend stepped up to me. She looked over at him and asked, "Andre, who is this little freshman girl and why does she think she can talk to you like that? Do you need me to check her?" She stood there waiting on her man to say something. I knew if she was as tough as she was trying to put on, she wouldn't ask for permission to go off. I was used to dealing with her type though. It was always girls like her that assumed because I was reserved, I couldn't get rowdy. Little did she know, she was about to get acquainted with Katrina da Don. The girl was much bigger than me but there is truth in that old saying, "The bigger they are, the harder they fall." She obviously didn't mean much to the guy she was putting herself in danger for because he still hadn't answered her question. I interrupted our staring contest to warn her. "Girl you couldn't check me if you got paid today." Andre's friends instigated, "Oooohhhh Sharice, you gon let her talk to you like that?"

"Sharice doesn't have a choice." I said matter of fact.

Andre still hadn't spoken up and kept his eyes on me. I could feel him burning a hole in me from the side, but I refused to look back. His wannabe girlfriend was frozen. She was probably used to talking crap and getting away with it. Dealing with me, she was gon have to back up all that mess she was talking. Sharice's face said it all, she was an imposter. I almost felt sorry for her. She looked over at Andre again, but he was intentionally avoiding eye contact with her. Finally, Andre interjected himself.

"What's your name shawty?"

"My name ain't shawty!" I said.

"Well, what is it?" he asked.

"Nunya!"

"Nunya what?"

"Nunya business!" Britney said as we dapped up laughing. Andre walked closer, so he was now directly in my face. "When you're done laughing, I'm still waiting on your name." he said. He was being so intense. He didn't even crack a smile. My heart started racing, and I couldn't help but give in.

"My name is Katrina." I told him.

"That's a pretty name Katrina. You wanna know mine?"

"I don't need it, and I heard your funky lil girlfriend say it anyway." I looked over at Sharice, waiting on her to speak up for herself since she had so much mouth earlier. She smacked her teeth but didn't say anything.

"You're solid. I like that." Andre said laughing.

"Boy whatever." I tried to turn my head away but couldn't hide that I was blushing.

"Ummm Hellooo." Britney interrupted while waving her hand in Andre's face.

"Sup Britney." he said dryly.

"Y'all two know each other?" I asked.

"I know him." Britney said with an attitude.

He ignored her shadiness. "Katrina, are you going to ask me my name, so we can be properly introduced?"

His smile was innocent but intriguing. I looked into his eyes and it was the first time in my life I ever felt hypnotized. I didn't even know what color they were, but I knew they were different. I had never seen anyone with eyes like his. I swore I saw them change colors too. Before he put me in a trance, I found my voice. "I don't need to know your name to know you got a problem with your vision. Next time, watch where you're shooting the ball please." Me and Britney went to walk away, and he ran up behind us. I could hear Sharice call out to him. "Andre, where are you going?" He waved her off and kept towards us. He followed me to the other side of the gym and left his boys and one-woman fan club right there on the court.

Andre walked with me while I walked Britney to class. She leaned in and whispered, "Careful with that one K. He's out of your league." She laughed it off as she entered 4th period, but I could sense the seriousness in her joke. When Britney left, it was just he and I. Andre didn't waste any time getting all up in my business. "So, where are you from? You got a man? What do you like to do for fun?" He studied me, waiting for my answer. I normally clammed up when boys got anywhere near me, but for some reason with him, I felt a sense of comfort. More importantly, I felt like he wanted to get to know me, and I had never had a guy interested enough to even ask me my name. I told Andre I was single by choice, which was a lie, but it sounded good. When we got to my class he didn't want to leave. I smiled at him and walked into Math class only to get screamed at for being late. Andre heard Mr. May yelling at me and peeked his head in the door. He waved, "I'm Sorry Mr. May it was my fault." Andre smiled like it was his get-out-of-jail card. Mr. May wasn't impressed by his charisma. "Get out of my classroom Andre!" He shouted. The whole class laughed. I could tell he had a reputation. Andre winked and smiled at me as he scurried out the door.

I thought about him the entire period. What did he see in me? Ms. Plain Jane with nothing to offer a guy like him. Even though I felt it was a stretch that he would be interested in me, I had pictured having his babies and marrying him already. My mind had gotten caught in the rapture of lust within minutes.

When I left class, Andre was right there again. Britney was waiting for me on the other side of the hall as well. She looked at me with an annoyed look, waiting for me to choose between her and the new cute guy trying to get to know me. Surprisingly, it wasn't a hard decision. Not wanting her to feel put on the spot I whispered, "I'll catch you later Britney, cool?" Her eyes said it all. She smacked her teeth and waved me off. "Whatever Katrina."

"Britney, don't be like that." I tried to make light of the situation and reached for her hand, but it was too late. She was already halfway up the hall. Andre could sense that he had caused a rift in my friendship and tried to apologize. "I'm sorry. I was going to walk both of you to class. She didn't have to leave." I tried to play it off, although I was disappointed in myself for choosing him over her. I knew that if it were me, I would not have wanted Britney to pick some new cute guy over our walks to class together. Andre interrupted my thoughts asking me, "Can I walk you to the rest of your classes, now and forever?" He stuck his arm out, and I grabbed it. He walked me to every single one of my classes that day and was outside the door after every bell. I didn't see Britney anymore, but I couldn't help how intrigued I was by him.

When the school day was over, Andre offered to pay his homeboy to take me home. "Why are you being so nice to me? You don't even know me like that." I asked him. Part of me was skeptical of him initially. Andre confessed that he saw me weeks ago and had been crushing on me. Claims he was waiting on the right opportunity for us to meet. I looked into those eyes again, and I knew right there after knowing him less than a day, I wanted him around me forever. I may not have been clear in what capacity, but I knew that I needed his energy. I had never tried drugs before then, but that's what I equate the feeling to, and you know what they say about your first high, you'll chase that feeling forever.

I called Britney when I got home to tell her all about my day. She picked up the phone with an attitude. "What Katrina?" I ignored her tone and went on with my story.

 "Hey best friend! I called to tell you all about Andre. Girl, I think I'm in love." I was stoked, but Britney was obviously not impressed. "Katrina, I don't want to hear all about your new friend. You know he's just out to get another notch under his belt anyway. I can't believe you're falling for it."

Even if that were the case, it didn't feel like it, and I wanted to give him the benefit of the doubt. "Britney, you know I'm not stupid. If that's his intention it will come to light, and I'll be the first one to call him on it." She took a deep sigh. "Ok, if you say so. Are we meeting in the morning or what?" she asked, changing the subject. Just then, I remembered that Andre said he would have his friend pick me up in the morning. I couldn't disappoint Britney again, so I told her we were still meeting at our usual spot.

The next morning, I met Britney at the bus stop as I typically did so we could catch MARTA to school. Before the bus got there, Andre had pulled up with his homie and asked me to get in. Britney looked at me annoyed. "Really Katrina. You gon ride with him and leave me here?" Before I could say anything, Andre jumped in, "Chill Britney! Katrina already told me you were riding with us. We're here to scoop both of y'all." I was so happy he was quick on his feet. Britney turned all giddy. "Well, in that case, get out and open the door for us." She was all of a sudden extremely confident. Andre hopped out, winked at me, and opened our door. She got in first behind the driver, and I slid in behind Andre. He introduced everyone. "Mont, this is my girl Katrina and her friend Britney." Britney leaned over to me and whispered, "The driver is mine." We dapped it up and I was relieved that she would have a distraction so I could focus on Andre. Britney and Mont chopped it up while I sat in the back too shy to say anything in front of an audience. Ten minutes into the ride, it was clear we weren't headed in the school's direction. I leaned over to Britney, "I hope they don't think we are about to skip school with them."

"If we are skipping it's cool. One day ain't gon' hurt your 4.0 GPA Katrina." Britney spoke loud enough for them to hear us. Her whole vibe had changed, and I didn't like it. She wanted to be viewed as cool in front of the older guys but at my expense. Mont overheard us and interrupted, "Nah' we ain't skipping school ladies. I'm going to pick up my girlfriend first." I could see his dimples in the rearview mirror as he smiled at us both. The backseat shook from Britney's heart dropping to her gut. She looked over at me and mouthed, "Girlfriend? What the hell?" She started visibly pouting and I urged her to get it together so she wouldn't embarrass herself.

A few minutes later we pulled up at Mont's girlfriend's house. She was waiting outside, and I could tell by the expression on her face, and the one hand on her hip, she was pissed that there were not only 1, but 2 girls in the backseat. Andre hopped out the front and left the door open for her to get in. She looked at Britney and me in the back seat and asked, "Good morning. Who y'all?" Andre answered for us. "This is my girlfriend Katrina and her friend." Britney jumped in and said, "Her friend Britney." Mont's girlfriend wasn't amused by Britney's assertiveness and turned around to look at him. If looks could kill, Mont would be dead. Andre squeezed in the backseat with us. He put his arm around me, and I could feel the steam coming off Britney. I had never seen my friend be so jealous and it wasn't a good look.

We stopped by this breakfast spot, and Andre bought Britney and I 2 Bacon, Egg, and Cheese biscuits. When we pulled up at school, we only had about 3 minutes before the bell would ring. I tried to run off, but not before Andre asked for a hug. I smiled and gave him a hug and kiss on the cheek. Britney stood there with her arms folded. "Aww, you want a hug too?" Andre asked with his arms out. She smiled and reached in for a full-body hug while Andre uncomfortably embraced. He and I looked at each other, and I knew without him saying anything it was a situation I'd have to address. She and I went off to homeroom, where we both had Mrs. Daniels. I wanted to talk to Britney about her being off balance but didn't know how to approach it without her getting defensive. When we made it to class, she asked what we all were doing later. I knew by "we" she meant her, Andre, and me. Although Andre was playing nice, I knew he was only doing it so she wouldn't feel left out. I needed to set clear boundaries because it was seeming that Britney was thinking we were going to roll as a trio. I threw a subtle hint at first. "Andre and I are probably going to hang out after school. What are you going to be doing?" I separated our plans so she would catch on. She caught the hint but wasn't happy about it. "Well, I guess since you'll be busy with your new man, I'll just find something else to do. Maybe Bre and I

22

will go hang out." she lied. I knew Britney was being shady because her and Bre hadn't hung out much since Bre started acting out and hanging with the wrong crowd. We hardly even saw Bre, and although they were sisters, Britney finally decided that sometimes blood ain't worth losing your identity for. I didn't rebuttal and decided to let it go. Britney and I didn't talk for the rest of homeroom, and when the bell rang for first period, she dashed out of the door before I could. When I got to the hallway, Andre was there with a confused look on his face. "What's wrong?" I asked. "What's up with Britney? I've really been trying to be nice to her, but her vibe is throwing me off. She knows you my girl, and she's pressed." Andre was so confident calling me his girl after only knowing me for 2 days, and not once did I correct him. I was just fine with my new title.

After school, I made one last-ditch effort to fix whatever weirdness was going on between Britney and me. I asked her if she wanted to catch the bus downtown to Underground and grab something to eat from the food court. She was down and told me she'd meet me after school at our usual spot. I told Andre that I would catch him later instead of riding with him as I had promised.

Britney and I caught the MARTA train to Five Points station. We headed downstairs and grabbed some items from the dollar store. We looked around at a few other stores where we knew we couldn't afford anything. It was like we were prolonging getting to our destination.

Finally, we got to the food court and took samples from everywhere while we chatted about everything but the elephant in the room. We settled on our usual Chinese food special for $3.99 that came with 1 meat and 2 sides. When we got to the table, I finally built up the nerve to speak about what had been going on. "Britney, are we good? I know it's only been a couple of days, but it just seems funny between us since Andre came along. I don't want it to feel like you

23

and I aren't cool just because he's gonna start being around more." She laughed in my face. "Katrina, I can't believe you're taking someone like this serious. Why would he want to talk to you?" Britney was being harsh but before I could go off, she tried to clean up her statement. "I just mean y'all from two different sides of the track. Why would he come on your side unless he has something to gain?" she asked. My face said it all. I knew what she meant. I wasn't Andre's type. Between the two of us, Britney always got the attention of boys. They would walk up to us and not even speak to me. It was usually all about her. The one time that I got picked over her, she couldn't believe it was genuine. Instead of being happy for me, she seemed to be jealous. I understood her feelings because truthfully when guys ignored me and gave her all the attention, I was jealous too, but I never took it out on her. I wanted to put a bow on the conversation so I reminded her I could think for myself. "Britney, I'm not stupid. If he's in it for the wrong reasons it will come out. Just give me a little space to get to know him. He's gonna prove you wrong, watch."

Britney smirked. "Ok Katrina, I'll follow your league on this one, but when he shows his true colors, don't say I didn't warn you." She and I wrapped up and headed outside towards the buses. On the way to our neighborhood, I thought about Andre. Now that I straightened everything out with Britney, I was hoping I wouldn't have to address the situation again.

When I got home, I called my new boo. He asked me how my day with Britney went, and I told him it was cool. I liked that he cared about my friendship with her, but I didn't want him to feel obligated to her as if we were a package deal. He asked me if I wanted him to pick us up in the morning. I declined because I didn't want to make Britney feel some type of way. I told him that I would catch him after first period instead. Before we got off the phone, he played Usher's "Nice and Slow," and made his best effort to sing to me. With each day, my interest grew.

The next morning, I got up and headed to the bus stop to meet Britney like I always did. When I got there, she wasn't anywhere in sight. Most days, Britney beat me to the bus stop or I at least could see her approaching from up the street. I waited 15 minutes then pulled out my minute phone which only had about 20 minutes left on it. I called her, but she didn't pick up. I was angrier that her line went to voicemail and used one of my minutes. If I knew Britney, I knew she was still in her feelings. Unless she was sick, she always met me at the bus stop. After 30 minutes of waiting, I accepted that she wasn't coming and caught the next bus. I called Andre and told him what happened. Of course he rubbed it in. "See, I told you something's up with your friend. She's mad that we're together." I felt the same way, but I couldn't let him think that about her. "Nah she's probably just going through something and projecting her anger on me. It'll blow over." I said.

"Well, if it doesn't blow over, don't say I didn't tell you so." Andre had no idea Britney had issued me the same warning about him. I hoped neither of them would eventually be proven right.

I made it my business to spend more time with Britney over the next few days. It wasn't what I really wanted to do, but I knew I would have to find a way to balance the 2 relationships if I wanted them both to stay intact. I went above and beyond, but no matter how much time I spent with Britney, when I wanted to break away to go with Andre, she would catch an attitude.

After a few weeks, Britney started hanging with the "In" crowd. She always had friends outside of me, but she never hung with them before. Now that she had more time on her hands, she got herself some insurance.

I was surprised when she told me there was gonna be a party at this guy Eric's house. Britney asked if I wanted to roll with

25

her, and I figured what better way to get our vibe back than to go out, break curfew, and cut up in Eric's parents' basement. I was down and looking forward to a Friday night party.

I asked Andre if he heard about the party, and of course he had. Andre said he didn't want to go because he had practice early Saturday. He said he was ok with me going, but his body language said otherwise. I started to push for him to come but if I brought him with me, I knew Britney would really be a bitch about it.

Instead of going home that Friday, I went straight to Britney's house. I went through her closet and found a nice blouse to go with my jeans. I brushed my hair up, threw some gel on my edges, and that was the extent of it. Britney invited Bre, and they both had gotten all the way done up. I almost felt underdressed but remembered Andre wasn't going to be there, so I didn't have anyone to impress.

After everyone was ready, the girls and I headed out. We walked the 6 blocks to Eric's house. Bre kept the convo going reminiscing on old times. It had only been a month since we last cut up, but it did seem like forever. Britney took out a cigarette and lit it. "What! Are you smoking cigarettes now?" I asked her. "Na, it's just for fashion. The older guys think it's cool. Here, take a hit." Britney passed the cigarette to me. "Uh uh girl. It stank. I'm good." I pushed her hand back. Even the smell of the cigarette smoke made me sick. I could tell Britney was annoyed that I wouldn't give in to her peer pressure, but I wasn't going to feed into her energy.

When we made it to Eric's house, we could barely get down the stairs to his basement. It was wall to wall and hot. There were strobe lights and smoke everywhere. I knew it was about to be epic. Eric had some big ol speakers in each corner, and Juvenile's "Back that a** up" was blasting. The girls were going crazy. The fellas were crowding around trying to grab something to get behind. Bre had dipped on us as soon as we got there. Britney was mingling with her new friends. I found a wall to put my back on and just grooved to my own beat. I was enjoying watching everyone else.

An hour later, Britney came and found me. She dragged me upstairs with her so we could chill with Eric and some of the other kids. They had gotten their hands on some beer and wanted to get the "real party" started as Britney put it. I recognized some of the kids there. Andre's friend Mont, who he rode to school with most mornings, was there with his girl Nene. Steven, Britney's lil boo was up under her, and then there was Eric. He was cool but obnoxious. I knew as soon as I walked in the room everyone was up to no good. "Oh snap, you came." Eric said excitedly. Everyone was booed up, and he was the only one without a partner. "You can sit here if you want." he said, motioning for a seat next to him. I felt like I was being set up, and I wasn't with it.

"So, as I was saying, in this group who would you Sex, Marry, Kill?" Nene asked. As luck would have it, it was Eric's turn.

 "I would Sex Katrina, Marry Katrina, and Kill the rest of y'all." he said. Everyone was laughing except me. I was uncomfortable. I looked over at Britney who just shrugged her shoulders like she had no clue what was happening.

Steven suggested we play spin the bottle instead. I definitely wasn't going to be kissing anyone but decided to stay around for a couple spins. The first spin landed on one of the Seniors and the guy that was sitting next to Eric. He was so anxious to kiss her, I was surprised she did it. The next spin landed on me and Steven, Britney's boo. I figured it was understood that it would be a pass. I got up from the circle and headed straight for the door. Steven jumped up and blocked the doorway. "You can't back out after the bottle spins!" he said.

"Boy, you better get your big ass out of my way before I tase you!" I threatened him.

"I ain't going nowhere. Rules are rules. If you wanna leave, then you need to bring them lips here girl." He leaned into me heavily, and I could feel myself shrinking. No one spoke up for me. Everyone looked like they were enjoying my torment. Eric was laughing, Mont was on his phone, and Britney looked like she wanted to speak up, but she was too scared to have the room turn against her. Steven taunted me. "I'm waiting brown skin. I ain't got curfew, but I know you do, so let's get this over with." I told Steven to close his eyes because I didn't want to have to look at him. He closed his eyes, and I slowly moved closer. He even had the nerve to pucker up. As soon as I was close enough, I punched him right in the nose. He was stunned. Steven grabbed his face as blood seeped through his hands. I was able to open the door and run out of the room. Once I made it out of the house, I started crying. I was embarrassed. Steven was one of those popular guys who thought women were supposed to kiss the ground he walked on, and I refused to be his victim. I stood under the carport trying to catch my breath. I could hear a loud commotion near the door. It was Steven. He was looking for me. I looked for somewhere to hide. I pulled at the handle of Eric's mom's car, and luckily the door was unlocked. I hopped inside and got low. Steven and some other boys came outside. "I'm bout to walk up the block and find this chick." Steven said.

"Let it go man." I could hear Mont trying to convince him.

"No! I know that's your man's girl, but no one hits me in the face. I don't give a damn who they are." Steven got more hype as more kids started coming out of the house. Mont steady tried to calm him down. "You know if you touch her you gotta deal with Andre, right? You ain't ready for that man."

Steven couldn't be restrained. He was talking big mess. "I don't care about Andre. That boy can't beat me one on one no way." he bragged. I had cracked the window and was looking out of the rearview mirror. By that time, all the kids from the party were outside, and I was wondering if I would be stuck in that car all night. The kids were in the yard, all watching Steven carry on. The only one that tried to reason with him was Mont. I figured it was the least he could do since he and Andre were friends. There was a group of kids coming through the cut from behind Eric's house and I was hoping they wouldn't see me in the car. One of them was almost jogging trying to get to the crowd. He had on a hoodie, and he ran up on Steven. The kid hit him so fast and so hard, no one even knew what happened until the body dropped. Mont swung on Eric, and he and the other kid started sizing a couple other guys up in the crowd. The kid pulled his hoodie back, and I saw that it was Andre.

The kids went crazy like we had just won a game.

"Yo Mont, appreciate the call homie. Where my girl at?" Andre asked.

"I don't know man. I was waiting for you to get here so we could go look for her." Mont said.

Right then, I opened the car door. Andre saw me and looked relieved. "Come on bae, I got you." I hugged Andre's neck. "How did you know all of this was going on?" I asked him.

"I told Mont to keep an eye on you. He hit me up as soon as it started going left. He told me we were gon have to fold some niggas because they up here playing with you. I was on my way as soon as he hit me. These niggas need to know how I'm coming bout you." Andre said it loud enough for the entire crowd to hear. He waited for someone to challenge him. Mont stood there looking at Andre like a proud big brother. Andre kicked Steven in the ribs, and he cried out in pain. "Lame ass nigga got my girl hiding in a car. I should beat you again." he said.

"No, let's go baby." I pulled Andre away, but not before he looked over and threatened Eric. "I heard you were over here on that slick shit too. You better have ya guard on at practice tomorrow because I'm gon drop your ass."

Eric put his head down and didn't say a word. Britney stood next to him, embarrassed that her man Steven was still on the ground trying to get up.

 "Y'all knew she was Andre's girl. I don't know why y'all tried it." Nene said. "Right. You niggas would do the same to Nene if I ain't around and I'm not Dre, I don't fight. I'm gon shoot one of you niggas bout mine." Mont said. He grabbed Nene, and we all hopped in his Cutlass and burnt out.

In the car, Nene asked, "What's up with Britney? I thought that was your friend. Why didn't she speak up for you?"

"I keep trying to tell bae Britney ain't her friend, but she thinks I'm tripping." Andre added.

"Well, I don't trust her, and she definitely wouldn't be my friend leaving me in the cold like that. You need to watch her. That's not what a real one would do." Nene reminded me.

We ended up going to Waffle King and kicking it the rest of the night into the early AM. My mom thought I was sleeping at Britney's house, but I wasn't messing with her now. Mont lived in his mom's basement and could come and go as he pleased so he offered Andre and I to stay over. We slept on the floor, and no lie it was the best sleep I ever had in my life.

I went home the next day like nothing happened, but I felt like a grown woman having spent my first night with a boy. I was starting to think the big fight and the fall-out with Britney was a sacrifice for such bliss.

Early on, Andre was the perfect gentleman. He would bring me gifts to school, decorate my locker with hearts, and even wrote me love letters every week. It was so easy to fall in love with him. I never had a boyfriend before and after being with Andre, I was not interested in finding out what was out there as my mother had suggested. She hated that I fell for the first boy that gave me the time of day, and I often felt like she was in disbelief that he fell for me too. My mom had the worst luck with men. She had never in her whole life set a positive example for me of the type of man I should date, so she wasn't someone I relied on for advice. She seemed to be so hateful towards men. I used to wonder why she wouldn't just be a lesbian. Her main concern for me was that I didn't bring any baby's home. She would even say, "If you bring a baby into my house, you're gonna be living on the street with it!" I never thought it to be a scare tactic and wholeheartedly believed that she would put me out if I did get pregnant. The more my mom tried to scare me away from having sex, the more intrigued by it I became. We didn't have the greatest relationship in the first place, and her attacking the only man that ever showed me some decency made me angry. It was like she didn't believe someone could truly like me for me. I remember telling Andre the first chance he got, I wanted him to take me far away. He promised that one day he would.

Until Andre was able to honor that promise, I had to settle for school being my get-away from home. Since Britney and I had stopped hanging, I didn't have anyone to keep me occupied but Andre. I wanted her and I to mend the friendship, but I didn't know where to begin. It's like the closer I got to Andre, the more she and I drifted apart. Bre had even started treating me funny. I tried to act like it was

31

nothing at first and I still called her. I even went to her house a few times just to be left on the porch knocking. I felt like Britney was in the wrong, but it was only me trying to fix it. I got tired of chasing her, so I left it alone.

In school, kids thought I was odd because I didn't try to fit in. Even as a freshman, I was focused on graduating. I was smart, and I always knew if I kept my grades up, I could go to college for free. Going to college meant getting away from my crazy mama. I thought of it like a paid vacation. I figured the better my GPA, the better vacation I could pick. I would watch shows like "A Different World" and "Fresh Prince of Bel Air," imagining being on a campus with other black women just like me thriving to get a piece of the pie. Andre loved that I was all about academics and always encouraged me to stay focused. When I didn't have anyone else's support, I had his. He was never ashamed to put our love on front street and I had drama with a lot of girls because of it. He made quite a name for himself in the 3 years before I got to South, and a few girls still had lingering feelings for him. He was known to break hearts and keep it moving. When he and I got together, he changed his game or as he always says, I changed the game.

From the outside looking in, you would think that I was lucky to have Andre. He could have had any girl at that high school, but he chose me. No one could understand why a popular, fine boy like him, who could have the pick of the litter would want a freshman. I had short, thick, kinky hair that I always wore pinned up. I was flat as a pancake in the front and the back. My style was reminiscent of Aaliyah who I idolized. I was most comfortable in a bun, some baggy clothes, and sneakers. I wore big clothes so I could look curvier than I was and still, no one ever checked for me. Andre on the other hand didn't have any issues with puberty or style. He was tall, dark, and handsome. He had a low-cut Caesar. His lean frame could rival any professional Basketball player and his style was one word, FLY. Even if you took all of that away, he could still kill you with his eyes alone. They changed with his mood. When Andre got hot for me, his eyes would turn amber; when he was happy, green; in the sun, they appeared to be hazel, when he was angry, fiery. He was perfect if I ever imagined it. Andre turned me on and made my body feel things my 14-year-old self couldn't understand back then.

It was hard, but I managed to hold on to the one thing I had control over, my virginity. It was my ace in the hole and I held on to it more so out of insecurity than morals. I questioned what Andre saw in me too, and I didn't want to end up being anybody's fool. Andre said he liked me because I was different. I stood for something. He couldn't get past the surface with most girls because they were too busy trying to be like someone else. I marched to the beat of my own drum. He didn't pressure me about sex and respected my decision of wanting to wait. We messed around a few times with clothes on but never went beyond that. I felt safe and comfortable with him. I told him my darkest secrets and even confided in him the issues I had with my mom. He never made me feel like I was alone in my world. He grew up completely different from me, but I never felt inferior. He was my air and the closer we got the more obsessed I felt.

When it was close to the end of the school year, Andre went away to visit his future college. He was accepted on a full-ride basketball scholarship to FSU in Florida. I was scared to lose him to the city of a million beautiful women, but he assured me that I had his heart. I had no choice but to trust in his word.

The girls at school must have had a countdown going because it hadn't been a whole week that he was away visiting his school before the vultures came out. They used Andre and I being apart as an opportunity to try and get in my head.

The leader of the pack was Sharice. She never got over me embarrassing her the day she tried to check me over Andre in the gym. I later learned their history and it turns out she had been crushing on him since they were kids. Andre said he never paid her any attention because she was too busy. Every guy in school had a story about her. She was 17 and had been kept back twice because she never came to class and she had the nerve to have the worst attitude. All that being said, she was still one of the most popular girls at school. Sharice would follow me up and down the halls calling me names and saying things like, "Your boyfriend isn't here to save you no more, we gon get in that ass." I never knew the "we" she was referring to, but I was ready for them.

One day I was walking to class and someone shoved me so hard from the back I fell forward. Before I could get up, Sharice was on top of me swinging. I fought back, but it happened so fast. Kids had surrounded us, and everyone was cheering Sharice on. Sharice's friend Tisha kicked me while Sharice was on top of me. I caught a glimpse of the crowd and saw Britney breaking through. She was my glimmer of hope. I knew no matter what we were beefing about she wouldn't let me get jumped. We hadn't spoken in a while, but if the shoe were on the other foot, it wouldn't even be a question for me. I just needed her to get Sharice off me so I could get up, then it would be on. I knew Britney and I could take the girls easily once I regained my footing. We had done it before, just like when we first met.

When Britney did get to the front of the crowd, she stood there and watched me get beat up. She looked at me with a cold dead stare while I was on the ground. She was enjoying it, and the fact that Andre was at the center of my conflict made her feel even better. I was fighting for my life, but everything went still for a moment. It was officially over. Britney and I could never come back from that. She was just as dead to me as the girl on top of me. I covered my face trying to protect what I could. I kicked until I was finally able to get Sharice off me.

The administrators came to break the fight up. I saw that there was blood on my shirt. I ran into the bathroom to see that Sharice had sliced the side of my face from my ear down to my chin. I collapsed to the floor and the next thing I remembered was being in the hospital with my mom talking over me.

"You see, I told you that boy was going to get you in trouble. He went off to college and got you out here fighting these chicks over him while he probably moved on to the next. Look at your face Katrina. That girl damn near cut you in half." It was the last thing I wanted to hear while lying in the hospital bed with 30 stitches in my face. Although I didn't like my mom, if she could have just hugged me and told me it would be alright, it would have meant the world to me. I already had Sharice to worry about and the one person that I could count on was away. My mama dug the knife in deeper. "Where was your so-called friend Britney? I thought y'all always rolled together. Why didn't she help you? I told you these heffas ain't ya friends. You had to learn the hard way." I turned my head trying to hide my tears. I hated to say it, but my mom was right.

I stayed out of school for a few days after the incident. My mom didn't want me to go back since it was so close to the end of the year, but I had a score to settle. It never once crossed my mind to let Sharice get away with what she did to me. She had given me a permanent scar on my face, and the price she would have to pay wasn't anything her ass could afford.

When I did go back to school, I was disappointed to learn that Sharice had been expelled for the remainder of the school year. I was still going to beat her ass, even if I had to wait a little while longer. I wanted to get my revenge in front of everyone, but it would be fine either way if I got my hands on her. I exercised patience and waited for the perfect opportunity. Finally, I got it on the very last day of school.

Sharice decided that she would buck and come to school grounds on the last day to celebrate with her friends. We were all outside when I spotted her. I couldn't believe she was crazy enough to come to school when she had been expelled. On second thought, anyone who would run up on me didn't have good reason or sense. I went inside the building to put my things in my locker. I grabbed my brass knuckles and said a prayer. I knew once the first punch was thrown, I'd blackout and was hoping I didn't kill anybody. I walked outside and calmly approached. I was nervous, but I always got nervous before fighting. My uncle said nerves were good. It meant you were in touch with your power.

My stitches were still raw and when Sharice's homegirl Tisha saw me she taunted. "Look who it is y'all, slice and dice." I laughed, but I wasn't laughing with her. As soon as Sharice was in arms reach, I stole on her with a quick right. I grabbed her ponytail with my left hand, wrapped it around my fist, and started pounding her in the face. Her friends were in such shock they didn't move. I threw her to the ground and started kicking her. When I was done, she was on the floor curled up in pain. I looked over at Tisha and before she could run, I grabbed her by the shirt and slung her down too. She was just as guilty as Sharice. I caught her with a couple of blows, and she was down for the count. It was too easy. A crowd had gathered, and everyone's mouth was wide. I looked back at them as they looked at me with Sharice and Tisha's blood all over my clothes. I know they thought I was crazy, but it was worth it. I could see the crowd start to separate and figured it was the school resource officer breaking through to snatch me up. To my surprise, it was Andre. His eyes were so big they could have popped out of his head. He ran over to me. "Katrina baby what happened? Are you ok?" Andre pulled me close to see if any of the blood on my shirt belonged to me. "What happened to your face?" he asked in a panic. I didn't bother telling Andre what happened at school in the first fight with Sharice because I knew he would have thrown his entire future away to make it even. He was away getting ready for college, and I didn't want to trouble him, besides I could handle my own business. I smiled and said, "I'm alright baby." I looked down at Sharice with her face all disfigured and asked, "Now how you like it bitch?!" She still didn't win the man and the only thing we had in common was scars, her's more hideous than mine.

As usual, Mont was waiting for us in the cut with the Cutlass. I left school after that and whatever my consequence would be was going to have to wait until after my summer vacation.

Chapter 2 I'll take care of you

When the summer was over, I did have to face my consequences. The principal at South said I was a threat to other students after what I did to Sharice and Tisha. I was expelled from all public and county schools. The only choice left was to go to an alternative school. I thought the girls at South were bout it, but the girls at alternative school were fucking Spartans. I got into a fight every day of my first week. If it wasn't someone attacking me for thinking I was too good, it was because I was too damn quiet. All in all, it was just people testing my gangster and learning the hard way that we move in silence. In alternative schools, you didn't get suspended for fighting. They let you fight, and when you were done, you took your ass back to class. I hated it there!

My mom blamed Andre for me getting off track, and she reminded me every chance she got that if I had listened to her in the first place, I wouldn't be in the predicament that I was in. Andre and I remained close while he was away at college. I didn't get to see him as much, but we did see each other every chance we got. He knew I hated my new school. He tried to make me look at the brighter side of things like the fact that I was the top student in the entire school. It wasn't hard to be in a place full of hoodlums. I was my teacher's favorite student because I listened and had good manners. A lot of the kids in alternative school couldn't care less about listening to anyone, let alone a teacher. Still, it was my goal by my senior year to graduate from South because I knew I'd have a better shot at college coming out of there. There was a rehabilitation program that would give me a chance at getting back into South if I could complete it. It was 6 weeks long, and I would have to take anger management, commit to 100 hours of community service, and pass an exam. I was all in.

The first few weeks were easy. It was all about not allowing myself to be triggered when tempted. I had been in the program for 4 weeks when I got the ultimate test. The teacher said we had a new student joining us, and she wanted all of us to make her feel welcome. After she gave her speech, Sharice walked in. All the blood in my body had rushed to my head, and I was mad all over again. Last I saw her, our moms were about to fight. Her mom wanted to press charges against me for assaulting Sharice, and my mom argued that we were even. They went back and forth for a while, but finally, both parents agreed to drop it. Our moms told us to stay away from each other, and my green ass thought that was it.

When Sharice saw me in class, we locked eyes, and I knew it was on. All that I had learned in anger management flew right out the window. "Imma kick your ass Katrina!" Sharice called me out. Our teacher, Mrs. Stallings, a frail little white lady from Alabama had turned pale, and I could tell she was reaching for her panic button. There were panic buttons in every classroom and for damn good reason. Sharice leaped over 2 desks and flew at me. I stood up and flung her even further than she intended to go. Sharice tumbled into the desks. She got up quickly and tried to come back towards me. I picked up my Anger management book, full of scenarios to avoid and started pounding her with it. The book slipped out of my hand, so I started punching her in the face with my fist. The administrators finally came running in the classroom and pulled me off her. I was up 2-0. "It ain't over!" she shouted. "We're going to fight every time I see you! Andre aint off-limits either! Both y'all better watch your back!" She threatened standing there with two puffy eyes. "Sharice, you're the one bleeding, I don't have to watch shit!" I was laughing at her to keep from crying because although I won the fight, I lost the war. I let my anger win and I wouldn't get the one thing I wanted, and that was to go back to South.

Later that day in the office, Principal Ward expressed how disappointed in me she was. I tried to explain to her that it wasn't my fault, but she didn't want to hear it. She told me to get comfortable because I blew my shot at going back to public school. I left her office and bumped into Mrs. Stallings. She didn't make eye contact with me, and I figured it was because I scared her when I went Rambo on Sharice's ass. I was walking to my next class as the kids in the hall cheered me on. I had officially become a member. I was one of them. It wasn't any sense in me acting like I didn't belong because I did.

I was sitting in an economics class when I was called to the office again. I was nervous because I knew it couldn't be good. This time when I walked in, I was greeted by Principal Ward, Mrs. Stallings, and my mom.

My heart dropped because I knew my mom was going to flip on me for fighting again. I darted my eyes at Mrs. Stallings. I just knew she had thrown me under the bus. Principal Ward had already shown me where she stood, so I was waiting to be attacked. A tear rolled down my cheek and my mom snatched me up and pulled me out of the office fast. "Katrina, stop crying. You ain't did nothing wrong, so wipe your face." She grabbed a Kleenex off the assistant's desk without even asking. "Now they already called me and told me the deal. I know this is the same girl from last time, and I'm deading this mess today. Fix your face and come on. I got you."

My mom stormed back into the principal's office and it was clear who was controlling the room. "So, who's gonna start?" my mom asked. Mrs. Stallings was understandably nervous because my mom was intimidating. I decided no better person to tell the story than me since I was in it.

"I was sitting in class minding my business, and Mrs. Stalling said we had a new student. As soon as I looked up, Sharice threatened me. I didn't even have time to say anything before she was on me. I did what I had to." I looked at my mama the whole time because she was the only one I cared about convincing. The Principal, not believing a word I said, suggested we let Mrs. Stallings give her point of view.

"Well, what Katrina just explained is exactly what happened." Mrs. Stalling attested. "The new girl Sharice came into my classroom, and when she saw Katrina, she threatened her. She then hopped over a ton of desks trying to get to her. Katrina was simply defending herself." I was so shocked that Mrs. Stallings had my back. I mean, she was simply telling the truth, but I wasn't expecting that. The principal still tried to argue that I took it too far by hitting Sharice with the book, but then my mom stepped in.

"Ain't no rules to fighting. That could've been my baby getting beat with a book, but the odds were in her favor today. When you start a fight, you don't know the outcome until it's done, if you're blessed enough to see the outcome. You know how many people thought they were going into a fight and ended up dead? Did y'all know this girl is the same reason my baby is in this jacked up school in the first place? What are y'all doing about that? This same girl keeps coming for Katrina. Did y'all not do your research before putting them in the same class? Now if I were to tell my daughter to attack this little girl every time she sees her, how the hell would y'all like that?" My mom had her head cocked hard to the right waiting for the principal to explain herself.

Instead of addressing the issue, Principal Ward threatened my mom that if she didn't calm down and stop cursing, she and I would be escorted out. Little did she know, my mama wasn't the one to be threatening. Moms leaned in towards the principal. "Put me out then. I'll have the Board of Directors in here faster than you can finish your paperwork. You can explain to them why you put 2 students with a known history of fighting each other in the same class. Even the teacher told you Katrina had no choice, and you sitting here all high and mighty like if it were your child you wouldn't have wanted her to do the same. I had to leave work early for this mess today, so we're gonna settle it TODAY! What do you wanna do?" My mama had big energy, and although I was nervous for the people in the room, deep down I was secretly smiling. Mom and I were a team, and we were winning. Principal Ward tried to reason with her. "Mrs. Green." My mom quickly corrected her, "It's Ms. not Mrs."

"I'm sorry Ms. Green, if we could just calm down and try working something out." Principal Ward asked. My mom smelled blood and went in for the kill. "Ain't nothing to work out because you're unreasonable. My daughter is in the rehabilitation program to try and get out of this damn school. You're trying to penalize her for defending herself? You know most of the kids in here are not rehabilitated. You wanna give one of the good ones a hard time?" I sat back and let my mama do all the talking, not like I had a choice, but she was on it. Mrs. Stallings sat in her chair waiting for her turn to speak again. "Mrs. Stallings what do you think? Does Katrina deserve another chance at the rehab program?" Principal Ward asked her. Mrs. Stallings didn't get a chance to speak. My mom answered on her behalf. "Principal Ward, you're asking Mrs. Stallings for her opinion as if hers or yours will be the deciding factor. You're going to put Katrina back in the program, and she will graduate from South High School. You can give the head nod, or the Board of Directors can do it for you. Those are the options on the table before I go over your head." One thing Jasmine Lashaun Green didn't do was make empty threats. Principal Ward must've sensed it because she gave in. "OK Ms. Green, you're right. Katrina is a great student, so this one time I'll make an exception." She looked over at me, and I could tell by her smirk she was still fighting for power in a room that had been taken over by my mama. She just had to try and say something. "Katrina, you can continue the program, but next time this happens…" My mom put her hand up and hushed the principal. "You should know not to go into the Lion's Den to chastise a cub. Katrina is my cub, and we're in the Lion's Den. I will correct my own child." Principal Ward was shut down once again. "Katrina, get back to class and keep out these girl's way. You do what you gotta do to get the hell up outta here. I'll take care of the rest." My mom darted her eyes at the principal.

"Yes ma'am Mama. I'm staying out of the way."

We did a secret handshake I taught her when I was a kid, and I headed back to class.

My mom stayed behind in the office after I left, and if I knew my mama, she was about to dig in their ass some more for making it so hard on me in the first place.

The rest of the year was a breeze. I stayed out of trouble and word got out that I didn't take no mess. I didn't have to fight to prove myself anymore, and I completed the rehab program. I would be back at South High as a senior. I couldn't wait to go back and show them how much I had changed.

Summer couldn't pass fast enough. Every weekend I would go to the mall and cop a new fit with one goal in mind, crushing them the first week of school. Unlike most girls I didn't have a clique to kick the door down with. My ace boon was still not speaking to me. The day before school was set to start, my heart got the best of me, and I walked down to Britney's house to try and make amends again. I still felt like it was her fault that we weren't friends anymore, and I couldn't forgive her for watching me get jumped, but I was beyond the blame game and just wanted my friend back. I couldn't believe we really hadn't spoken in almost 2 years.

I took a deep breath and said a prayer before I knocked on the door. I did 3 soft taps hoping the person on the other side would know I came in peace. Britney's mom flung the door open rudely. "You got some nerve bringing your ass down here girl." I was confused why she was talking to me like that. She had always been so nice before. "I was just coming to check on Britney. Is she here?" I asked.

"Britney and Bre went to stay with their father in Jacksonville 2 summers ago. If you were any kind of friend, you would have known that. And I know you were right along with them when they had boys in my house so you can turn around and take your ass back home too." she said before slamming the door in my face. I stood there for a minute, thought twice about knocking again, then I remembered how crazy Britney's mom could get so I dipped. I walked away feeling silly for avoiding someone who had not been there the whole time. It sounded like Britney's mom finally had enough and sent them south. If I had to guess, it was Bre that had got them caught up. If Britney and I were still hanging out she probably could have at least saved herself.

By the time I became a senior in high school, Andre was a Junior in College. I went from Pancake Katrina to *Plenty Cake* Katrina. I started to fill out, and all the boys that typically didn't look my way started undressing me with their eyes. It was uncomfortable at first, but afterwhile I got used to it. My hips had spread, butt had grown, and my breasts were on swoll. My mom would say, "Katrina, I know you been having sex with Andre because your ass is getting big and that only happens when you having sex." She was wrong. The truth was I still had my V-card, and I was one of the only people I knew with it. I thought about sex all the time but used my energy to focus on other things like keeping my grades up and looking cute.

I had a part-time job at Mickey D's and my mom started letting me use my money to go to the beauty salon to get my hair done. I had learned a few things about make-up and was coming into my own. I would go to the track after school and run laps which kept my body on point. It was an exciting time for me, but Andre didn't like it. He felt like he was losing me. He became jealous and it brought out the worst in him. He started acting crazy and insecure. I never saw that side of him before, so I didn't know how to deal with it at first. He would call me every day all day, even while I was in class. He would make me leave the phone on while I slept and would pop up on me all the time. He never caught me with another guy, but he still accused me of cheating. At first, I thought it was cute that he cared so much, but that got old quickly. Once, I was at the salon getting my hair done and he blew my whole spot up. He came in and shouted at me in front of everyone. "Katrina, I know you see me calling your damn phone! Where the hell have you been all day?" Andre grabbed my arm trying to pull me out of the chair.

"Get outta here with all that Andre!" I tried to push him off, but he wasn't having it. He pulled me outside with him. I remember looking back at my stylist Goochee who was frozen with the flat irons in his hand. When we got outside, Andre wanted to argue.

"Why are you playing with me Katrina? You see me calling, why can't you answer the damn phone?" he asked.

"See, that's what I'm talking about right there. I'm busy and if I'm busy I don't have to answer my phone. I will call you back when I'm not busy!" I shouted.

Andre started pacing back and forth talking to himself.

"Look Andre, I gotta get my hair finished. Are you going to be ok?" I asked. I turned to reach for the door to go back inside.

"I'm Ok Katrina. Just pick up the phone when I call." He had a cold look in his eyes.

"Yea ok. My phone is on the charger. I didn't even see you calling. You're bugging out!" I told him.

Andre looked back and saw that there were mostly women clients and stylists in the shop. Everyone was staring through the windows looking at him being the young, overzealous, stereotypical boyfriend you hear about on the lifetime channel. He was being foolish, and he didn't even apologize for embarrassing me. I thought that would be a turning point for us, but it wasn't. We still fought quite often over his jealousy. It got so bad, I made a call. I called it quits. I had been with Andre for almost four years and breaking up with him was the hardest decision I had made in my life, but it needed to be done. He had become too much to deal with, and I didn't like the man he was growing into.

 I tried to get adjusted to being alone again. It was hard because I hadn't been alone in years. Ever since I met Andre, it was he and I. I missed him, but he hadn't called me, so I wasn't going to dare call him. I spent a while sulking in my misery, but decided it was time to start enjoying my senior year with or without him. I started dressing cuter and made some new friends. I had even become a part of the IT crowd, although deep down I never fit in with any of them. I started going to some of the football games, and it was at one of those games that this guy named Chris, who was a sophomore in college and an old associate of Andre's, confessed that he had feelings for me. Initially, I was not open to the idea of talking to anyone associated with Andre, but Chris told me that he and Andre weren't close, so it wouldn't be violating any man code for us to get to know each other. Chris got accepted into a college near home, so he came to the city every weekend and every holiday. We didn't have much chemistry, and he wasn't my type, but I still entertained him. I didn't have my type down to a science, but

I knew he wasn't it. After our second date, Chris tried to kiss me. I told him I was only interested in being friends. He took the letdown well but stayed persistent. He called me all the time and was a great distraction from my heartbreak. He introduced me to bike riding, and he and I would wake up on Saturdays and ride around Piedmont Park. Afterward, we would grab a bite to eat from The Pizza Shop. Chris and I got really close over the 2-month period that we chilled, and we started to catch a vibe. I stopped worrying about what Andre would think if he ever found out and just started focusing on enjoying my time with someone else. It wasn't long before word started getting out that I was hanging with Chris, and I would hear whispers that it made its way back to Andre.

Midway through his Junior year, Andre abruptly transferred out of Florida and enrolled in G Tech so he could be closer to home or however you want to spell *ME*. He and I still hadn't spoken when he moved back, but something in my gut told me it wouldn't be the last I'd heard from Andre Billups. I heard rumors that he had a new boo thang hanging on his arm. It stung but I was determined to let it be. I still cared for him, but if he was crazy enough to try living without me, I was going to make him stand on that.

One weekend, I was at Magic in Greenbriar. Magic was the theater all the high school kids hung out at. I had a bad feeling about going there with Chris out of fear we'd see one of Andre's friends. It was the premiere weekend for "Paid in Full", and it was all anyone could talk about. Chris convinced me if we did run into one of Andre's friends there wouldn't be anything to worry about. Just my luck, we hadn't been there 15 minutes when I spotted him. It was worse than I thought. Andre and some chick were hugged up near the game room. I was so hurt, but I was more concerned that he didn't see me and who I was with. I tried to go the other way with Chris, but before we could get out of view, Andre spotted us. "Katrina, what the hell are you doing here with Chris?" he shouted. Chris and I looked at each other, and I could tell he was scared. Chris told me I didn't have anything to worry about if we ran into one of Andre's friends, but we never discussed what would happen if we ran into Andre. Andre left his date standing there and started charging towards us. He greeted Chris by shoving him in the chest.

"You're supposed to be my boy and you're here with her."

"Her got a name!" I snapped at him.

"Katrina, you better stay out of this before you get fucked up too!" Andre screamed on me while pointing his finger at my forehead

Chris chimed in, "Too? Who you gon fuck up in the first place my G?" Physically Chris didn't stand a chance against Andre, but he still had his pride.

Andre walked closer to him. "Oh, you a tough guy now. My bad, I ain't seen you in a while." Andre stood over Chris in an intimidating stance. I felt bad for him, so I tried to grab Chris' arm and pull him away. "Come on Chris, let's just go. He ain't worth it." Andre snatched my hand away from him. Like the ref at a boxing match, he stood between Chris and I and refused to let us touch. "Oh, I'm not worth it? How do you say something like that to me Katrina? You got me messed up if you think you're leaving with this fool." Andre stood toe to toe with me, but his eyes were pleading. Pleading for me to choose him. I stuck to my guns because I knew Chris wasn't brave enough.

"I can do what I want Andre. You don't own me!" I tried to reach for Chris again, and Andre pushed him back with even more force this time.

"Not in front of me you can't. Try and grab this nigga hand again and see what happens." Andre was threatening me, but

I knew that meant he would take it out on Chris. He was so mad.

Andre's date walked over and made it clear that she was vexed that Andre was all up in Chris' and I's face while he was on his own date. She calmly asked him, "Andre take me home please." He pulled his wallet out, tried to hand her 40 bucks and said, "Take a cab." She walked around to face him. "I'm not taking a cab. You brought me here, you're going to take me home or do you want me to explain to my daddy why you are trying to send me home in a cab?" she asked him. I didn't like how she sized him up, but it wasn't my place to say anything, and she was right, Andre was being a jerk. She stood there waiting for him to make a move. He looked over at me. I turned away. I wasn't going to say anything, but I was waiting for him to respond to her. Deep down, I was hoping he'd make the right decision, so I didn't have to show out and reveal that I too was jealous as hell that he was there with another girl. Andre poked his chest out, "Look Deidre, my apologies, but I can't take you home tonight. Matter of fact, I ain't taking you home no more. We're done!" He looked at me as he spoke to her as if I was feeding him his lines. Deidre didn't like that and turned on me instead. "Oh, you showing out for some high school chick? Boy you so lame, I don't know why I even gave you the time. She's probably more your speed anyway."

I knew Deidra was undercutting me, but I figured Andre had embarrassed her enough, so I'd let her get her shit off, but I wasn't going to give her much more courtesy before I rocked her like a baby. "Deirdra take the $40 and go before I hurt your feelings." Andre told her. Woman or man, Andre didn't like anyone messing with me.

"You can't hurt my feelings boy. Look at me, do it look like I got feelings for you?" I couldn't believe she was what Andre had resorted to dating. She was nothing like me and although she was really pretty, she was stank. Not in the sense of the smell but the stank attitude, and usually Andre hated girls like that.

"Look Deidra, take this $40 out of my hand or you gon pick it up off the floor. It's up to you." Before Andre could countdown, she slapped him so hard the crowd reacted. I jerked almost hitting her out of reflex, but instead I let Andre get his Karma stamp. He still held the $40 firmly in his hand waiting on her to grab it. She smacked her teeth, grabbed the money, and finally left. A crowd started to gather around us. Andre grabbed my hand and led me outside. Chris reluctantly followed.

When we got outside, Chris tried to flip it. "Come on man we boys. We can't fight over a female." I couldn't believe that was his approach. He was the one that convinced me I wasn't violating because he and Andre weren't that cool. Now he wanted to cop pleas about them being boys. Andre knew it was bull and called him out on it. He shoved Chris to the ground, "Don't play with me! You know Katrina ain't just some female. You, your mama, and everybody at that school know she's off limits! So why the hell are you here with her? You ready to get your ass beat over my woman?" I looked over at Andre. "Your woman! Last I checked your woman just left in a cab. I ain't nobody out here woman." I tried to walk away from them both and Andre ran up behind me. "Katrina, I'm ready to stop playing. I'm telling you right here right now I want it to just be us. I don't care about that girl or Chris Punk ass. I love you and I know you love me so let's both stop this bullshit. I'm sorry for accusing you of cheating, but you know how I get when we're apart. I'm sorry. Do you forgive me?" It was hard to say no to Andre while looking in his eyes. They were Amber and I was slowly melting in the fire. I turned to look at Chris who couldn't even make eye contact with me out of fear. He stood there with his head down. The truth was, I didn't want anybody else but Andre. Even though he had proven to be temperamental, I liked that he was willing to fight for me. I wanted someone who no matter what would never let me go and Andre was him. I grabbed his hand so we could jet. We left Chris to be alone with his thoughts and forgot all about catching that movie.

Andre took me to one of our favorite spots instead, Cascade Skating Rink. I always loved seeing Andre on skates. He was so smooth. He could skate backwards, and he could dance. While all the girls would be in there sweating him, he always would slide right up on me to let it be known who he belonged to. Andre grabbed my hand and led me onto the floor. Outkast's, "I'm sorry Ms. Jackson" was playing. Andre and I caught a rhythm and started bouncing together. I smiled because I missed my baby. I could tell he missed me too and we were right where we should have been all along. The DJ started mixing in Zapp and Roger's "Computer Love." Andre and I started grinding together. I wasn't as good a skater as him, but he taught me what he could.

"Girl, I can tell by the way you're grinding on these skates, you're gonna feel so good when we finally do." he whispered in my ear. I melted inside and almost lost the feeling in my legs. Andre leaned in for a kiss, then we both went tumbling down. I looked into his eyes, took a deep breath, and quickly stood up. I always got nervous when we had moments like that. I went to turn my skates in, and Andre followed. When we got outside, he forced me to look at him.

"Katrina, why do you always do that? You act like just because we look into each other's soul we gon end up having sex. I'm allowed to look at my girl ain't I? Even if I'm lusting, it's the least you can let me do. I'm gonna marry you so I don't see why we're waiting anyway." he pouted. I leaned on his mom's car that he borrowed for the night. "Andre, I'm not waiting till marriage. I'm just waiting till I feel the time is right. I don't ever wanna regret my decision or the person that I make that decision with." Andre was a man, and he wasn't a virgin, so he didn't relate to my sentiment.

"I understand baby and there's no rush. I don't mind waiting. If I know when you are ready you wanna share that moment with me, I could wait forever Trina." Andre kissed my forehead, my nose, then my lips. It was so intimate, and something came over me in that moment that helped me make up my mind. "I'm ready now." I said, looking into his eyes so he knew exactly what I meant. He didn't ask any questions. Not even 5 seconds later, we were on MLK at the stoplight listening to Andre 3000 murder Lloyd's "I want you" remix.

"So where should we go?" Andre asked me. "Wherever you wanna go." I said. We laughed because Andre and I were near grown, yet so shy about finally going all the way in our relationship. "We can go to my house." he suggested.

"No! We can't go to your house. What if we get caught? I'm not fighting your mama tonight. You know how she is about you. Let's get a room." I insisted.

He turned his nose up.

"Katrina, I'm not taking you to a hotel room, not for our first time. Why not my bed, my house, so I can sleep with the memory forever. I can smell you when I miss you. Come on baby, what's more special than my house, my room, our bed?" he asked.

I couldn't argue with him. Andre had a point. If we did get a room, there would be nothing special about it, and strangers have sex in hotel rooms. Andre and I had history. There was no better place than his bed.

When we got to his house, he went in first to make sure the coast was clear. He came back out and told me to meet him at the back door. I snuck in through the back and went straight into Andre's room. He put on Jagged Edge's, "J.E Heartbreak" and I tried to relax, but I was sitting on pins and needles, mind running a thousand miles a minute. Andre suggested we just watch a movie, and if it happened, then it would happen.

He put on his favorite movie, "Belly." There was a sex scene, you know the one, and I felt myself getting hot all over. I started to feel Andre up and finally got the courage to seduce him for once instead of the other way around. He was enjoying every minute of it. I grabbed a condom off the nightstand and attempted to climb on top of him. I caved in as I tried to sit on it. He giggled and flipped me over on my back. I was so embarrassed. "Don't be embarrassed baby, it's supposed to be tight. I got you." Andre assured me. I believed everything he told me. We kissed passionately and I gave him the final piece to my puzzle. I didn't go home that night and I knew my mom was going to get in my ass for it, but it would all be worth it after the night I had.

Andre and I woke early the next morning. We wanted to be up before everyone else in the house so he could sneak and drive me home. Just as we got to the door to open it, Andre's mom came from the kitchen and asked, "Katrina, are you leaving before breakfast baby? After the night you had, you at least deserve breakfast?" She shoved Andre out the way. "Excuse his rude ass. Move boy!" She grabbed me and led me into her room. She went into her drawer and handed me a towel and washcloth. "How do you feel baby? Are you ok? Young boys don't know how to make a girl feel special the first time around, but I'm hoping my son was at least a gentleman, and I'm hoping y'all used protection?" she asked. "Yes ma'am we did, and Andre was a perfect gentleman." I said. "No matter what happens after this I want you to know my son loves you, and I know for a fact he never loved any other girl." she said.

She gave me permission to use her master bathroom to shower. Before she left, she said "You can wash last night off you, but a mother always knows. If I were you, I'd tell my mom the truth. She probably gon kick your ass, but if you're grown enough to have sex, you grown enough to deal with the consequences, and if an ass whooping is all you got coming, consider yourself lucky baby." Her and I laughed, and I figured it was her way of giving me her blessing.

After I showered, the three of us had breakfast. Andre's dad was home too, but he never engaged with anyone outside of his wife. He stayed in his mancave. He barely even talked to Andre. Andre's mom was grilling us and asking questions that no one wants their parents to ask them. "Katrina, are you on birth control?" Andre butted in before I could answer. "Ma, come on, that's weird. We'll talk about it later."

"Boy, how are you bold enough to sneak a girl in my house and stick your Ding-a-ling in her but you're too shy to talk about something that might end up saving your life?"

I jumped in because I thought I knew what she was getting at.

"Mrs. Billups, I don't have any STDs. I've never even had sex before last night, so Andre's life isn't in danger."

She chuckled, obviously being sarcastic.

"Katrina, you know the number one killer of people ain't STDs, it's stress. Stress from kids, life, and having to take on responsibility you are not ready for. I'm more scared for Andre to walk in here telling me he got a baby on the way and he ain't finished college yet vs. him telling me about his woody burning. One I can take him to the clinic for, the other I might end up taking care of. You see the difference baby?"

"Yes Ma'am." I said. It was the most Mrs. Billups had ever talked to me and I loved her brutal honesty.

"Ma, can we talk about this some other time?" Andre asked.

"This is the last thing I'm gonna say. If y'all wanna do grown folks' stuff, then I only ask that you be responsible when doing it. You wanna have sex, use a condom. You don't like condoms, get on birth control. If you wanna play house, go buy one." Mrs. Billups gave us a serious look and we both understood her point.

Andre cleared the table and I offered to wash the dishes. Mrs. Billups took the news better than I expected she would. The big test was going to be what my mom would say. I didn't know what she would beat my ass for first, not coming home or finding out why I hadn't come home.

When we pulled up at my house. Andre and I sat in the car for 30 minutes. He turned to me and said "I'm sorry for keeping you out late. I wish I could go in there and take your beatdown for you." We laughed and I started to get out of the car to face my fate. Before I walked up the porch, I leaned into him. "I love you Andre."

"I love you more Katrina." He pulled off, and I started to pray.

I didn't creep in the house because I knew my mom would be on the other side of the door waiting with a big stick. I swung the door open hoping to mistakenly catch her off guard and knock her out cold, but there was no one standing behind the door. I went and knocked on her room door and she didn't answer. The house was eerily quiet. I walked to the back and checked the kitchen. There was no one there either. I went to my room and flopped down on my bed. I smiled after I realized I had the house to myself. I was finally able to be alone and think about what I had done. I thought back to what Mrs. Billups said about how she knew Andre loved me and only me. I felt high. Andre always made me feel high. I was on a cloud that no one could knock me off. I sat up on the bed to turn the TV on and saw a note that I hadn't realized was there before. It was from my mom.

"Katrina,

Be back in a few days. Food is in the fridge. Curfew is at 8:00pm.

P.S Don't have that boy in my *damn* house!"

God was always on time. I hurried over to the house phone to call Andre and ask him to come back over. He was back in my driveway before I could hang up. When he walked in, we picked up where we left off. This time, in my bedroom.

Chapter 3 Are you still down

As time went on, Andre and I got stronger. We had disagreements here and there but nothing bad enough to call it quits. I thought we had put all the jealousy and distractions behind us until it was my turn to go off to college. I got a full scholarship into GSU and opted to major in Marketing. I always dreamt of being a lawyer, but I felt that my life would eventually get too demanding to spend the time needed in law school. I didn't even realize at 18 I was already making sacrifices for love.

Andre was trying to find his way and it took a toll on him. While I was excited about what was to come and busy thriving, he felt like he was burning out. He was a senior and didn't really have any career prospects. Instead of spending most of his time finding a job or apprenticeship, he spent it hovering over me.

My freshman year, I had a big class project where the professor put us in pairs. The assignment was to come up with a unique company and find a way to market it to the masses. I was paired with Malik, this fine brother that was focused and determined just like me. He and I were cool, and I respected him because he was a young black man fighting to overcome what society said he couldn't. We were in the library working on a strategy for our company. We decided to create a website where customers could design their own clothes. Instead of shopping for clothes that anyone could buy, you would instead build your own design, and we'd manufacture it for you. If other consumers like what you created, they'd have to get your permission to purchase the design, and we would give you a percentage of the profit made from the sale. Malik and I had a good working chemistry, and I knew we would ace the project and presentation. This day in particular, Malik wasn't his usual engaged self. It seemed something heavy was on his mind. I asked him what was wrong, and he confided in me that he and his girlfriend were arguing about him not having any time for her lately. She thought he was cheating, but the truth was he was working 2 jobs to pay for school, and he helped take care of his sick brother. Malik didn't have any time for himself let alone his girlfriend. He had so much on his plate, and I had a newfound respect for him after hearing his story. He wasn't even 21, but had to take care of an ailing brother, an elderly father, and work 2 jobs to support his family. It made me feel better to know I wasn't the only one going through personal problems. We took a 10-minute break so he could get his feelings out and vent. When it was all over, he took a deep breath, and I could tell it was just what he needed. Malik reached in for a friendly hug. Just my luck as we embraced, Andre was walking up the aisle.

He eyed Malik up and down before looking over at me. "See what I mean, you always moving funny. I thought you were supposed to be studying." There I was in the library with textbooks open on the table, yet Andre was insinuating I was there for something else. Malik picked up on the vibe and told me he'd give us a few minutes.

"You can leave bruh." Andre stepped in.

"She can tell me that herself bruh." Malik responded, looking right past Andre and directly at me. "You gonna be OK Katrina?" I liked that for once Andre was getting checked by another man. Malik was from Philly and Andre's tough guy persona didn't intimidate him. They were face to face and neither of them winched. I knew my man was crazy so it could go either way. I pulled Andre by his arm and tried pleading to Malik who was the more levelheaded of the two. "Malik, please walk away. I'll see you tomorrow." My voice cracked. I feared what would happen to my scholarship if anything went down in that library. What Andre was doing had little to do with Malik anyway. It was all about his busted-up ego. He didn't want to retreat in front of his woman, and I was hoping Malik would give him a pass on the strength of me. Finally, without saying a word, Malik winked at me and walked away.

Andre turned around to look at me and before he could say anything, I laid it to his ass. "Why do we have to keep going through this? You're insecure and that's a YOU problem. You at my school with this foolishness knowing the kind of trouble I could get in. You can't pay for my classes if I lose my scholarship. This macho shit is not going to keep me here. Get it together Andre or I'm done!" I grabbed my books, bookbag, and left him right there in the library. His jealousy was on track to ruin us again.

My prayers for Andre to ease up were answered during my junior year. Andre got the opportunity of a lifetime. He was offered a position at McNeil's, the best sports agency on the East Coast. He would have to travel a lot, but I was all for that. It would give us the time we needed apart and hopefully show him there was more to life than me. Most women would want their man to be all about them, but I felt space was the best thing for us at the time.

Just as I expected when Andre started working things got better. He still had his moments, but we were making progress. The time we spent apart taught Andre that he was going to have to trust me, or he'd lose his mind trying to keep up. To keep the flames burning, he sent a different floral arrangement twice a week. His mom and I would have Sunday dinner together and he'd have her make enough food for me to take a plate back to school. I tried inviting my mom to dinner with me a few times, but the only thing she hated more than Andre was the fact that his mom and I had gotten so close. My mom didn't want anything to do with the Billups family and it caused division between the two of us. Any time I would talk about Andre, my mom would change the subject or make me feel foolish for loving him. I enjoyed talking to Mrs. Billups because she was open to sharing advice with me. I never had a woman like her in my life. She was the complete opposite of my mom. Mr. Billups took advantage of her, but it never changed how she treated people. I wanted her and my mom to become cool, but it didn't work that way.

Mrs. Billups and I's relationship eventually came into that of a mother-in-law, daughter like connection. I confided in her the issues I had with Andre which was his jealousy and possessiveness. She confided in me that Andre's biggest fear was that I would one day realize how much more I deserved. I didn't understand that then because I felt I deserved him, and he was the best man for me. I told Mrs. Billups that I couldn't see myself with anyone else.

 She and I were out shopping for his 23rd birthday gift and she took me to the jewelry store. She had the jeweler pull out these beautiful Sapphire earrings. She asked me if I liked them because I would need something blue for my special day, hinting at the old tradition of something old, something new, something borrowed, something blue. She stood behind me as I admired the gems in my ear. The Jeweler offered to give us a moment. It was just me and Mrs. Billups in the store. She turned to face me.
"I'm glad my son chose you. I knew when he brought you home you were exactly what he needed. I want to tell you something about Andre that I think will help you in the long run. Growing up he used to be a playboy so it's hard for him to believe that girls like you exist. He tells me all the time, *Mama, Trina is too good to be true. She the type gon break my heart and I won't see it coming.* He fronts like he's the man, but girl you his kryptonite. I know he's jealous, insecure, and sometimes downright stupid when it comes to you, but be patient with him. He's still growing up. I'm only telling you this because I know Andre's your first love, and girl you gonna do all you can to hold on to

him, but don't lose yourself and never be scared to start over. I had to have a forgiving heart for Mr. Billups and baby you gonna need one for Andre too. In the end, your love story will make sense." She smiled and welcomed me to bury my tear-filled face in her shoulder. I didn't grasp the underlying meaning of what she shared, but it felt good for someone to root for us. I took her words to heart and held on to them. I knew she would play a vital role in Andre and I's future. Too bad God had other plans. Mrs. Billups passed away shortly after that.

When she passed, it hit Andre and I both like a brick to the face. We didn't know she was sick and didn't discover she had been battling breast cancer for 5 years until Andre's dad told him. When Andre found out what his mom had been dealing with, he exploded. It was the first time he put hands on his father. He knew that his dad mistreated his mother throughout the marriage but finding out that she was sick on top of it all set him off. He accused his dad of being responsible for her death because of his neglecting her. Around that same time, Andre battled a bout with depression. He never talked to me about it, and he coped by smoking a lot of weed, drinking, and hanging out in the clubs. I let him do him, because not only was I mourning as well, but I also needed to focus on finishing school.

During my Senior year at GSU, I found out there was truth in what Andre's mom had told me about men and their culpability lurking in the shadows. All the accusing Andre had done to me turned out to be his guilty conscience getting the best of him. Andre's dad sold the house, and I went over to help pack up Andre's room. I found letters in his nightstand from a girl who signed her name as "lil baby." She talked about how much she cared for him and how what they shared would be forever. She even referred to how good he felt which absolutely crushed me. She said he was the best thing that ever happened to her and I just couldn't understand that. I sat there and read them all trying to piece together who she was. She never signed her name, just "lil baby." So many thoughts ran through my head. Why did he still have the letters? Who was she? When did they hook up? The letters didn't have dates, so I tried analyzing how old the paper was to get an estimate of how long ago it was written. My stomach was in a knot. I felt like my best friend stabbed me in the back. Andre promised me that of all the things to worry about, him messing around with other women wouldn't be one of them. Based on the letters, he had done more than messed around. I thought about that girl Deirdre from back in the day that I caught him at the theater with. Could it have been her? Every woman who had gotten near him was a suspect.

I confronted Andre later that day and asked about the letters and who the mystery girl was. He claimed he didn't know. I wondered how many girls he had been with to not know who would be sending him love letters. He said it was probably some crazy stalker and he only kept the letters because he was trying to figure out who she was. My gut was telling me differently.

"How many times Andre?" I had to know.

"How many times what?" he asked.

"How many times did you sleep with her?"

 He paused for 5 seconds. "Katrina, it was years ago, and it was a mistake," he confessed. I still wanted to know who, what, when, where and how, but he said it was the past and refused to tell me. It upset me that he was protecting her identity when I figured she knew who I was. I always felt like she could be someone in plain sight or even worse, a friend. Every girl who took a second glance at me was in question. I would always think, *is that her*?

I started to struggle with my identity around that time. I should have been excited about graduating college and starting my new life, but I didn't know if I was coming or going. I felt like I didn't have my man secured, like I wasn't attractive or enough for him. I was questioning everything that I used to be sure of. Although Andre insisted he was young and dumb when that happened, it didn't make the pain any less excruciating. He was still a little young and dumb, so I was scared he'd make the same mistake again.

After the cheating scandal, Andre tried his best to make it up. He worked in town as much as possible, we went on dates every weekend, shopping, and we started going to church. I appreciated his effort, but there was a permanent internal scar that he couldn't heal with any gift in the world. Nonetheless, he tried, and he tried. I was such a young girl back then, I couldn't articulate that it wasn't gifts I needed but reassurance, and proof that he'd never betray me again. Not sure if that was even possible but I wanted him to try, every single day, even if I shut him out.

I ended up having to confide in my college roommate Alicia what was going on in my relationship. I didn't like putting people in my business, but after Mrs. Billups passed away, I didn't have anyone else to talk to. Alicia and I were close enough and she was the only person I did feel comfortable opening up to. Besides, I felt I owed her an explanation of why I was moping around. Alicia was from Florida and just like the sunshine state, she always had a way of looking at the brighter side of things. She told me she had been through the same situation in her most recent relationship. She could've fooled me because she didn't seem sad or anything. I asked what she did to get over it and was hoping she knew a secret formula that would just kill the pain. I found out there was no such thing.

"Katrina, some pain ain't meant to get over. Pain is just a point of reference. Sometimes it's a reminder of what not to do, and sometimes it's a reminder that you're doing everything right." Alicia didn't stop putting on her make up as she preached to me. She wasn't telling me what I wanted to hear but she had a point. The ghost of Andre's past would probably burden me the rest of my life.

"There is one thing you could do to make yourself feel better tonight, but it'll only be a temporary fix sis." Alicia stuck her tongue out and batted her lashes. It was what she did when she was about to invite me to trouble, and she had my attention. "So, what do you suggest?" I asked her. My roommate was wild, so I knew if nothing else she'd suggest something fun. "Well, there's a party going on tonight for the new line of Zeta Phi North and the brothers they got in are fine." she bragged.

"Nah, I'll pass. The last thing I need is a bunch of obnoxious frat brothers around me." I told her.

"Katrina, these brothers are different. This fraternity is new, and the brother who started it is something serious. He's not with all that rowdy, disrespectful, macho crap. He's all about business and smart as a whip. He's majoring in law, and it's only a matter of time before he takes over this entire city. You should come down with me and let your hair down." Alicia started doing the snake trying to get me to loosen up.

"I don't know Alicia. Andre would have a fit about me going to a frat party." I admitted.

"See that's your problem right there. Always living for what Andre wants. What about Katrina? No one says you have to hook up with anybody. We're just going to have a good time. Nothing more, nothing less." she said.

Alicia was right. I was always keeping Andre in mind when I moved around, but he damn sure didn't keep me in mind when he was cheating. I decided to go to the party after all. I threw my hair in a high ponytail and put on some popping red lipstick. I wore a pair of low-cut jeans that showed the dip in my waist and a cut off shirt that said, "K is for Katrina."

Alicia and I headed to the party 2 hours after it was scheduled to start. She said only women with nothing better to do showed up to parties on time. When we got there, it was more than I imagined. Fine ass men wall to wall, beautiful women everywhere, red cups all over the floor and that Atlanta music that turns any party out. YoungBloodZ, "Damn" was playing, and everyone was doing the A-town stomp. Alicia and I cut through the crowd and found a corner to post up. She went and got us some drinks from the punch bowl, while I protected our 2 square feet of floor space. It was 30 minutes into the party when I realized I hadn't thought a peep about Andre. Alicia may have been right. Getting out was just what I needed.

By drink 3, I was on the dance floor doing the laffy taffy. Alicia came over and tapped me on the shoulder and shouted over the music. "Trina, this is my boy I told you about. He started the fraternity and he's gonna be the next Johnny Cochran. This is Malik." I knew exactly who he was. "Malik! How have you been? Why didn't you tell me you were starting a fraternity? We worked on that marketing project together all that time and you didn't even mention it." I said, happy to see him. He reached in for a hug and he smelled so good I could've licked him.

"My bad Katrina. You know my headspace was crowded back then. It's good to see you. You got that possessive man up off you yet or did you have to sneak out tonight?" he asked.

"Oh, you got jokes huh. I could say the same for you Mr. I'm too busy for my girlfriend. Does she know you're here?" Malik stopped smiling when I asked that question. "She and I aren't together anymore. She doesn't understand my vision right now, and I can't focus on all the extra stuff. I got big plans for my life and I'm not losing myself in a relationship."

Malik was so confident in what he was saying. I wish I was set up that way, where my career took priority over my relationship. Instead, I always considered Andre before I made any life changing decisions. "Well, I'm gonna leave you two to it. I see my boo just got here and I'm trying to get my booty rubbed on." Alicia said walking away.

Malik and I stood there staring at each other. For the first time in my adult life, another man gave me the tingle. Nothing major, but I felt it, and I know he felt it too. He had grown since I last saw him. He had more muscles, and his beard was dark and full. The DJ got on the mic, "We gon slow it down for this next one." he said. He put on Lil Jon, Usher, and Ludacris, "Lovers and Friends." Malik asked me to dance. I took his hand in mine and we did a sexy two-step. I laid my head on his shoulder while he positioned both hands on the small of my back.

"Katrina, I miss having you around. You were one of the only females in my life that kept it real with me. Most of the chicks I know just agree with everything I say because they're scared of making me angry or they're not confident enough to challenge me. I've always liked that you had your own mind and never been scared to let ya boy know what's up." he said.

"You miss me huh? Could've fooled me the way you just disappeared after our freshman year was over." I tried keeping the mood light.

"Yea, I know, but I was going through a lot at the time with school, my girl, and my family." Malik explained.

"Speaking of which, how is your brother doing? Has anything improved?" I asked.

"Actually, my brother passed away back in March." Malik revealed.

"My God. I'm sorry to hear that. I know that's gotta be hard on you." I regretted asking the question.

"No, it's all good. Everything happens for a reason and he's in a better place now. No more suffering." Malik put on a brave front.

He pulled me closer to him. "Katrina, I got a confession. You know why I distanced myself from you freshman year?" He asked.

"No, why?" I always wondered why Malik and I got estranged suddenly.

"I started catching feelings for you. Your man knew it too. That's why he ran down on me." Malik said.

"What do you mean ran down on you?" I was confused because it was my first time hearing that story.

"It was him and another guy in a cutlass. They rolled up on me one day when I was leaving the gym. We got into it, he told me to stay away from you, I told him to make me. It was about to get out of hand, but then some guys I knew from school rolled up and they broke everything up. I knew then, a lot of trouble would come with me pursuing you, so I didn't. If he never rolled on me like that, I think you and I would have been as close as I wanted us to be." Malik confessed.

I stopped dancing so I could look into his eyes to see what he was really feeling. The eyes never lied. "What do you mean as close as you wanted us to be Malik?"

"Katrina you must be crazy not to know I was crushing on you back then."

"Well call me crazy Malik because I never knew."

"Well, your boyfriend knew. That's why he was on my head about you. I had just moved to Georgia and didn't want to make any enemies because I didn't have any family and friends. It's part of the reason I started my own fraternity. I wanted brothers, specifically from the North down here for school to feel like they had a support system." Malik shared.

I didn't want to leave Malik out there to be open alone but what could I say. I felt bad that my boyfriend had threatened him, and I knew the only person crazy enough to roll with Andre on a mission like that was Mont. Mont probably encouraged him because he was always ready to be in the mix of our mess.

"Malik, I didn't know he did that. I'm sorry." I wasn't responsible for Andre's stupidity, but I still felt the need to apologize for it.

"It's cool Katrina. Things happen. I'm over it now, but tell me something, is he still around or not?" Malik's deep voice sent vibrations through my body.

I wanted to deny my relationship status to avoid losing the bomb ass vibe Malik and I were on. If I did admit Andre was still in the picture, would it mess up the night? I wasn't trying to make Malik my man, but I was enjoying the ego boost and having the creator of Zeta Phi North show me all the attention. I didn't have to say anything. I guess I took too long to respond, so Malik knew what was up.

"It's all good lil mama. I'll see you next lifetime." Malik winked and kissed my hand. He tried to walk away but I went after him.

"Malik, wait. Andre is still in the picture, but tonight I don't wanna think about him. To be honest, I found out he wasn't who I thought he was, and I'm struggling with that. In the meantime, I just wanna do something that'll make me feel better." I was flirting with him and he knew it.

Malik smiled, showing off those pearly whites. "OK, so you're just looking for a little distraction or a big one?" He looked down and his smile was mischievous.

"I think you know exactly what I'm looking for." I said.

"Come on." Malik grabbed my hand and led me to the master bedroom. I looked back down the hallway and made eye contact with Alicia who was dancing with her boo. She mouthed to me, "Have fun Trinaaaaa." I knew what she was thinking because I was thinking the same damn thing. What's going to happen when we get to the room?

Malik walked in behind me. I heard him turn the lock on the door, but I didn't turn around to acknowledge it. I went over to sit on the bed while he grabbed a bottle of Grey Goose from the closet. He pulled out some shot glasses, then took his shirt off. "It's hot in here. Feel free to get comfortable. I won't bite, not this time." he said.

I was so damn nervous. Malik was sexy and smooth. I couldn't help but compare him to Andre. They both were tall, dark, and handsome. Malik had a bit cockier build than Andre and he definitely was twice as smooth. I wanted to push the limits, but I didn't want to go all the way. I was hoping he wouldn't ruin the night by pushing up on me too hard and just letting something beautiful happen organically. He asked if I wanted to play truth or dare. "What's the rules?" I asked.

"It's simple. You pick truth or dare, and if you're too scared to answer or do the dare you have to take a shot." Malik explained. Sounded innocent enough.

Malik kicked it off. "Ok Katrina, truth or dare."

"Dare! I ain't never scared." I bragged while Bone Crusher, "Never Scared" blasted in the background.

"Ok, I dare you to kiss me on my chest." Malik made his right peck jump. *Damn,* I thought to myself. He didn't waste any time getting to the good stuff. Little did he know, I was down for a little touching. I scooted over to him and not only kissed but licked and caressed his nipple.

"Damn girl you tryna get it crackin. Ok your turn." he said.

"Ok Malik, truth or dare."

"Dare." he answered quickly.

"I dare you to run around the house in just your boxers." I knew he wouldn't do it and was hoping I could make him take a shot instead. Malik poured a double shot and gulped it down.

"Scary ass." I was just teasing him.

"I ain't scared, I just don't wanna leave this room right now," he said. His Philly accent turned my insides to lava. After a few more rounds, Malik and I were both buzzed. It was his turn again. "Truth or dare Malik?"

"Truth." It was the first time all night that he chose truth, so I wanted to make it good.

"Tell me the truth about something you've lied to everyone else about." I challenged him. Malik got quiet and his face was all serious.

"I have a secret that I've never told anyone, but I don't know if you can handle it," he said.

"You can tell me anything Malik. I won't say nothing. I promise."

"Katrina, I'm serious. If you tell anyone, it could ruin me, and shit will never be the same."

"Well, if it's that deep you don't have to tell me. It's just a game anyway." I didn't want him telling me anything he wasn't comfortable sharing.

"No, it's not just a game anymore. Honestly, I've been needing to get this off my chest, but I can't trust anyone to share it with." Malik sat up on the bed.

"What's up Malik, just say it," I urged him.

"Remember when I told you my brother was sick and I had to help take care of him?" he asked.

"Yea I remember that."

"My sophomore year he took a turn for the worst. My family was telling me I would have to quit school because he needed full time care and his insurance wouldn't pay for it. I couldn't afford it either, even with working 2 jobs. My grades dropped, I was about to lose my financial aid, and I didn't know what to do. Before my brother got really sick, he took out an insurance policy on himself that was worth $100,000 and he made me the beneficiary. I talked to him about it and he and I both agreed that him staying here would be too painful to bear. I mean he couldn't walk, couldn't keep his food down, he was losing his bowels on himself. My brother didn't want to live like that." Malik stared at the ceiling as he spoke.

I could only assume he was about to incriminate himself and for someone majoring in law, he knew better.

"Malik, I think you should stop. Maybe I shouldn't know this. Some things you should take to your grave." I tried to warn him.

"Katrina you don't understand. This has been eating me up. I need to tell someone." Malik started crying. I knew part of it was the liquor but drinking only pushes out what's on the tip of the tongue already.

"Dont finish what you're about to say Malik." I wanted him to stop.

"I gotta get it out Katrina. My brother asked me to do a mercy killing and he suggested I use the insurance money to pay for school. I didn't want to do it, but he said if I didn't, he would kill himself and that would forfeit the insurance money. I agreed to do what he wanted, but I can't help but feel guilty about it. Sometimes, I wish it was me instead of him." Malik put his head in his hands.

I was astounded. I couldn't believe Malik killed his brother, let alone confided in me about it. As crazy as the story was, I knew I would never tell anyone his secret. I still wish he hadn't told me. I held Malik and wiped his tears. I told him everything would be ok. The party ended, but Malik and I sat there in silence until the sun came up. It was a special moment between the 2 of us and it was unspoken that it would never be shared with anyone else.

The next morning, he walked me back to my dorm. "Thanks for everything Katrina. You have no idea what this means to me. If you ever need a lawyer just know I got you, and it's on me."

"I'm gonna hold you to that Malik."

"I'm serious Katrina. I got you for life. Take care of yourself." He leaned in and kissed me on the cheek. I watched him head off, then I headed upstairs.

When I went in the room, Alicia was sitting on the bed giving me the, *I know you got some cutty last night* look.

"So, have you been thinking about Andre?" she asked

"Not a peep." I said.

"Cool." she smiled. We dapped it up, and she didn't pressure me for details. Alicia asked if I wanted to go to breakfast, but I was tired. I told her I'd catch her next time. When she left, I pulled my phone out and saw that I had 50 missed calls. I already knew who it was but didn't feel like answering to him. I still had Malik on my mind for more reasons than one. I put some music on and hopped in the shower. I stayed in longer than usual while Destiny's Child, "Temptation" played on repeat. I knew I had to call Andre back, but wasn't looking forward to it. When I got out, I picked my dirty clothes up and could smell remnants of Malik. I still didn't know how to process what happened between us. My professor in African American studies once told me that if a black man confides in you, that's him baring his soul, and there's no greater gift he could offer.

I pulled my phone out and made the call I had been dreading. I hated keeping secrets from Andre, so I planned on telling him about my night. I would leave out the details like me kissing Malik's chest or even seeing him at the party, but I would admit to going to a frat party.

"Hello." Andre's voice was calm but agitated.

"What's up Andre?"

"What's up baby where you been? Are you ok? I was worried."

He wasn't really worried, but he knew he better not come at me wrong because he was already on thin ice. "I'm ok. I just went out to clear my head last night and the time got away from me." I said.

"Went out. Where, with who?" he asked frantically as if I went out against my will.

"Calm down Andre. I just went to a frat party with Alicia."

"Frat party!" he shouted.

"Boy if you don't calm your ass down!" I warned him.

"Ok, you're right. It's just you're not usually into those, so I'm surprised you went is all."

"You know what Andre, I'm still learning what it is I'm into. Things I thought I was sure of, I'm not so sure of now." I told him.

"Baby, I know you're still mad at me, but Katrina I promise that was a long time ago and it was a mistake. Don't let that girl ruin what we have now." Andre's emotional immaturity was showing, and I was starting to take exception to him for it.

"No Andre, that girl didn't ruin anything. You did!" I reminded him.

"Listen baby, I don't want to fight. I'm trying to do whatever I have to do to make this right. I'm not even the same man I was back then. The man I am today wants to be with you forever. No more mistakes Trina."

"I don't know Andre, but right now I'm tired so I'm gonna get some rest." Andre wanted me to reassure him, and I couldn't do that, or maybe I was being stubborn because he never did it for me. I ended the call and went to take a nap.

It was a couple of months before I let Andre touch me again. One evening, after I was working late in the library Andre asked me to come over. When I got there, he had a candlelit dinner set up in his little one-bedroom apartment. He cooked Spaghetti, and he and I spoke about our dreams for the future. Andre asked if I could see a future with him, and despite his mistakes from the past, I couldn't see a future without him.

I told Andre I wanted him around for as long as he wanted to be, but I couldn't play second to anyone ever. Andre swore it would never happen again. After that, he got on one knee and popped the question.

"Katrina baby, will you marry me?"

He pulled out the ring and my eyes could've popped out of my head. I started shaking, and it felt like I was about to have a panic attack. Andre kept my hand in his, and it kept me from getting over-anxious. He asked again, "Katrina baby, will you be my forever?"

I answered it without a second thought. "YES!" Andre put the ring on my hand, and I didn't weigh the good and the bad. I didn't think about his cheating. I didn't think about what it meant for us to make such a big commitment at such a young age. I only thought about my feelings at that moment. I thought about all the love I felt over me, and I wanted the feeling to last forever. I also felt like what better way to prove I'm number one in his life than to have his last name.

I was 21 then, and Andre was 24. We had been together 7 years and each day brought a new testament to the love story we were creating. We had more than a few bumps in the road, but we dealt with it as best we could being a young black couple in love with not a healthy relationship in sight to learn from. Andre's father wasn't the pillar of a man and never taught Andre how to properly love a woman. My family was no better. No one was married, my dad wasn't in the picture, and my mom had a horrible relationship history. To top it all off she stopped talking to me. When I told her Andre cheated on me, she ridiculed me for being too weak to leave instead of supporting my decision to stay. She accused me of being *dick whipped* and called me names no mother should ever call her daughter. My mom had always had a vicious tongue, but I couldn't forgive her for kicking me while I was down. I just wanted her support, and she couldn't understand that. She says I let Andre come between us, but I say she chose hatred over love and grudges over forgiveness. In my eyes it was her in the way, not Andre.

After Andre and I's engagement, I agreed to let bygones be bygones. I wanted us to start fresh, so I put the cheating behind us and agreed not to bring it up anymore.

When I graduated, I landed a great job at a marketing firm that I previously interned at. Andre had settled into his career as a Sports Agent. He was great at what he did, and his pay was starting to reflect that. When he started bringing in the big bucks, we planned the wedding. He told me to spare no expense and he didn't have to tell me twice. We rented out an event space and Andre and I invited all our college friends, work colleagues, and people we had met over the years. The day truly was beautiful and any doubt I had was eased on my wedding day. Andre and I were connected at the soul and I was honored to take his last name. Neither of us had family at the wedding, but we did not let it ruin the meaning behind the day. Our family would be who we made it to be going forward.

After the wedding, it was moving time. We were on the hunt and we had been to house after house, condo after condo, and nothing was standing out. The very last house we went to see was a 4-bedroom, 4-bathroom, Craftsman style home. I fell in love with it the moment I walked on the porch. It was a new build with marble countertops and dark hardwood floors. It was something I could only dream of. I turned to Andre and mouthed, "This is the one." We hadn't even made it up the stairs. He smiled and held the keys out. I ran and jumped into his arms and felt like the luckiest woman alive. I was able to decorate how I wanted and really took my time to customize everything about my home down to the numbers on the house. It took more than 2 years to get everything exactly how I wanted it, but it all came together. I even had my dream car thanks to Andre. Anything I asked for was at my fingertips. From the outside looking in, I was living the life that women envied. I often asked myself if I had left him early on because of his indiscretions, would I have ended up with someone who was worse off or better. Most of the women I knew were having their own issues in marriage. If their husband wasn't a cheater, he couldn't find a job, or he struggled with addiction, but it was always something. I learned that with every man there is a flaw and with some men there are more flaws than one. Andre was the lesser of evils in the world or at least that's what I told myself. I found comfort in knowing that the bad in him was all a part of the past.

After we surpassed a decade, we were super locked in. It was way too late for either of us to leave. We had invested so much into the relationship. I was head over heels in love. Our marriage was unbridled, but it was us. A beautiful painting and we added brighter colors every day. I was about 24 at the time and still finding myself as was Andre at 27. Marrying young is a beautiful thing but staying married while going through growing pains was a constant battle. We were still growing in life as we tried growing together, so it caused a lot of head butting. Most of the time the arguments were silly, and we fought because we both were stubborn. I had my mood swings and Andre had his own personality issues. As we learned how to deal with the growing pains of life it brought us closer together.

I didn't have a perfect marriage, but it was the thing I cherished most. My mom may say I settled, but I made a choice. She couldn't make sense of it but show me a relationship that makes sense all the time and I'll show you a couple putting on a good front. I did find myself doing some senseless things for Andre over the years, but I never questioned why because I knew why. I loved that man. He loved me too, but he was flawed. I didn't give up on him because I understood when we got married that he and I both were a work in progress. I married him anyway. I married Andre Potential Billups and hoped one day to get a return on my investment. I accepted my consequence either way and was willing to live with it.

I was younger than Andre but more mature by a long shot. I was able to deal with guys hitting on me all the time without taking the bait. I secured the Senior Marketing Specialist position and I worked with powerful men every day. You haven't seen anything until you've had a rich, obnoxious man hit on you. Something about successful women turns them on. I've had men offer ridiculous amounts of money just for a night with me or for me to run away with them. I never even thought about taking the money. The love I had for Andre wouldn't allow me to even consider it. There wasn't any man that could hold a token to him and no amount of money that could make me betray him. I always felt like when you're truly in love with a person, nothing in the world could make you intentionally hurt them. I knew me being with another man would hurt Andre, so I didn't do it. I never wanted to see my man broken, on his knees, crying out to me because of something I did to hurt him. Andre didn't share my logic. He believed as a woman, I was made to endure certain heartache. He would even say, "Katrina, I don't know what I would do if you were as weak as me." He took advantage of the very thing he admired about me, my strength.

I had to check Andre's ego more than a few times. Him working around athletes all the time also meant he worked around a lot of groupies. Andre's buddies knew he was married, but that never stopped them from trying to tempt him into having a little fun, as they would call it. Andre tried to convince me that a little flirting was good for business but insisted he knew not to cross any boundaries.

No matter how much I loved Andre, that chip on my shoulder would pop up occasionally. I still held a grudge because Andre never told me who the girl was he messed around with. We could be watching a movie about a cheating husband and he and I would get into a fight about it later. We could be out, and I would feel like he's looking at a woman because he's sleeping with her. I'd have an attitude for the rest of the day. Crazy how a situation could haunt you for a lifetime. Sometimes, I would be so lost in thought, I wouldn't realize he was in the room with me. Andre tried his best to convince me that he had changed, but for me forgiveness didn't mean forgetting.

Chapter 4- Try Again

Ever since I was a little girl, I've always wanted to be a mom. When Andre and I were confident enough in our careers and bank accounts it was time to make that dream come true. We had a lot of fun trying to make a baby. We brought books and watched documentaries on what positions to try in order to get the gender you wanted. I wanted a girl because I felt like older sisters were more mature than older brothers and she would be a good way to start the Billups legacy. Andre wanted a boy because he felt like he could protect the younger siblings. All in all, we really wanted a healthy baby, and it wouldn't be a disappointment if it were a boy or a girl.

After 6 months of trying, we still could not get pregnant. I was sure to monitor my ovulation days, and we would have sex twice then. I hadn't been told of any infertility issues at my yearly checkups, but nonetheless I was worried. Most of my friends from college and work colleagues my age were having kids and I was on the outside looking in. I didn't want to admit to myself what I had been thinking, but eventually I came to grips with the fact that maybe I had some issues I didn't know about.

I didn't tell Andre when I scheduled the doctor's appointment because I was ashamed. I felt like part of my responsibility as a woman was to bear children and if I couldn't then what? Looking back, I treated myself and my body so unfair based on a dumb ass outdated stereotype. I even went to a specialist because I needed them to do a thorough examination. They pulled blood, urine, and even swabbed my vagina. I was in my mid twenties, and there was no reason I could think of that would prevent me from conceiving. I prayed their answer would give me clarity and a solution. When the results came back, they called me to come back into the office, so I knew it was bad. Dr. Semaj explained to me that I had 3 large uterine fibroids, which would make it extremely hard for me to have a baby. I panicked thinking it was something I had been doing wrong with my body or even worse something Andre had caused. The doctor explained it's affected by hormones. As if finding out I had fibroids wasn't enough, Dr. Semaj also told me that I was in fact pregnant. She said it would be a high-risk pregnancy and I would possibly need surgery to save the baby if the baby could be saved at all. I was 16 weeks and had no idea. I even still had the flow.

When I got home, I had to tell Andre about my visit, and I knew he would be upset that I went to do something so life changing on my own. I cooked his favorite dish hoping to soften the blow.

"Baby, do you like the chicken?" I asked while Andre ate like it was his last meal.

"Baby one thing about it, you ain't never been nothing to play with on this fried chicken." he said with his mouth full.

"Well, I have to tell you something. I went to my doctor today." Andre stopped eating and I really wish he hadn't because now I had his undivided attention and that meant he would be able to process every word I said. "What's up baby? Is everything ok? Why did you go to the doctor and why are you telling me after the fact?" he asked. I told Andre why I didn't tell him about the visit beforehand and what transpired while I was there. He and I both went through a series of emotions, but we were happy that we were closer to the one thing we felt we needed to feel complete.

I scheduled another doctor's appointment for the following day to get an ultrasound and see what we needed to do to make sure our baby would be ok. This time, Andre was right by my side. He held my hand tight, and I could tell he was excited and nervous. Dr. Semaj came back into the room with a defeated look on her face. My husband and I tensed up as if we were bracing for impact. I remember hearing the doctor say we couldn't save the baby because a fibroid had ruptured, and I had to go in for emergency surgery if I didn't want to die.

I woke up 2 days later in the recovery room surrounded by Nurses. I looked for the first person I wanted to see, and he wasn't there. I asked one of the Nurses where my husband was, and she rubbed my hand and said "These situations can be hard on fathers. He should be back soon." I didn't know what the hell she was talking about, but it didn't sound good. I looked around for my purse so I could get my phone to call him. Before I could, Andre came stumbling in with flowers and chocolate. He reeked of alcohol and could barely walk.

"Hey baby. You awake, I missed you." he said, falling across the bed at my feet.

"Ok sir, let us help you get in the bed." The nurse from earlier said. There was a bed on the other side of the room that she and a male nurse helped Andre get into. He laid back and closed his eyes immediately. The nurse came over to sit my flowers on the table next to the bed. "Like I said Mrs. Billups, these things are hard on both parents. Moms and dads cope in different ways." She tucked me in. "You'll be discharged after 5. I'm Nurse Nia if you need anything." She cleared the room and closed the door to leave Andre and I alone. Andre was snoring as I lay in my bed fighting tears. I couldn't believe he left me and came back drunk. I was going to let him rest, but I had so many questions for him.

When Andre woke up, I asked him where he had gone. He told me I needed to focus on getting better and not starting fights. I had only asked him where he'd been, and he accused me of starting a fight. I knew from experience that meant he had something to hide. He was right, I needed to focus on getting better, but I also didn't need to be stressing about what my man was doing to cope with our tragedy.

When we checked out that day, Andre and I both left a piece of ourselves in the hospital with our angel baby. We didn't talk on the ride home and when we got there he left shortly after. I had never lost a child before, but I imagined that the parents would come together to help one another get through it. That's not what happened with Andre and me. He distanced himself from me, and I let go because I didn't have any fight left in me after what I had just gone through.

We hadn't recovered from the first loss, but Andre and I were already trying again. As soon as the doctor cleared me, it was on. I tried again and again, and I lost baby after baby. Once, I made it to 6 months with what seemed to be a healthy baby boy. I felt blessed. Andre stopped drinking and even started going to Lamaze classes with me. We decorated the room beautifully. We chose Gray and Blue for the colors. A cherrywood crib and rocking chair to match. I would go in there sometimes and sit in the rocking chair for hours anticipating what many of my future nights would be like.

March 17th, I was at home sleeping when I woke up with extreme cramps. By that time, I was so familiar with the feeling of miscarriage, I knew something was wrong. I called Dr. Semaj and she agreed to meet us at the hospital. When we got there the doctor told me I was too far dilated, and we would need to deliver the baby immediately. I wasn't even able to get an epidural.

Andre Billups Jr. who we would call AJ for short was born fighting. My body felt like I had been hit by a Mack truck, but it was all worth it seeing my baby boy. I couldn't hold him because they had to immediately take him to the NICU. He was hooked up to all types of machines. Big Andre was freaking out asking if it all was necessary. The doctors explained that our baby needed help breathing because his lungs weren't fully developed. The physical pain my body felt didn't compare to what I felt emotionally watching my baby suffer. Wondering how he could be feeling with all the machines and tubes running through his tiny little body. I started hating myself for wanting a baby so bad I would risk bringing one into the world that would have to endure such pain. I asked myself what type of mother would do such a thing. I couldn't express those emotions to my husband because he had checked out on me. The hospital gave me my discharge papers 4 days after I gave birth to AJ, but I never left. There was no way I was taking my eyes off of him. The nurses and I had become well acquainted, especially Nurse Nia and I. She would always sneak me in even after visiting hours. She would break the rules and let me sleep there so I appreciated her.

After 2 weeks, I was finally able to hold my baby on my bare chest. I could cry thinking about it now. It was the purest feeling. Andre was scared to hold AJ because he thought he would hurt him. I would never be scared to hold my baby, but Andre was. Sometimes he wouldn't even stay at the hospital. He would bring my bag and toiletries, stay for an hour, then leave. I never left. Not since AJ was born. I washed up in the hospital bathroom and I ate in the cafeteria. I slept where I could. I stayed because I wanted to spend every moment with my son.

Like the faint smell of rain before the storm, I could sense that my time with AJ was limited, but I never prepared for it to end. 21 days after AJ was born, he passed away. I thought about checking myself into a mental institution. You always hear people say I'm going crazy, but you have no fucking idea what going crazy feels like until you lose a child. In my mind, I was failing at everything that mattered. I was failing as a wife and a woman. All that happened had taken a toll on my body and the doctor told me if I got pregnant again, I'd likely die or do permanent damage to myself. I wasn't even

30 when my dreams of being a mother had come to an
end.

Andre again distanced himself and coped by doing whatever
he did. I started turning a blind eye to things because I was
coping in my own way and fighting with my husband would
have made it worse for me. He and I both had become 2
independent entities living under one roof. I told myself
when I was able to get over losing my babies, then I'd try and
get my husband back.

Chapter 5 Hurricane

On Andre's 35th birthday I planned him a surprise vacation to NY. I took off work on a Friday so we could fly out that afternoon and catch Michael Baisden's, "Men cry in the dark" live in Harlem. Andre had been wanting to see the play, and I knew he would be so excited to catch it in his favorite city. He loved the food, the arts, the scenery, and something about the hustle and bustle inspired him. I loved the city too and was so excited for us to get away. We both had been working hard and hadn't had much alone time together. The past few years were the rockiest in our relationship. The trip was to celebrate him and to set off the fireworks in our marriage again.

I heard the front door open and went to get in position. I hid in our master bathroom because the first thing Andre did when he got home was drop his kids off at the pool. I couldn't wait to jump out with the plane tickets in my hand and hopefully make his day.

I could hear him come into the bedroom talking loudly on the phone with someone. He was pleading with them. "I'm sorry I've been busy. You know I wouldn't avoid you. I know you want me to tell her, but I need more time." Of course, I was all ears, curious to know what it was Andre needed more time for.

"My birthday is this weekend, and I don't wanna ruin anything. I think she's planning something nice. Just let me handle my situation. I love you, but Katrina and I got over 15 years in this. I still wanna do things the right way because I don't wanna break her heart again. I promise I'm going to do it, but I need more time. You gotta trust me." he said. I was infuriated listening to him refer to me as a "situation." I peeked through the crack in the door to see Andre slowly pacing the floor while he spoke. He rubbed his hand over his head like most men did when they felt overwhelmed.

"Why don't you come over again? This time I'll cook us some breakfast and maybe we can watch that movie you told me about. I'll set something up soon baby." He ended the call after, and even though I couldn't hear what the other person was saying, it was clear that he was seeing someone else. From the sound of it, his side piece wanted him to tell me about her. I was more concerned with why the hell she wanted to be known. There was only one reason side chicks would blow their cover, and that was for a promotion to be the main chick.

I sat in the bathroom quietly rocking back and forth on the edge of the tub, contemplating what approach to take. It wouldn't be his first time betraying me, but this sounded serious. I still had the tickets in my hand which I had gripped so tightly they were nearly balled up. In my head were the whispers of him repeating that he loved her and admitting to having her in my home. I clenched my teeth and threw the tickets down on the bathroom floor. When I couldn't stand it anymore, I burst out of the bathroom. Andre looked like he had seen a ghost. "Hey baby." he said nervously. I didn't say a word. I walked up and slapped the piss out of him. I never put my hands on my husband, but the nice, non-confrontational girl that he had known long ago was dead. Andre played me for the last time. I was tired of him taking advantage. "What the hell you slap me for?" he shouted while holding his face.

"You ain't gonna be satisfied until I snap and kill your ass. All these years and you still fucking me over like this?" It was a rhetorical question, but I looked at him like I was waiting on an answer.

He had a stupid look on his face. The same one he had when he got caught before.

He asked me again. "Katrina, what are you talking about? Don't come in here slapping me and don't even tell me why I'm being slapped.

I slapped him again. "Stop playing with me Andre! You know what you did. I heard the whole story about you and your little bitch. You're sorry you haven't made time for her right?" I stood there waiting for him to try and lie his way out of it. Andre's jaw was in the basement, eyes wide open, and there was nothing he could say. He reached out to touch me, but instead I backed away and tossed the first thing I could find at his head. He ducked and the remote crashed into the wall. He tried to apologize,

"I'm sorry Katrina. I messed up baby. It's not what you think, but I screwed up and I'm sorry. I didn't want you to find out like this. I don't know what else to say, but please give me a chance to make this right." Andre sat on the bed and put his face in his hands. There really wasn't anything to say. I cried, I yelled, I warned him not to do this again, and I thought the last time Andre cheated would be the last time Andre cheated. Part of me wanted to ask what I did wrong, if he lost his attraction to me or if there was anything I could do to make it right, but I refused to be that woman. The one blaming herself for a no-good ass man's evil ways. The one always trying to change into the woman he needs only to get left for the woman he wants. I couldn't stoop lower than I had already done with him.

  Andre had so much to lose but clearly the other woman was worth it. He bought her into our home and had developed an entire relationship with her outside of his marriage. Andre had never fully gained my trust back from the first time I caught him cheating, but I still couldn't foresee him doing me that dirty.

 I always hear people say, once a cheater always a cheater, but I wanted to believe my husband was an exception to the rule. I wished he could feel what I felt, hurt like I hurt. If I had lived like he was living, I would've been a single woman a long time ago. There was no way to put my shoes on his feet, but I was damn sure going to try.

"Andre, how would you like it if I went out and slept with other men? Look at me, you know I can do it." I spun around to show off the figure that Katrina the grown woman had blossomed into. Slim waist, pretty face, nice bump in the back and hips that would make Shakira wave the red flag. I treated my body like a temple and went to the gym 4 days a week to keep it intact. My body was in the best shape it had ever been in. I could see Andre's eye's changing colors. He was getting upset. I wanted to dig the knife deeper, so I walked over to my purse and grabbed my phone. "You know what Andre, I'm gon set me up some new dick tonight since you think you're the only one that can have some fun around here. I actually met someone last week and I think I'll take him up on his offer for dinner." I dialed the number to the restaurant up the street and held the phone to my ear. I prayed that Puerto Rican Papi with the sexy accent picked up because he always flirted with me. Andre stared at me waiting for me to hang up the phone, but little did he know I didn't have any plans on it. Papi loved talking to me and we talked about everything from his family to him recently getting his citizenship. Papi had a beautiful wife named Maria that also worked at the restaurant with him. Her, Papi, and I would laugh and share stories when I went in for my weekly slice on Thursday nights. Papi was a flirt, but it was very innocent. He only had eyes for Maria. We would speak Spanglish to each other, and Maria would just crack up laughing at us. I even helped them market their business for free when they first came to our neighborhood. Papi tried to offer me free pizza for life for the favor, but I told him the favor was him giving the community somewhere delicious to eat.

The other line was finally answered and immediately I could tell it was Papi. I put on my sexy accent and flirted as much as I could without being inappropriate. I didn't want to disrespect Papi or Maria. I asked him in Spanish about his specials and giggled as he read them to me.

Papi and I didn't get far before Andre had snatched the phone from my ear and cursed Papi out. He ended the call, and I snatched my phone back. I tried to call the restaurant again and apologize to Papi, but Andre walked up in my face and said, "I dare you." His ego had him acting like a typical man who could dish it out but couldn't take it. He couldn't even handle me talking to other men let alone sleeping with them. He was in my face, but I knew he wouldn't hit me, I mean he hadn't before. I would tell Andre, "If you put your hands on me, I'll be the last woman you see." That wasn't a threat and Andre knew it. We had gotten in heated arguments before and he would threaten me, but I'd always say, "you sealing your fate nigga not mine!" I ignored his threat and called his bluff. I dialed the number anyway. We were now chest to chest as the other line rang.

"If he picks up, I'm fucking you up Katrina!" Andre said, breathing on my neck.

"That's the only thing you've been good at lately, fucking things up." I replied, taunting him.

The look in his eyes was something serious, but I wasn't scared. He had done the worst to me 10 times over and he couldn't hurt me no more than he already had. Andre was standing toe to toe with a woman who had nothing to lose, and that was my advantage.

The phone rang and Andre got closer and closer to my ear to hear. When his face touched mine, I mushed him off me.

"Get out of my face Andre!" I ended the call and he felt like he won so he boasted. "No, call Papi back and we are going to be moving furniture around this motherfucka tonight! Katrina, don't disrespect me as a man. I'm still your husband." he said boldly.

"As a man?!?! What the hell are you talking about? Ain't no man standing in front of me. Men don't disrespect their families over and over a-fuckin-gain!" I snapped at him. He didn't deserve respect from me. He didn't show me any. He didn't even have rules for how he cheated. Most men would at least make the house off limits, but Andre didn't even try and keep that as sacred ground. I put my phone in my pocket and realized it was silly dragging Papi into it in the first place. Besides, I didn't need him to fuck with Andre. I could do that myself.

"Andre, I'm trying to spare your pride. Now back the fuck off me or we going to have to take this shit all the way, and you know you not ready for me to take this shit all the way, you never have been." I warned him. He stood his ground. "Katrina, I ain't backing off shit. Watch your mouth before you say something you regret, and I mess you up in here."

Andre had tried the fuck out of me. I'm a Taurus, you can't try a Taurus, and you damn sure don't look a bull in the eyes during a standoff. I wasn't giving in so there was only one way to go from there, up in flames! I told him I was done! "Andre, I'm out. I'm going to find some new dick to replace your weak ass. I'm going to find a man who loves and appreciates me. By the time you realize what you had, I'll be gone forever. You, that whore, and whoever else you got playing part in your circus can enjoy being clowns because I'm clocking out." I went to walk away and just like the other times when we'd have a heated argument, he grabbed me, looked into my eyes, and tried to use that dick as his secret weapon, but I wasn't feeling that. I was emotionally exhausted and wanted out. Instead of letting him trick me into having angry sex and forgetting about his screw up, I grabbed my keys and left the house to get away for a few days. I told myself when I got married it would be forever, but I was ready to throw in the towel.

I took a ride around the city and tried to calm down. The quiet storm didn't make it any better because they kept playing songs that reminded me of him. First it was "We belong together" by Mariah Carey, then "Get it Together" by 702, followed by "Let's stay together" by Lyfe Jennings. I changed the station, but it was Monica's, "Why I love you so much." I was so confused. I had fallen in love so long ago, and I didn't even know how to live without Andre. It was easy to watch movies about other women going through similar situations and criticize them for staying, but looking at my own life, I was no different. If I had to name my relationship after a movie it would've been "Why do fools fall in love" because that's what I felt like, a fool.

I stopped at the Marriott downtown and tried to get a room, then realized I left my purse at the house. I was defeated realizing I had no choice but to go back home. I couldn't call my Mom because she would judge me and give a whole bunch of I told you so's. I didn't talk to her anyway, so she probably wouldn't answer. As unsupportive as she had been of my relationship, she was who I wanted to call but I knew I couldn't. I sat in the parking lot of the hotel thinking of alternatives, but I knew calling someone and asking for help would require me giving them a front row ticket to my shit show and I wasn't ready to reveal what was behind the curtain.

I headed back home and let the waterworks flow. You'd think when a person betrayed you the way my husband betrayed me, the love you have for them would turn off just like that, but it wasn't that way for me. I hated Andre, but I still wanted him, furthermore I didn't want anyone else to have him.

When I pulled up the weight of the world resumed its position on my shoulders. I used to feel butterflies rolling into my driveway knowing my husband was inside waiting for me with God knows what type of gift, or my favorite, when he'd be naked at the top of the steps, dick hanging. Those happy days were far in our past at that point. I was only 32, but Andre had made me feel older with all the stress he had put me through. Dreadfully, I got out of the car and went inside. Sneaking around my own home, I tiptoed in the room. It was silent. I squinted to see in the darkness and there he was, sleeping like a baby as if he hadn't just turned our world upside down. My thoughts started running wild. I wondered why he wasn't awake and worried about me. If I had broken someone's heart who I loved, I wouldn't be able to sleep, but he was knocked out and appeared to be at peace. He didn't even call me when I left the house to ask if I was okay or beg me to come back. I knew I was done with his ass because he was dead wrong and wasn't even concerned about making it right. All the time we had invested in each other and he was willing to throw it away. I was devastated. There's no pain comparable to watching something you want so badly crumble right in front of you.

My thoughts were getting the best of me. I wanted them to stop, but I couldn't make the little voice inside stop speaking up for me, even when I didn't have the heart to speak aloud for myself. Watching him lay there all content when I had no idea what sleeping content felt like, I was bitter. A lot of my nights were sleepless worrying about where he was and who the hell he was with. I couldn't get my time back, so I wanted revenge. I wanted him to pay for his mistakes, but I didn't want money.

I went into the master bathroom and closed the door. I sobbed quietly and wiped my tears with the hand towels. I felt so alone. My husband was just a few feet away and I felt like I was in an empty house. I tried thinking back to the last time we were happy and healthy. It was one thing to be in love, but a healthy relationship is just as important. I didn't know what happened that had driven us so far apart from the day he laid eyes on me in that gym. I opened the medicine cabinet and found my sleeping pills that I had disguised in an Advil bottle. My doctor had prescribed them to me when I told him I couldn't sleep. I would take them with a glass of wine on rough nights or when Andre would get bold and decide not to come home at all. I took 2 pills and closed the cabinet back. I caught a glimpse of myself in the mirror and the tears started flowing all over again. *What have you done to yourself Katrina*? I just wanted some peace by any means necessary, some sleep. I wanted the pain I was feeling to stop. I opened the medicine cabinet again and took 4 more pills out. I ran water in the mug I kept in the bathroom and took them by 2's. It was too late for me to save my marriage, so I wanted to check out. It only took a minute for me to regret taking so many pills. I stuck my finger down my throat and spit the pills back up. I didn't want to die, I just wanted the pain to stop. It was scary to think about being alone. When we were kids, Andre and I would say we wanted to die together, so we didn't have to live without each other. I hadn't seen that Andre in a while, the one who was just as lovesick about me as I was about him. I could always think of a reason why I stayed, but I had run out of reasoning. I had hit a wall and it was starting to feel like I wasn't in love, just in stupid. I wondered if my mom was right.

I left the bathroom and when I looked over, he was still sleeping like a baby. I turned the light out, walked out of the room, and headed to the kitchen to get the biggest knife I could find. I turned on the radio to muffle any loud screams. The quiet storm was still playing. This time, it was H-town's remake of "A Thin line between love and hate," and that's exactly how I felt. I walked back toward the bedroom with murder on my mind.

I peeked in the door, and for a minute I just stood in the doorway crying. I was having flashbacks of the times when things were good. Like when Andre and I would make love all night long, all over the house or when I found out we were having A.J. Those times were some of the best of my life. Unfortunately, for every good thought there were more devastating ones to remind me that I wasn't living a fairytale. Andre and I hadn't been intentional about making our marriage work in years. I saw it crumbling, but I was on a cliff and we were moving too fast for me to jump out of the car.

I snapped out of it and walked over to the bed to stand over Andre. It was dark, but I could tell he was still knocked out. With the knife clenched tightly, I raised both hands above my head. I was shaking. I wanted to kill Andre to prove my hurt to him, but I hated that he wouldn't be around for me to see if it had any effect. I was willing to sacrifice all I had built for myself in the name of love and in one night it would all be over. I tried to bring my arm down, but something was holding me back. My eyes refocused into the dark night and I made one last attempt to find a reason to change my mind, but there was none. I swung my arms down and stabbed him. The first stab didn't feel deep. The second time I came down hard. By the third stab, I had my rhythm. I was frantic and I lost count after 10. I just kept going and going until I figured it was enough. He wasn't moving, so I knew he was dead. He never saw it coming and didn't get a chance to scream. I spared him which is more than I could say he had done for me when he was alive. I backed away and fell against the wall. I cried and fought to breathe. I still had the knife clutched in my hand and couldn't believe what I had just done. I did my best to get a grip. I got up to get into bed. I wanted to lie with him one last time.

I went to pull the sheet back, and suddenly the lights came on. "Damn Katrina, you really stabbed me! I can't fucking believe you!" I fell to my knees in shock. I was choking on my words and couldn't get them out. Was I hallucinating? I looked back at the bed and saw there was no blood on the sheets, and Andre sure as hell didn't have any on him. "What if I had been in bed? You really could've just killed me over this." he said. He went to pull the cover back and revealed that pillows and clothes were stuffed under the sheets where he usually sleeps. I crawled over to his feet crying. "Get away from me!" he screamed.

"I heard your ass in the kitchen messing with the silverware. I knew you were on some bullshit." he went on. I didn't know if I was happy that he wasn't dead or disappointed. He sat on the floor next to me, "Katrina, you really want to see me dead? I know we've been through a lot, but you really want me out of your life for good?"

"I'm tired Andre. I never was one to give up but you got power over me and you abused that. You created this monster." I tried to make him understand while I gathered myself.

"You really want it to be over?" he asked again, reaching for the knife. He took a deep breath and started to cut his wrist. I didn't say anything at first because I didn't believe he would hurt himself for real. Andre looked into my eyes and continued to cut. Blood started to drip down his hand and I still didn't utter a word. Part of me wanted to see how far he would go. He hadn't made me feel like he cared either way about the marriage, so I wanted to see if he would really die to prove his love. He pushed the knife deeper against his skin and I still watched. There wasn't any sense in stopping him. I could see the pain starting to show on his face. "Katrina baby, you're not going to stop this?" he asked. I didn't utter a word. I couldn't bring myself to say anything. Finally, Andre stopped cutting his wrist. I sneered at his failed attempt. Woozy, I tried walking, but I could only stumble toward the door. "Katrina, don't do this. Don't leave again." Andre begged, dropping to his knees. "Just let me go Andre. You have wasted enough of my life." He still had the knife in his hand. He grabbed my hand with his other. "Katrina, please baby. I can't live without you. I won't." Andre's eyes had turned fiery. He was angry, and I was scared. The next thing I knew Andre shoved the knife in his thigh. Horrified, I screamed, "Andre, what did you do baby?" Frantic, I grabbed the knife and started to pull it out, but more blood came gushing out. "Ahhhh that shit hurts!" he cried. "Andre why the hell would you do this stupid?" It may sound crazy, but I was upset.

"You want me to die anyway. Here you go." He pulled the knife out of his thigh and went to stab himself again. I grabbed his arm and stopped him. "Please Andre stop! You're gonna kill yourself." He looked at me confused. "You don't want me to kill myself, but you just tried to off me?" He didn't get it, but me killing Andre and him killing himself were two different things. Although the outcome would be the same, I couldn't stand by and watch him take himself out. I still wasn't sure if he knew how much trouble he could be in if an artery was hit. The way he was bleeding I knew it was serious. Andre had to be a fool or really trying to prove that he couldn't live without me. He moaned, and he sat there. The blood was coming out fast and his hard breathing was making it worse. I ran to the phone to call 911.

 "NO, what are you going to tell them?" he shouted.

"I'm calling an ambulance Andre! You're crazy." I dialed 91 and stopped. It was true, I was the one who brought the knife in the room in the first place. How would I explain to the cops what happened without one of us going to jail or a mental institution? I jumped up and grabbed my first aid kit. I was first aid certified, but I had only used my training for Andre's minor injuries. He was accident prone, and I was always stitching and bandaging him up. I made him move to the bathroom and get in the tub so I could see better and check if he had any real damage. I cleaned around the wound first. I could tell he hadn't hit any organs, but the knife wound was still deep. I grabbed towels, suture, alcohol, and some Hennessy. I poured him a glass of Henn, and while he sipped, I cleaned and patched him up. After I was done, there was blood all over the tub and floor. I couldn't believe what just happened. Andre sat there fixated on me, and I couldn't tell what he was thinking. I got up to go clean off, and I came back with a warm towel to clean him up. He was going to be ok. I wiped the blood away, and we made eye contact for a moment. He had me. It was like he cast a spell. Andre's eyes were my entrapment. My mama used to say, "Don't trust him Katrina, he has eyes like a snake. Like the serpent in the garden."

His eyes were Amber, looking right through me. I tried looking past him instead of directly at him. He knew when I was trying to avoid eye contact because he knew what his eyes did to me. He grabbed my face and forced me to look at him. He rarely showed vulnerability, and I could tell he was scared too. Had I finally gotten through to him? I rubbed his face, and he grabbed my hand and squeezed it. He started to cry and so did I. He walked out of the room briefly, and I could hear the music being turned up. The Isley Brothers started to serenade me, in "Journey to Atlantis." Andre came back into the bedroom. I walked over to him, and we started to dance. He could barely stand, but it felt like old times again. I felt like Andre truly regretted what he did even if just for that moment in time. I put my head into his shoulder, and it felt so good, him holding me tight while I let all my pain out. I was glad that he wasn't dead. I knew it was going to be a long road ahead, but I wanted us to be together on it. I closed my eyes and slipped away.

I hovered over my body bemused. I saw a light that felt like a magnet, but I didn't want to go to it. I wanted to know why my body was on the floor, and why my husband was screaming, but I couldn't hear him. I looked back at the light, then back at Andre, it started to make sense. I tried to scream, but nothing came out. I hit Andre, but he couldn't feel me.

The next thing I remember is waking up in the bathroom with Andre on top of me pumping my chest shouting "What did you take baby?" He stuck his finger in my throat, and I started throwing up. He ran water on my face and kept slapping me asking me to stay awake. Andre started going through the medicine cabinets. He found my pills and threw them. He shouted at me again, "Baby how much did you take! Please Katrina, tell me baby! Don't die like this. I'm sorry! I fucked up, but don't make me live without you, you know I can't do that." I could hear Andre but was too paralyzed to even move my lips. I thought I had thrown up all the pills earlier, but I still overdosed. Andre picked my head up and placed a towel under it. "Please Katrina, I swear on my life I'm done. The women, the lies, all of it. I'm done, just don't die!" Andre sat me up and stuck his finger down my throat again. I threw up more and was gagging uncontrollably. I laid there on the cold tile floor with Andre behind me in the spoon position. He pulled my hair out of my face and we cuddled quietly until I was able to stop gagging. I was still very tired but awake. I could feel something wet on my back and turned around to see that Andre's leg started bleeding again. I got up and my legs were so wobbly I fell back down. Andre tried to help me as I crawled over to get him a towel. I put as much pressure as I could on his wound. We locked eyes again and I could see the man I fell in love with all those years ago. We both were terrified of losing the other. He took the towel I used to stop his bleeding and wiped my face and neck with a clean area of it. He slid my nightgown off which was covered in water and vomit and threw it in the sink. He turned the shower head on and we both climbed into the tub. As the blood washed down the drain, Andre tried cleaning me off with one of the hand towels that I vowed were only for decoration.

It had been too long of an evening. Afterwards, Andre and I limped over to the bed to lay down. There was a moment of silence, then Andre rolled over and started to kiss me. He started at my lips then my neck, my belly and everything below. He slid two fingers in me as he played around my clit with his tongue. In and out slowly at first, then fast, then slow again. He pulled them out and came up face to face with me. He stuck his fingers in my mouth and I could taste my juices and his saliva. Andre cupped my ass and pulled me as close as gravity would allow. He lifted my pelvis up toward him and just like that we were one, him inside of me and my soul being penetrated by the only man I ever loved. I started to moan but then stopped him because for a moment I felt like I shouldn't be making love to him after what we had just gone through. The fact that it felt so good, and I was enjoying it, made me feel psychotic. It was dangerous what Andre did to me. It would drive any sane person crazy and was one of the reasons I wanted to kill him in the first place. He looked at me and said, "Baby let me show you how sorry I am, please." He went back down and started rubbing his beard along my inner thigh then in between. I was at the point of no return and just like that I went to paradise and came all over his face and the sheets. Andre stood over me and wiped his beard with his hand. His womb was still bleeding through the bandages, and he looked so rough. Andre was a savage, but he was my savage and I just wanted him to act right. I didn't want to leave, I just wanted him to do right by me. We were in love and war. That night, love won.

Andre went into the bathroom, and I started moving pillows around on the bed to make room for us to sleep. As I moved the pillows out of the way I could see the stab wounds and couldn't believe that less than a couple of hours ago I was trying to kill him. Andre came out and saw me in a daze. "Don't worry about it baby, tonight is for new beginnings. This isn't your fault. I have been a bad husband to you for a long time, and I brought you to your breaking point. I'm man enough to deal with the woman I turned you into, and I'm gonna be around for when you find yourself again. I know it's going to take a long time to build your trust back, but I want to try even if I fail." Andre said wholeheartedly.

I laid back on the bed and motioned for Andre to come over and lie down. He fell fast asleep, but I was wide awake. I felt like we had a breakthrough and wanted to savor the feeling. Although it felt good, I learned that I couldn't take Andre's word for shit, and I would have to let his actions show if he meant what he said. I prayed to God for serenity, courage, and wisdom. That was all I could do before I eventually dozed off.

Chapter 6 Waiting in vain

The next few months were a dream. I couldn't believe how great Andre and I had been doing. It only took for him and I to almost die for him to have an awakening. It was hard for me to think about the night I almost killed us both, but Andre didn't make me feel guilty about it. He claimed to have understood why I did what I did and said if he were in my shoes, he would've broken a long time ago. I didn't know if it was the truth, but whatever the case we had been on great terms, and I wanted to keep it that way.

I was at work when Andre popped up with lunch and said we needed to talk. He hadn't brought me lunch to work in ages, so it was a pleasant surprise, but usually when he wanted to talk there would be no good coming out of it. We went to a park near the job and sat in the car eating sandwiches. "Are you still down," by Jon B and Tupac played on the radio. Andre leaned over and kissed me. I grabbed his face and kissed him back. Andre had been married to me for a decade but was still figuring out his place as a husband to me. Maybe I was a fool for giving him so much time. Andre and I laughed while we reminisced on a more innocent time in our relationship.

"Katrina, I should have told you this a long time ago, but when we met in the gym that day, I knew I couldn't save that ball." Andre said.

"What do you mean?" I asked him.

"I mean, I knew I couldn't save the ball. It was gonna go into the bleachers, but I wanted to save you from getting hit with it. I wanted to protect you. I always want to protect you, even though I know you can protect yourself." he explained.

Andre always managed to create some metaphor to avoid talking about the real issues at hand. Sometimes I just wanted to say *cut the bullshit Dre,* but that would make him shut down. Instead, I joined him down memory lane sharing one of my fondest memories of us.

"You remember Da Black Hamlet, the play I was in at that alternative school? I told you not to come because I knew no one else would be there. I didn't want you to see that I only had two lines, but you came anyway. It was you and maybe 10 other people in the audience. You made such a big deal after and brought me roses and balloons. No one had ever showed up for anything I had at school, so I never expected that. We went out to eat after and you celebrated with me." I reminded him. Andre's support of me back then meant so much.

"I remember that." Andre smiled.

After we were done dwelling on the past, Andre got serious and said he had something he wanted to talk about but felt we needed a mediator. He suggested we go see a counselor. I was usually the one who suggested counseling and Andre was always against it. He said it was for crazy people and white folks. I guess he was feeling crazy because he damn sure wasn't white. He asked me if I knew anyone who could refer us somewhere, and I knew exactly who to call.

I reached out to my homegirl Alicia. She ended up marrying one of the guys from Zeta Phi North, even though everyone told her frat boys were promiscuous. She shared with me that they had gone through a rough patch. I remember her mentioning a counselor that worked wonders for them. Alicia's husband had been sleeping with her family member behind her back and somehow the counselor helped them through that. If he could save her marriage, he could help Andre and I. Alicia gave me his information and wished me and Andre luck. I contacted Dr. Jonas and told him that I was referred by his previous client Alicia. He asked me 2 questions, "Do you want to save your marriage, and what do you expect from counsel that you haven't been able to get on your own?" I liked him immediately. I set the appointment and it was a go.

Our first visit with the Doctor was very interesting to say the least. Dr. Jonas felt it would be best if Andre and I started at the lowest point of our marriage and worked our way to where we are currently which if you ask me, was the lowest point. Andre hated reliving the past, but I knew the only way for me to truly heal would be to deal with all the pain once and for all. I would always tell Andre how bad he hurt me, but after he apologized, he expected me to dead the issue. There were so many questions I wanted to ask. Andre thought I was hurting myself by asking for details, but that didn't stop my curiosity.

Dr. Jonas asked me to express to Andre what bothered me the most about his betrayal, and he asked that I describe the pain in my best words. I turned to face Andre.

"Andre, I feel like I lost my best friend. We used to do everything together, we told each other everything. You were the first and only man I've ever loved. I don't expect you to be perfect, but you're supposed to always choose me. I never really got over the first mistake you made, then after the second one I tried to make myself numb. I wouldn't have survived any other way. At times, you're emotionally unavailable and that makes me feel like I'm alone even when we're together. When I had those miscarriages, you checked out. Andre Jr. made it into the world, but he wasn't the only baby I lost. There were 5 Andre. 5 babies, and I felt like I was dealing with that pain by myself. I wavered in my faith and looking back I'm dispirited at how I let my pain define me. I was dying inside, and you didn't even notice. When you lie to me, I hate that the most. I relive the worst scenarios all over again. You get caught up and you're never honest about it. The other day you were caught red handed and you tried to convince me that it wasn't what it seemed to be. No matter how bad the news, I just want you to tell the truth. I don't want people walking up to me telling me shit I don't know about you. Do you know how humiliating that is? You don't because I would never embarrass you." Andre stared into my eyes but was masking his emotions. I kept talking because I felt it was probably the only time I'd ever get it out. "Andre, I'm always carrying myself as if I'm a representation of you while you're out here acting like you don't even have a woman. Every time I think you're changing for the better you take 10 steps back. If you don't want to be in this marriage you need to say that because it's not going to work if I'm fighting for it by myself. You treat me like an option. Maybe I've made you believe that was OK, but I'm choosing me over you from here on out. I'm OK with this story ending." My body language had gotten tense. I wasn't OK with our story ending, but I needed Andre to know if he wanted to leave, he could.

The Doctor tried to calm me down. "Mrs. Billups, I like that you are being open about your feelings, but I want to encourage you to remain calm for your own sake. I find that when couples tense up, the communication becomes less and less effective. Also, threatening that the story can end sets a precedent that you're not here to fight for this relationship, and I know that's not true. I want you to try this. When you get upset, express how badly you want this marriage to work, not how willingly you are to allow him to leave. Andre doesn't want to leave. It's why you both are here."

I wanted to snap at the doctor, but I wouldn't dare be the blame for our therapy session going sour. Instead, I just let the tension flow all through my veins. Dr. Jonas looked over his glasses at Andre to encourage him to speak up for himself. "Mr. Billups, this is the Safe Zone, and whatever we talk about here will be used as stepping stones to better the relationship and not for y'all to throw at one another." The

Doctor looked at me requesting I acknowledge his statement as well. I nodded. If Andre would tell the truth when I asked, we wouldn't have to keep reliving these awful situations. I had so many unanswered questions about things that happened in our past because Andre lied about them to begin with. The Doctor asked Andre and me to hold hands. I reached for Andre's and he was reluctant. "It's your turn Andre." Dr. Jonas nudged. He reached out, and I knew whatever he wanted to say was going to be heavy. The little voice in my head said *deep breaths*. I surely didn't want to act a fool in the doctor's office, so I just kept inhaling, exhaling. I let Andre talk and promised myself not to interrupt him.

"Katrina, I love you. I ain't never loved another woman the way that I love you, not even my mama. You mean so much to me and despite what I've done, I think you're amazing. You're independent, driven, poised, headstrong, and you know I think you're the most beautiful girl in the world. I've made a lot of mistakes and most of them were because I was young and dumb. I fell in love with you when I was a kid, before I even understood the true meaning of what love was. I just knew I didn't want to live without you, and I thought that was enough. When we lost Andre Jr that was a lot for me to deal with too. You acted like you were the only one affected. You shut down on me when I wanted to talk. When I touched you, you'd flinch. That made me feel awful. On top of that, I felt like us losing all the babies had a lot to do with me and my genetics." I squeezed Andre's hand tighter as tears welled up in his eyes and he confessed. "I was born prematurely and almost died at birth due to a genetic heart condition passed down from my father. Doctors told my mom I would have a very complicated life ahead. She said the doctor used the words *bad seed* like something was wrong with me. Then when you started having complications, I just figured it was me passing that bad seed down that I never told you about. I wanted to talk to you, but you shut down. I needed you Trina, but you wouldn't let me in, so I looked for comfort from somewhere else. It's like we both were hurting but didn't know how to express it to each other. You went and threw yourself into work, and for an entire year we were strangers sharing a home. I needed an outlet. That's when I started talking to other women. I wanted a way to get your attention, but you didn't fight for me, you let me go. You appreciated me having a distraction so you could be left alone to do whatever you wanted to do. You went to work and carried on like it was nothing. I even thought you were seeing someone. It started with me trying to get your attention, then it turned into a competition of who could care the least. Things went further than they were meant to go. I put myself in a bad position and made an even worse mistake. None of those women meant anything to me. I didn't comprehend the damage that was being done because we didn't speak about it until you'd had enough and snapped. I didn't wake up until we had that incident that night at the house. Almost losing you was enough to show me how stupid this whole thing has been. I've loved you for too long to not make this work. When you almost died, all I could think was, what the hell would I do without you. To be honest, I've done so much dirt sometimes I feel like walking away from you is the best gift I could give, but I can't live without you. I can only pray my past doesn't come back to haunt us. I can't change what happened, but I can promise you from this day forward, I'm a changed man." Andre was relieved after laying it all on the table.

Dr. Jonas was speechless and so was I. I didn't know my husband felt that way. I still had questions and I wasn't taking credit for Andre's indiscretions, but I did understand where he was coming from. I never said I was perfect, but I wasn't a cheater. I've been devoted to my marriage and that should count for something. Dr. Jonas broke the silence by asking what Andre was referring to when he said the "incident that night." Andre and I looked at each other and without saying a word agreed to not talk about what happened with Dr. Jonas. "That's a sleeping dog we'd like to leave sleep Doc." I said, speaking up for the both of us. He didn't press the issue and instead told us that we could wrap up for the day. Before we left, he made us both promise to not use the stepping stones as weapons. I smiled at Andre, and he smiled back, that was our agreement.

On the way home, Andre asked me how I felt about our first session. I told him it was ok, but I felt since we revealed so much in the first session the next few would be even harder to digest. Andre agreed and said that he felt more comfortable talking with the Doctor in the room. I was willing to do anything to try and make it work so it was a no brainer if I was down to go back.

Andre made a detour before going home and said that he was taking me to this nice restaurant that someone he knew owned. When we pulled up, Andre valet parked his Mercedes AMG and led me into this gorgeous place that looked more like a palace than a restaurant. A handsome man came down the steps and he and Andre embraced. Andre introduced me.

"Yo Ty, this is my lady Katrina." Ty reached for my hand. "Oooh, this is Katrina." he said, while gazing into my eyes. "You're beautiful." He turned to Andre. "No disrespect my man, but you got yourself a real trophy. I thought I had all the trophies in Atlanta." he flirted. "How are you doing Ms. Billups?" The cute rambunctious man asked. Andre stepped in between us. "That's Mrs. Billups Ty. Don't make me beat you down in your own damn restaurant." They laughed, but I caught the warning to Ty in my man's playful jab. Ty waved one of his people over. "My man, give these 2 the best table and the best bottle of wine we have, on the house. I want you to personally take care of them as if they were my family, hell they are my family." Ty winked at Andre and pushed us off with the waiter.

The waiter led us over to a dimly lit, cozy corner. I didn't know who Ty was, but he seemed cool. He was clearly very young and successful, a little cocky, but seemed like he had the right to be. I asked Andre where he knew him from. He thought about it then said, "Long story, we'll talk about it in the safe space." I giggled thinking back to Dr. Jonas' reference. I figured that meant Andre had met this guy while he was doing some dirt. I wasn't going to ruin the mood, so I let it be. The waiter brought over a bottle of Dom Perignon and poured us 2 glasses. After my first glass, I felt all giddy inside like a schoolgirl on a date. Andre and I toasted to many more moons and love filled nights with each other. I wished moments like that lasted forever.

My husband and I feasted and drank until we were spent. We stayed at the place until it was near closing. I excused myself from the table to go to the restroom. When I came out of the stall Andre was there with that look. He hit the lock on the door and without saying a word, he bent me over the sink and slid under my skirt. "You see what I'm on?" he asked me, as he stroked long and slow. "I love you Katrina, you're the most beautiful girl in the world." he said in my ear. Within 2 minutes I could feel him cuming inside of me. I always loved when he stayed inside. "Don't make it obvious." he said, kissing my neck before leaving. I couldn't wait to get home and have cake with that icing. I got back to the table and Andre asked for the tab. The waiter said there wasn't one. Ty had taken care of everything. He wouldn't even let Andre leave a tip.

Andre asked for my hand across the table. He looked like he was working his nerve up to say something. It was such a good day, but Andre had been unpredictable lately. He said he wanted me to meet someone and asked me to wait at the table while he went to the back to bring them out. I immediately thought the worst. First counseling, then dinner, and now a special guest. He was on a roll, and I was starting to get concerned about his motives. I was tipsy. I straightened my clothes out, wanting to be sure no one could tell me and my husband had just finished getting busy. I watched the door to the back area hoping to get the drop on the special guest before they'd notice me.

Suddenly there was this loud commotion, and I could hear Andre yelling at someone. I couldn't make out the words, but he was screaming. I went to see what was happening, and Andre came rushing out of the back damn near knocking me over. His collar was stretched out, and he looked disheveled. He grabbed my hand, and we flew out of the restaurant and didn't look back. He didn't even say goodbye to his friend Ty. On the way home, I asked him what that was all about. He had the nerve to smirk at me. He placed his hand on my thigh and started caressing me. He was being passive aggressive again. Clearly something happened at that restaurant because the look on his face when he came out of the back said it all. I wasn't going to let it go that easy. "Andre, just cut the shit! I don't need to be caressed. I need to be informed on what the hell is going on with you." I snatched away from him and called him out. He looked at me like I was the one who had just caused a scene in a restaurant. "Katrina, let it go please. I've had enough for one day," he said, as if I caused any of the issues he had going on in his life. My husband was a piece of work, and I had been the fool putting in all the hours.

We rode in silence for about 10 minutes. We were almost home when his phone went off. It was late and due to past experiences with him, his phone ringing after 11:00pm set off my PTSD. It was never a good thing when his phone rang that late. I looked over at him, and he looked back at me. It was the same look he'd always have when he had something to hide. I looked out of my window and shook my head.

"Are you going to answer her?" I asked.

"It's not like that Katrina. I promised you since that night, I'm a changed man, but I got some unsettled business." he said.

"Change your fuckin number." I offered him an option.

"I'll do it next week." he proposed, not taking his eyes off the road.

"No, you'll do it tonight! Why next week? By then you would have contacted all your exes. Is that what you're trying to do Andre? You wanna let all your bitches know you trying to work it out with your wife, so give you some time?"

"Katrina, can we please not do this tonight. Would you give me the benefit of the doubt just this once? I'm not doing any dirt baby." He didn't sound any more convincing than he usually did.

"Whatever Andre."

When we pulled up at the house Andre got out and came around to open my door. I was still upset but didn't want to fall back too far into the hole we had just gotten out of. I went and opened the front door to walk in, and Andre didn't cross the threshold with me. I looked back at him to see what the problem was. He couldn't even look me in the eyes. "I'll be back Katrina." And just like that, I knew the bullshit was starting again.

"Really Andre! Are you kidding me! Today of all days? You can't even be straight today! Whatever it is, why don't you just tell me so we can deal with it and move on? I can't keep doing this high and low shit with you. You're a fucking joke and a disappointment." Frustrated and on the brink of tears I ran upstairs. I could hear Andre close the front door. A minute later I could hear his car pulling out of the driveway.

Andre didn't come home that night and I felt stupid. It didn't make sense that of all the days to relapse he would pick a day when we were making headway. When I woke in the morning and his side of the bed was empty, it was another blow. Now I felt like the joke. A complete fool, and Andre knew it, otherwise he wouldn't be so bold. I had to work, so I got dressed, put on some heavy makeup to cover the bags under my eyes and prepared to start a new day. I'd deal with Andre when he did decide to come home.

Chapter 7 Love TKO

When I first got the call, I thought it was a prank. I even hung up on the detective initially. He called back 3 times and finally I picked up the phone yelling at him. "What the hell do you want and why are you playing on my phone?" The voice on the other end was somber. "Mrs. Billups, this is not a prank. I need you down at Grady hospital right away. Your husband has been in a serious car accident." The room suddenly got cold. I forgot that I was mad at Andre and just prayed to God he would be ok when I got there. I grabbed my keys and flew out the door.

I almost wrecked at every turn and couldn't get there fast enough. I parked illegally and ran inside the hospital. The place brought back so many hurtful memories thinking about the babies I lost there. I finally spotted the emergency room staff. "Where is Andre Billups's room," I screamed, scanning the area looking for any clues that would lead me to him. One of the nurses ran over to me. "Detective Stone is waiting for you." she said. She walked me over to a room where the Detective was alone with a Doctor. They immediately went silent when I walked in as if I interrupted a secret conversation. I looked at the nurse and demanded, "Take me to my husband. I want to see my husband!" My stomach was starting to sink. I couldn't understand why they wouldn't take me straight to him. The detective walked up to me. "Mrs. Billups, there's no easy way to tell you this, but unfortunately your husband succumbed to injuries sustained in a car crash he was involved in." The detective's lips kept moving, but I didn't hear anything after that. Everything went black.

I woke up and was hooked to an IV. One of my arms was restrained to the bed and my head felt like I had been hit with a brick. I started to panic, then the nurse came in all bubbly and said, "Hi Mrs. Billups you're up just in time for me to check your vitals." It was Nurse Nia, the same Nurse that helped me with my miscarriages. I asked her why the hell I was tied to the bed, and she explained to me that I passed out and woke up trying to fight everyone in the room. I had to be restrained by officers and during the struggle I hit my head on one of the waiting room chairs and was knocked out. As she told the story the pain was new all over again, and in that instant it all came back to me why I had come to the hospital in the first place. I started to cry and pull at the zip tie on my right wrist. When I started bleeding, Nurse Nia threatened to sedate me. She tried to reason, "I know this is hard but look at the good in this, your baby is alive, and Bella is as well. It's going to be a long road but you all will get through this together." I looked at her confused but before I could say anything, she went over to a Bassinet on the other side of the room that I hadn't even noticed before. She picked up a baby and my eyes got wide. She walked it over to me and at that point I didn't know if it was a boy or girl. When Nurse Nia handed the baby to me she asked, "What's her name?" I looked at the baby confused. Was it a dream? I didn't know whose baby it was, but I knew it wasn't mine. Nurse Nia snapped me out of my daze when she asked again, "What's the baby's name Mrs. Billups?" I knew it had to be some type of mix up, but I answered her anyway. "Her name is Sky." I could say it had meaning but the truth is my first thought was this baby just fell out of the sky so that's what I called her. The nurse commended me on having such a good little girl and bragged on her for barely crying while I was knocked out. I just kept staring in awe at this beautiful baby who had very familiar eyes. She had been scraped up from the accident, but it wasn't anything an aloe vera plant couldn't heal. I couldn't focus on her injuries because her eyes were so piercing and so familiar. Not just her eyes but her nose, lips, and cheek bones. I cried out as I came to the realization of who she looked like. Tears of anger, confusion, amazement, love, and disappointment all in one. I asked God to rewind time. I closed my eyes and begged him. When I opened my eyes that baby girl was still in my arms. Only a few months old but alert and looking right at me. The same mug I put up with all those years. She looked just like my husband. Nurse Nia rubbed my back to comfort me. "Mrs. Billups, I understand this is hard, but Sky needs you to be strong. You're all she's got. She's such a beautiful baby. She looks just like your husband." Nurse Nia didn't know the half. How would I be able to be strong after what was unfolding? The baby, my husband being dead, it was too much. The nurse went in her pocket and pulled out scissors. "Please don't try fighting me with your baby in your arms." she said, cutting the zip tie. I laughed through my tears and laid the baby on my chest as I stroked her hair.

I gazed off into space for a while. My thoughts were unclear, and it was only the beginning of how much my life was going to be altered by Andre's death. He had left someone behind who couldn't fend for themselves. I looked down at Sky who was drifting off to sleep. She looked so cozy laying on me. For a moment, I thought about the possibility of being someone's stepmother. I pushed the thought aside as I recollected where the baby had come from. She was conceived by his side chick. How could I get involved with her? I loved Andre, but I couldn't be responsible for his mistake even if it weren't her fault. I thought about the baby's mom. I shifted my attention and asked Nurse Nia for the full story on what happened when my husband arrived at the hospital. I acted as if the concussion caused some short-term memory loss and knew the less I talked the more I could listen. I asked the Nurse if Andre said anything about this Bella girl she mentioned earlier. Nurse Nia explained that he and Bella came in together and at the time Bella was unconscious and my husband was barely able to talk. He was only awake long enough to tell doctors that he was in the car with his daughter. Nurse Nia said that everyone was ejected from the vehicle. When they found Sky, she was upright in her car seat 50 yards away from where my husband and his mystery woman were found. The baby had minor injuries compared to the two of them. They weren't wearing seatbelts, so they went crashing through the window. The Detective was only able to call me after they found my husband's phone near the scene.

It was so much to digest at once. Sky couldn't have been more than a few months old and what she had survived was a miracle. I felt sorry for all parties involved including Bella. She was a homewrecker, but I wouldn't wish such a horrible situation on anyone. I asked the nurse if Bella was in bad shape. Her face went dim as she tried to sound optimistic. She told me Bella was in a coma with bleeding on her brain. The doctors were hopeful but advised that the family should be prepared for the worse. I asked if I could go see her. Nurse Nia agreed and got the wheelchair from the other side of the room. I slowly got up with baby Sky in tow, and we were wheeled over to the Intensive Care unit where Bella was being kept.

Rolling down the hallway with a baby in my arms felt weird being that I had never even gotten to wander around that hospital with my own baby. When we got to Bella's room, Nurse Nia rolled me over near her bed. I stared at her looking for her qualities in baby Sky. Outside of her sandy brown hair Sky didn't look anything like her from what I could see. Maybe Bella was so beat up I couldn't tell. I asked the Nurse to give me a minute alone with her. She stood right outside the door. I rolled closer to Bella. One would think I was praying over her, but I wasn't. I didn't know what to feel for her while I sat with her child in my arms. I had mixed emotions. I was sad over my husband's passing, anxious holding his baby, and mad that the reason I was holding the baby was because he had been unfaithful with this woman. Bella's eyes were swollen shut. Her lip was busted, she had a deep scar over her left eyebrow, and her head was wrapped in white bandage. I couldn't even tell where her wound was, but I could see the blood at one point or another starting to seep through. I caught chills thinking of the pain she must be in if she could feel anything at all. The nurse told me to be optimistic, but it was clear Bella wasn't walking out of that hospital. I looked down at the baby again. She had started fidgeting. She was so beautiful. I couldn't see myself leaving her there. It wasn't her fault that she had irresponsible parents.

I called for Nurse Nia and asked to be taken back to my room. As we headed up the corridors, she told me the detective would be back to talk to me about a few things and I would need to cooperate this time. She told me it was routine for detectives to question next of kin when there was a death by way of accident. She urged me to say as little as possible because Detective Stone was a hard ass and wouldn't take it easy on me just because of my loss. I thanked her for her advice.

Later that day the detective came back and asked some questions about where my husband was going and whether he was drinking. Andre and I both were drinking that night before we left the restaurant, but I knew mentioning that would cause trouble. I made up my mind that I wouldn't tell on Andre because I didn't want to give the detective any ammo against him. I didn't tell the truth, but I answered all his questions. I could tell he was suspicious of my story and my husband's reason for being out with Bella. The whole time he kept an intent eye on me like he was looking for something to be off. He always rephrased his question to ask it twice. When I would answer him, he'd pause and stare at me for a moment as if my answer would change. After we wrapped up, he handed me his card and said if I thought of anything else that I thought would be relevant to the "case" to contact him. "Case? You mean this is an investigation?" I asked.

"Yes, that's exactly what I mean by case." Detective Stone answered before walking off.

I watched him until he was out of eyesight, and just when I thought I would have a minute to myself the nurse came back and said we needed to go downstairs. I asked what for, but she wouldn't tell me. She took the baby to the nursery, and she and I took the elevator down to the basement floor of the hospital. It was cold, dim, and it smelled funny. It looked like a scene out of a scary movie. "I know there's no perfect time to ask you for this, but I need you to identify the body." Nurse Nia leaned down in front of me and said. I fell sick. There had to be a better way to spring that shit on me. I asked the nurse to take me back upstairs, but she insisted that it had to be done now. I braced myself to see my husband who I expected to look disfigured.

Nurse Nia rolled me over to the morgue where a woman was standing over him ready to snatch the thin sheet away and reveal his corpse. To her it was just a job. After she showed me my husband's body she would probably go on about her day and still be able to eat lunch. Meanwhile my forever as I knew it had just ended tragically. I looked at the sheet near where Andre's nose was protruding hoping I would see him breathe. Maybe he would breathe again if he knew I was there. Maybe my scent would wake him up. I knew none of those things could happen, but I had to try and believe so. If I had allowed myself at that moment to accept that my husband was dead forever, I would've collapsed. "Are you ready?" Nurse Nia asked. I wasn't, but I took it she was going to make me do it anyway. The woman lifted the sheet, and it took me out. I couldn't get to him fast enough. I needed to touch him. Nurse Nia tried to restrain me, but I got out of the wheelchair which I didn't need much in the first place and fought her off. I demanded she let me touch him. The last time I had spoken to my husband we were about to fight again. I needed to touch him to give myself some closure if there was such a thing. I hadn't done anything wrong, but it was hard not to feel wrong while he lay there dead. He wouldn't get a second chance at anything. The Nurse finally gave in and allowed me 5 minutes with him. Her and the Medical Examiner left the room and I just stood there. I looked around and there were so many lockers with more dead bodies. I looked at them all, feeling the energy of the countless people that would be affected by their passing. I rubbed my husband's hand. His face had been scratched up from flying through the window. I leaned down and kissed him. I just wanted to feel him one last time. I didn't think about his indiscretions. Nothing mattered to me anymore. I just wished I could tell him that all was forgiven, and I was sorry. I mourned for the only man I ever loved. I prayed that God would give me the strength to carry on despite the circumstances. I was inconsolable and even though I knew it was impossible I prayed that God would wake him up.

Nurse Nia came back in and said we needed to wrap up because another family was coming. Just as I thought, identifying bodies was only a job to the M.E. and she needed to get her job done. Nurse Nia and I headed back upstairs. This time, I didn't sit in the wheelchair. When we got back to my room, I asked her to go get the baby. She returned with Sky and left us to be alone.

I was finally able to think without distractions. I laid there in the hospital bed plotting my escape. It was far fetched, but could I pull it off? I was having second and third thoughts about taking Sky or leaving her. Would it be as simple as walking out with her and starting a new life? What if I started to resent her later? What if she turned out to be problematic? I knew if I accepted that child, I would have to love her unconditionally, but I wasn't sure my heart had the capacity to do that. I wanted to do the right thing, but I couldn't drown out my true feelings. I needed to get home. I could think better in the comfort of my own home. My head was still hurting but surely I was in good enough shape to be released, physically anyway. Emotionally I was still a wreck. I walked over to the bassinet and laid Sky down. I started looking around the room for my purse and belongings. As soon as I spotted my purse, Nurse Nia came back in and asked me what I was doing. I asked when I would be able to go home, and she suggested I stay overnight to have some test run. I told her I had enough for one day, and I just wanted to get home with my daughter to get some good sleep. On top of it all, I would need to start planning a funeral. I didn't want to wake up in the hospital another day. I knew she couldn't force me to stay so I asked for my discharge papers. She took forever but finally gave them up and asked when I would be back to visit Bella. I honestly didn't want to come back. I wanted to leave that hospital and run as far away with Sky as possible. I told Nurse Nia that I would be back in a couple of days to visit my "cousin."

It hadn't been an entire 24 hours that I was in the hospital, but when I got outside, I felt like I hadn't felt fresh air in forever. It was cold in Atlanta. Christmas was right around the corner and it was one of the coldest winters ever. I lived north of the city and the roads were icy. The hospital gave me a car seat since Sky's was now a part of the evidence in the case as Detective Stone put it. I strapped baby-girl securely in her car seat and walked around to get inside of my Range Rover. I cranked her up, sat, and waited. While letting my truck warm up I told myself if it wasn't meant for me to have Sky someone would come outside and stop me from leaving before it was too late. What type of hospital would let a mix up of this magnitude happen anyway? There were levels to mistakes, and they had made a colossal one. Luckily, I'm a good person who could never dream of harming a child. I was convinced that Sky's best shot was with me. Her father was dead, and her mom didn't look like she would be alive much longer. Even though I wasn't technically her family, who would take care of her if not me? She was Andre's child so rightfully so I should have some type of say in her wellbeing. I always knew I would be a great mother, but God had chosen to take that ability away from me. Maybe this was his second chance in disguise. I looked around one final time and glanced over at the hospital exit. No one had come for her, so I backed up and crept out of the parking lot.

Sky was as quiet as a mouse on the way home. I played smooth Jazz and took a slow stroll north. I was so glad I stayed far away from most of my friends. I didn't want to face anyone else for at least a few days. When I got home the house was warm, but it wasn't cozy. All I could hear bouncing off the wall was the last thing I said to Andre, *You're a fucking joke and a disappointment*! I couldn't feel more awful. No matter how much I tried to drown out the voices they lingered. I slowly walked up the stairs with Sky in hand and I had just the perfect treat.

It was the last door on the right and I strategically chose the room furthest away from the staircase for safety reasons. I opened the door, and it was just like I had left it. It felt a little stuffy because no one had been in there for a while. I moved all the stuffed animals out of the way to place Sky down in the crib and headed downstairs to get a bottle. Before I could reach the bottom of the stairs, I heard Sky screaming. I ran back up the stairs and she was wailing. I figured she had to be scared being in that unfamiliar environment with unfamiliar smells. I picked her up and took her with me to warm up some milk.

I didn't have any baby formula but figured a little fat free milk wouldn't hurt her. I prayed she wasn't lactose intolerant and would find out one way or another. I had read so many books about being an expectant mom that I was probably more prepared to take care of a baby than an experienced mom. I wanted to be as close to perfect as possible but never got that opportunity. Andre Jr. didn't even live long enough for me to take him home and lord knows that's all I wanted to do. I just wanted him to come home, so he could leave his smell. I wanted him to lie on my bed, the couch, and slop on my clothes. I missed him so much. I would need the same resilience I had with AJ to make it through what was to come with Sky.

Sky made it to the bottom of the bottle, and she was out again. I headed back upstairs and this time I laid her on my bed and decided she would sleep with me. I put on one of Andre's t-shirts hoping the smell would keep her content that someone familiar was nearby. I watched her in awe thinking could she possibly be all mine? As soon as I started to doze off there was a knock at my door. It was 7:00am, and I was sure it was the police. I started to ignore them at first but foolish me for not pulling my Range in the garage. I crept out of the bed hoping the baby wouldn't wake up. I went to the door, and it was Linda. Linda was my nosey ass neighbor who every time I thought I made it clear I didn't want her popping up at my house she would pop up again and prove me wrong. I opened the door and as usual Linda invited herself in without asking. She started with the waterworks, "Oh My God, are you ok Katrina? I heard about the accident on the news. I can't believe this happened to you. I am so sorry." The sun was barely up, and Linda already had the scoop. She really could run a neighborhood watch by herself. She grabbed me and gave me a bear hug. She was such a big woman that I was swallowed. I was shocked that Andre made the news and was hoping his family and other friends didn't see it because I needed time to get the story together. Andre's family would want to know who the woman in the car was and why he was with her. I didn't know what I was going to tell everyone about the baby that had popped up out of nowhere. I pulled away from Linda and said, "Please I just need some time to myself. I can't even talk right now." I put my hand softly on her back and started directing her towards the door. I closed it behind her and locked it. I turned off all the lights in the house except my bedroom. If anyone else came unannounced it would fall on deaf ears.

Chapter 8 Over My Dead Body

The next few days were a blur. I had been dodging people all week, hiding baby Sky, and on top of it all, I was planning a funeral. Detective Stone had still been in touch with me advising that the accident was still being investigated for several reasons. I couldn't imagine what could be so complex about a car accident involving a man and his mistress. It wasn't unique, and he was looking too far into shallow waters.

I planned the funeral for a Saturday to give most of his family and friends an opportunity to come. Although my husband had proven himself to be disloyal to me, I planned on putting him away with respect and dignity. I chose Murphy Brother's funeral home which was one of the best in Atlanta. It would be my last gift to my beloved. Andre wasn't all bad and I was determined to focus on the good in him.

I had written so many checks to make sure everything would go well. $10,000 to the funeral home, $800 for the caterer, I made a small donation to the church so I could have it there, and $3,000 for a head stone. Andre had insurance, but it would be a few days before that check cleared so I was stuck footing all the bills. The company that I purchased the headstone from called me to inform me the check I wrote them had bounced. I had never written a rubber check in my life, so I knew it had to be a misunderstanding. I went into the bank to find out what was going on. Amanda, who had been our banker for years, was there. I explained to her that I needed to talk about what was happening with my accounts. She called me in her office and pulled up my information. I had overdrawn my checking account by $2,000. I had always been on top of the money and based on my calculations, I should have had enough money for everything I had written a check for. Amanda printed a detailed copy of our statement which showed Andre had recently taken out $20,000. I asked her if she saw him that day and did he indicate why he was taking the money out. If she was trying to hide something, she was doing an awful job. I could tell by the look on her face she knew something. "Tell me Amanda, were you here that day?" I knew if she were there, Andre would have gone through her. "Katrina, you know I consider you and Andre to be friends of mine, and I don't want to get in between your marital affairs." she said, wearing her professional hat.

"Well he's dead now, so it doesn't matter. What the hell is there to hide?" I asked coldly. Amanda clearly hadn't heard the news. "He's dead? When did that happen?" she asked. I thought the word had gotten out, but it didn't make it to Amanda yet. She was so stunned to hear me say it with little to no emotion.

 "Amanda, he died last week, and his funeral is Saturday if you're interested in coming. Now, what happened the day he came into this bank and withdrew $20,000 behind my back?" Amanda finally gave it up. "He came in here with some girl and he withdrew $20,000 from the account. It was suspicious but not a crime. I wanted to call you as a friend and a fellow wife, but you know I can't cross the line we have in business. I can't tell on your husband when he decides to take money from y'all's shared account. I'm also the bank manager." I looked at her trying not to be mad because I understood she had a job to do, but I considered her to be a friend. "Amanda, how would you feel if your husband died, and while you're planning his funeral you find out you can't pay for it because $20,000 is missing from your account? I need answers. What can you tell me about this mystery woman?" I asked. Amanda said that the woman with Andre appeared to know him very well, but she didn't know in what capacity. "They seemed to be well acquainted but when Andre and I locked eyes he pulled away from her. I figured he was hiding something, but again he was here on business, so I didn't get personal." Amanda divulged. I heard enough. I asked her what the girl looked like, and sure enough she described a 5'0 tall woman with sandy brown hair. The fact that Andre withdrew money with another woman and had a baby with her led me to believe he was prepared to live a whole lie and another life. I left the bank feeling lower than I had when I arrived there.

I went over to Navy Federal where I had a secret account because every woman should have a secret account. If for no other reason, for when your husband does dumb ass things like what mine had done withdrawing $20,000 from our joint account. Had he had a secret account, he could have played with his own money in peace. Any time I would get a bonus check, I deposited it into my personal account. I had close to $50,000 and promised myself that I would save the money for a rainy day. It was raining, so it was as good a time as any.

I moved some funds around and got the money back in order. I went to the headstone company and this time gave them a money order since they would no longer take a check from me. Imagine that, a company turning down my $3,000 check. Andre was still embarrassing me even in death.

Saturday crept up quick, and the closer I got to putting my husband in the ground the gloomier I felt. I kept it together for the most part but thinking of putting Andre in the dirt seemed so final. Here I was embarking on a journey that he and I both had dreamed about and now just like that he was gone. I used to pray to God for a baby. I would even say, God, I'm willing to sacrifice anything. I didn't know anything would be my husband.

I needed someone to watch Sky and the only person I could think of was Christina. She was a girl I met while she volunteered at my company as part of her high school work study program. It was a 2-week assignment for her to learn the ins and outs of marketing. Not only did I teach her everything I knew, but we bonded in the meantime. She was only 17 and reminded me a lot of my younger self. I instantly took a liking to her and promised when she graduated from college if she still had an interest in marketing, I would have a job waiting for her. She asked if I would be her permanent mentor, and that turned into somewhat of a big sister little sister relationship.

I called her to ask for a favor. Instead of explaining anything, I came right out with it and asked if she would watch my baby. I knew she was confused but she didn't ask any questions. I told her how much I was offering to pay, and it was enough for her to agree. I took the baby over to her house and told her I'd be back later. After I got Sky settled, I headed back home to prepare for the funeral.

I was staring in the mirror when the doorbell rang. I was paralyzed for a moment looking at how the last few days had worn on me. I lost a few pounds, and it was clear I was stressed. I didn't remember the last time I had a meal and was on a coffee and alcohol diet.

The doorbell rang again and reality set in. It was time. I headed down the stairs and toward the door. I could see Andre's Aunt Nettie peeping through the window. I rolled my eyes because she was the last person I wanted to be alone with. I opened the door, and before I could get a hello out, Nettie started being rambunctious. "Well dang, how long were you going to leave me out there? I'm glad a dog wasn't chasing me or else I would've been bit chile." I was too tired to argue. Nettie looked at me, and she knew I just wasn't in the mood. Any other time, Nettie and I would go back and forth and give each other a hard time, but this time her timing was off. Nettie walked back over and gave me a hug. "I'm sorry Katrina, I know this ain't the time. You know I ain't got no manners." I appreciated Nettie getting the hint sooner rather than later. She went into my kitchen and put on some coffee. Nettie always made herself at home and this was one of the times I didn't mind. She pulled out two coffee mugs from the cabinet and poured us both a cup. There was an awkward silence and as if on cue, she asked, "So what happened?" I knew it was coming sooner or later, but I only wanted to tell the story once. I told Nettie I would explain when the entire family got there. I knew she had an attitude, but I didn't care. I wasn't going to be interrogated. I was going to tell the story once and that would be that. Andre's family never came to visit us so those acting concerned did not move me. It was a shame that we all would only be in the same room because of the tragedy that happened.

Everyone arrived within an hour of Nettie, and the funeral cars shortly after. I didn't know how the ranking in Andre's family went so I told them whoever was the closest with him could ride in the family car with me. Andre didn't speak to his father, but I still respected that he was the closest blood family member, so I did offer him a seat. Everyone else was cousins, aunts, and uncles. I sat up front with the driver, and there were 6 available seats in the back. Andre's dad, Nettie, and his cousin took the first seat. Nettie's daughter, her daughter's boyfriend, and a friend of the family took the last seat. As we pulled away from the house, I looked back at all the cars following and felt sick. Nettie and her daughter tried to make small talk, but after a few one-word answers from me they gave up and the rest of the ride was silent.

When we pulled up at Central Holiness, Andre and I's church, there were more people than I expected. I knew everyone loved Andre, but I was still surprised at the turn out. I didn't even recognize some of the faces there. There were a lot of people from our high school including Mont and Nene who were now married. Sabrina was there, and even a few of his exes. Pastor Epps did a wonderful job with the service and kept it short and sweet, just like I asked.

At the burial site it was the hardest thing ever watching my husband be lowered into the ground. It was the end of my forever, and it wasn't a dream. There was so much more for us to do. The best of our marriage was yet to come, and now I would never find out.

Afterwards, Andre's friends and a few members of the church followed us back to the house. I ordered Essie's catering, and the food was already set up when we got back. We ate, laughed, and reminisced about better times when Andre was alive. Sabrina pulled me to the side. "Katrina, I can't believe we beefed so hard in high school. Looking back, none of it was worth it. I have kids now, and Lord knows I wouldn't want my daughter to go through what we did. I just wanna say I'm sorry for everything and my condolences." she offered. "Thank You Sabrina. I appreciate that." I walked off quickly before she reached in for a hug. While everyone was distracted, I grabbed Andre's dad, Nettie, and a few of Andre's other relatives and brought them to my office area. I went over and sat in my chair and took a deep breath as I prepared to tell the most important lie of my life. They all looked on, wide eyed.

"I know everyone wants to know what happened. Some of the details still aren't clear as far as what caused the accident, but what we do know is Andre was driving with his co-worker, someone cut them off, and Andre lost control of the car. Neither of them was wearing a seatbelt, and unfortunately, they both were ejected from the vehicle and died. That is all I have for now. The entire situation is tragic, and I wanna start trying to heal at this point." When I was done telling the story I looked around waiting for questions. It was their one and only chance to ask anything they wanted to know. It wasn't guaranteed they would get the truth, but I wasn't going to talk about it anymore. I didn't mention Sky or the fact that Bella was still alive because they didn't need to know that. It would just cause more confusion. Everyone took what I said at face value, and that was it. Nettie was the only one who offered herself if I needed anything but she knew I wouldn't call her if I did. After the talk, I got up to leave. I knew they would stay there a few more minutes gossiping about me. I didn't care. As long as they didn't ask me any more questions.

I mingled around with the guest, hid in the room when I needed to, snuck a shot when the walls started to close in, and I had finally made it to the last few stragglers in the house. A few of Andre and I's friends and a couple of family members hung around talking about Andre as a child, and how he was always the one they knew would be someone special. I was thinking of a way to ease everyone on without being rude, but the bottom line was I wanted them all out of my house. A deep voice coming from behind approached and asked, "You need anything else?" I turned around and Ty was standing there in a black suit with a card. I hadn't noticed him earlier.

"No, I'm fine." I told him.

"Are you sure because I don't mind staying to help out if you need?" He asked.

"Ty, I'm sorry to be so forward, but how do you know my husband? He never talked about you until he introduced us the other night at the restaurant." It may have been indecorous, but Andre never got around to telling me how he knew Ty and I needed to know.

"Andre and I met at my restaurant. He used to come in with different clients." Ty explained. I knew by clients he meant whores. "They would eat lunch and he and I would chop it up about basketball and whatnot. We got really cool, and I told him anytime he wanted to come to the restaurant he could call me ahead, and I'd be sure to have a table waiting on him." Ty laid out. I knew he left out parts of the story that he thought would incriminate Andre, but I didn't push it. I was smart enough to put two and two together, and figured the restaurant was one of Andre's playgrounds. It wasn't Ty's fault that my husband was promiscuous, and I wasn't going to take it out on him. Instead, I smiled and thanked him for coming.

"Can I help you with that?" he asked, reaching for the dishes in my hand. I ran out of paper plates and cups earlier and the dishes were starting to pile up. I started washing the rest of the dishes, and Ty dried them with the dish towel on the sink and placed them in the dish rack.

"So unfortunately, Andre and I didn't get to talk much about you Katrina. Of course, he mentioned he had a beautiful lady at home, but I'd like to know more if you don't mind. I want to know about the special woman who locked my man down and see if she has any sisters." Ty joked. That made me laugh but really, I was fighting back tears. Why didn't Andre tell his friend more about me? Was he too busy playing Casanova? Ty could sense my mind wandering and he put the dishes down. He grabbed my hand, then led me over to the table to sit down. He said he was going to tell everyone else to leave so I didn't have to. He came back to the kitchen 5 minutes later and said everyone was gone. I thanked him and was waiting for him to see himself out as well. I wanted to go pick up the baby, and he was holding me up. He sat down at the table. I looked over and connected with his almond shaped eyes. I could still appreciate a fine man even while I was mourning.

"Katrina, do you have anything stronger than Coffee?" he asked.

"In the cabinet, there's Vodka." I said.

He had read my mind because I absolutely needed a drink. Ty got the vodka and poured us both a glass.

He toasted, "Cheers to Andre." There was something about him. He was smooth. Kinda reminded me of Andre. I felt guilty for thinking about it. I had been so tense and overfilled with emotions that I could explode in more ways than one. I knew what would make me feel better. When Andre and I made love the world would go silent, pain was no longer felt, and it was just he and I. I would never get to experience that again with him. I pictured Ty helping mask the pain. I needed to slow down on the drink because I was having wild thoughts.

Ty kept talking to distract me from getting lost in my anguish. He revealed some stories about Andre that I never knew, and I came to find out that the two of them were closer than I had known. With each drink I found out more flattering and not so flattering things about my husband. Ty probably assumed that like most married couples Andre and I talked about everything, but Andre and I hadn't had that dynamic in years. Ty poured the last of the bottle in my glass. There was an awkward moment of silence, then he stood up and asked me to walk him to the door. I asked if he was ok to drive, and he assured me he was fine, so I saw him out. He thanked me for my hospitality and leaned in for a hug. I hugged him back and we both embraced maybe 2 seconds too long. As he made his exit, I closed the door, and I watched through the window as he walked off the porch and headed to his car.

I went over to the couch and flopped down. I felt like there was something I should have said, but I didn't say it. My vulnerability was getting the best of me. I sat there rocking back and forth and biting a pillow. I didn't want to be alone, but then again, I did. I went to get my glass off the table and downed my last sip of alcohol. I was tipsy so I picked up the phone to call Christina and ask if Sky could stay till the morning. Christina said it was fine and I was happy to have the house to myself to sort out the weirdness I was feeling. I grabbed an aromatherapy candle and lit it. The label said the aroma was created to calm nerves and ease tension. I hoped that it would work. If the candle didn't work, the blunt that I was going to roll would. Earlier at the funeral, Brother Nelson from my church slid it to me, and told me when his wife died it was the only thing that helped him sleep. I smelled the package, and it was so strong. I was surprised Brother Nelson could tolerate it. "It's the good stuff Katrina. Just try it if you need to." he told me. I slid it in my purse and thanked him for his consideration.

I turned on the radio and they were playing "Two Occasions" by The Deele. It triggered another breakdown for me. "Two occasions" was one of my wedding songs and one of Andre and I's favorites. I laid down on the couch, lit the J, and snuggled under the blanket. The music played while I let my tears flow.

I fell into a deep sleep and was awakened by a phone ringing. It wasn't my house phone, or my cell phone, and I didn't recognize the ringer. I followed the sound to the kitchen table where the phone's caller I.D showed an unknown number that had called 6 times. I answered, hoping to find out whose phone it was. The voice on the other end was deep,

"Katrina, it's Ty. I left my phone. Do you mind if I come and grab it, or should I wait till the morning?"

"It's fine, you can come grab it tonight." I said.

"Ok, I'll be there in 20 minutes." He hung up abruptly.

I considered leaving the phone on the porch and playing sleep because I thought it best not to see Ty again. I wasn't in the best shape for company under the circumstances. I went over and opened the door and waited with Ty's phone. He pulled up faster than I thought. He cut the car off, and I wondered why because he was just picking up his phone and leaving. I walked to the last step of the porch and reached out to hand it to him. Instead of grabbing his phone he grabbed my hand, pulled me close to him, and kissed me. I didn't stop him, and I started to kiss him back. He didn't even take his tongue out of my mouth as he backed me up the stairs and back into the house. We didn't make it past the foyer before he had me pinned against the wall. I led him to my bedroom and stopped at the doorway. I looked at my bed, and I couldn't help but think about Andre. Ty told me it was ok and led me to the couch instead. It was like he could sense what I was feeling without me saying anything. We both sat down, and we didn't say anything at first. Then Ty spoke.

"I'm sorry. I couldn't stop thinking about you when I left. I know this is probably the dumbest thing I've ever done, but I had to come back and tell you what I felt because I felt like you might feel it too."

I didn't say anything because I felt wrong. I felt like I was cheating on my dead husband. Ty looked at me waiting on me to say something. Instead, I leaned into him, and this time I initiated the kiss. I imagined he was Andre, and he was giving me what I needed to feel better. I closed my eyes and climbed on top of him. I still had on my dress from the funeral. Ty unzipped the back of it and pulled it off me shoulder by shoulder. He asked me to stand up. I stood, and the dress fell to the floor. Ty grabbed me by my waist, lifted one leg, and rested my thigh on his shoulder as he sat on the couch. He pulled my panties to the side and licked once, I quivered. Twice, and I got goosebumps. By the third lick, I could barely stand.

Ty stood up and unzipped himself. When he pulled it out, I tried not to stare. He was well endowed and the look on his face said he knew he was. His eyes asked me for permission, but his hands didn't wait for me to say yes. He turned me around and whispered in my ear. "If you want me to stop, you're going to have to say it." I couldn't bring myself to say

133

stop or anything else for that matter. He stroked his dick up and down the crack of my derriere. I hoped he didn't hear my heart racing. He moved my hair off my face and slid inside of me. With every stroke, I could feel the tension releasing from my body. Ty asked, "Do you like that?" I loved it and felt bad that I did. I started to cry but tried to wipe the tears away before Ty would notice. "It's ok. Let it out Katrina. I know it hurts, let Ty make it better." He was already making it better with each backshot.

I stopped thrusting with him and stood up. I grabbed him by the hand and led the way to my guestroom. This time I didn't hesitate. I lay back on the bed and my body said use me. I was still crying but it didn't bother Ty. He kissed my neck and shoulders before nibbling on my nipples. He slid inside of me again and it was even better in the bed. I shed tears while Ty screwed me face to face. He was a fine man, but it was hard to look at him because he wasn't my husband. Andre wasn't coming back but I was still coping with that. The more Ty pumped, the more I cried. He had his lips on my ear, "It's ok Katrina, just let it out. Say what you want to say baby, I'm here."

"I want him back. I want my husband back." I mewled. Ty pumped harder.

"What else baby? Say it. Tell me what you want."

"I want Andre!" I called out his name and started to shake uncontrollably. Ty kept going. It didn't bother him that I wished he was my husband.

"Baby I got you if that's what you need right now. What would he say to you when he made love to you?" Ty asked.

"Andre would always tell me he loved me, and I was the most beautiful woman in the world." I could barely get it out in between orgasmic convulsions.

"I love you Katrina, you're the most beautiful woman in the world." Ty repeated. I locked my legs around him and screamed. It was the release I needed, and he had been the perfect man for the job. I lay in Ty's arms and for the first time since Andre died, I fell asleep with no problem.

Chapter 9 Diced Pineapples

The next morning when I woke, I felt on Andre's side of the bed, and Ty was gone. The sheets were still wet, so I knew it wasn't a dream. I didn't mind that he left, and it was probably better that way because I didn't want to face my mistake. I headed downstairs to put on a cup of coffee. To my surprise, Ty was in the kitchen cooking breakfast. I had enough of him last night, and now he was overstaying his welcome. I offered him coffee and sat down at my table nervous while I watched my dark roast brew. Ty was in boxers, and man, he was built like an African warrior. He was only 25 years old, but that body had some experience on it. He grabbed a plate out of the dish rack and brought it over to me. He had bacon and eggs in a pan. He made him and I a portion, then he sat down to join me. The feeling was all too familiar because Andre and I had shared many mornings over breakfast and coffee at the same table. I tried to come up with an excuse for him to leave.

"I've got some running around to do, so we'll need to make this a short breakfast." I mentioned, as he went for his first bite of bacon.

It wasn't that I didn't enjoy Ty's company, but our time was over. I wanted to go back to grieving my husband. I appreciated what he did for me, but it didn't mean I was going to be his new special friend.

I tried to explain myself because no one deserved to be used and thrown away even though it was all part of the game. "Look, what happened last night was something I needed, but I don't want to give you the wrong impression of what this is. I was vulnerable and needed comforting. You did that for me, and I appreciate you." I tried thanking him.

Ty gulped his coffee down. "Anytime." he said. He abruptly left the kitchen and came back downstairs within 5 minutes fully dressed and ready to dash out the door. He came over and kissed me on the cheek. "Next time, I don't mind you telling me to leave. You don't need to lie to me." He found me out and I felt bad. I thought about all the times I had said the very same thing to Andre about lying. I didn't want to be rude to him and that wasn't my intention. I suddenly felt a rush of guilt and ran out to the driveway to stop him.

"Ty, let me take you out for a drink later?" I proposed.

"Nah I'm good. You've got running around to do." he said, being sarcastic.

"So, how's 8:00pm?" I asked, ignoring his uncompromising attitude.

He couldn't hide his smile, and I knew I got through to him. "I'll see you tonight at 8 Katrina." he agreed.

Just like that it was set. I walked him out, then went upstairs to get dressed. There was something intriguing about him and I liked it, but I knew we couldn't let it go on much longer. I tried to ease my conscience by reminding myself that Andre slept around on me when he was alive so I shouldn't feel bad for moving on after his death, even if it was sudden.

I called Christina and told her I was headed to pick up Sky. I asked her if she would be available later that night because I needed to step out for a couple hours. I was hoping it would only be a couple of hours, but with Ty I couldn't be certain. I was so depressed, and he was a breath of fresh air. I didn't want to do anything serious, but I did want to be around someone that made me feel good.

I spent the rest of the morning and afternoon with Sky running different errands. I needed to keep myself busy, otherwise I would go somewhere and fall into a sunken place. On my to-do list was shopping for some clothes and baby necessities. We went to the mall and while everyone was going about their day it felt like I was in a world alone. I wondered if anyone could sense my desolation. Did anyone care? I made it to 2 stores before I had to leave. The walls were closing in and I suddenly wanted to go home.

When we got home, I put on "Matilda" and watched with Sky until she and I both fell asleep. I woke up to my alarm going off on my phone. It was 7:00pm, and I had overslept. Sky was still asleep as well. I went upstairs to get dressed. I decided to put on a black dress. I put my hair in a high bun and wore clear gloss. I packed Sky's bag, and we headed to Christina's house. When I greeted her at the door, we hugged, and I slid her a $200 tip. Her jaw dropped, but before she could thank me, I told her I'd be back soon and was out the door. She had really been a big help to me, and part of the reason she was so reliable was because I took good care of her.

Ty and I agreed to meet at Lisa's Groove, a Jazz restaurant in East Point. I had tried getting Andre to come with me, but he never got around to it, so I didn't feel any quarrels about being there with Ty. I arrived first, so I went in and got us a table. It was a corner booth with plenty of privacy. I watched the different couples move about. Not long ago I had a partner to do those things with, but there I was waiting on Ty. He finally showed up 20 minutes late, but he looked so good I didn't make a fuss. I stood up to hug him, and he had on one of my favorite colognes, Sean John "Unforgivable." I knew that scent anywhere. Andre had worn it since high school. It brought up so many memories for me. Oddly enough I was turned on. I ordered us 4 shots of Henny and an appetizer. Ty did a double take at how quickly I downed the 2 shots and requested 2 more. I urged Ty to drink up because I wanted him to loosen up. The more he drank the more he talked. He gave me the rundown on his past relationships and the current status of his dating life. When I saw my opportunity, I took it.

"Ty, what happened that night at the restaurant when my husband and I came to visit?" I asked, sliding more Hennessey over to him.

"Which night?" Ty asked, stammering over his words.

"The yelling in the back, the night of the accident." I reminded him.

"Why did my husband rush out of there like that?"

Ty looked like a deer caught in headlights, but I kept my game face on. I wanted to know the truth. I had dealt with the worst of the story already. Any other secrets that my husband had wouldn't kill me if the ones I already knew hadn't. Ty took another shot and leaned back in the chair. "You shouldn't worry about that. It's probably gonna cause more harm than good." he said. The fact that he wanted me not to worry about it made me worry more. "I'm a big girl Ty. Tell me what's up." I faced him head on, and he knew I wouldn't let up until he told me the truth. Finally, he confessed.

"To be honest, I'm not sure what was going on. All I can tell you is Andre came to the back to bring out this surprise he had been planning. There was a woman there who tried to confront him, and it went left. He kept saying *now ain't the time,* but the woman wasn't trying to hear it. I take it he ran out to protect you from that. I didn't get to talk to the chick after, but it seemed like she was upset about something. He called me later that night and said he was coming back to talk to her, but he never showed up. I figured he got intercepted by you." Ty explained to me.

I wanted to ask him if he knew about the baby, but I promised I wouldn't tell anyone about her. Just in case it ever became an issue, the less people that knew about Sky the better. I decided to lay off Ty. I had gotten enough out of him for one night. I focused my attention back to us. He was looking delicious sitting across from me. After hearing what my husband had done, there was nothing more I wanted to do then to take my frustrations out on Ty in my bedroom. He sensed my body was calling for him and asked for the check. He was young, but he understood body language very well. I was feeling like a cheetah and he was looking like prey. I tried to pay the tab since I offered to take him out, but he wouldn't let me. He paid for the evening and we were out. I rode with him back to my place and couldn't keep my hands off. "Gotta Get You Home" by Foxy Brown blasted through the speakers. The heated seats warmed my thighs. Ty gave me the once over and licked his lips. I could feel him throbbing as I caressed him through his linen pants. I was a woman in heat even though I was still in mental anguish. The only thing that could temporarily get my mind off reality was some good bodywork, and that's what I intended to get.

When we got back to my place Ty led me up my stairs as if it were his home. He laid me down. "This time, I want you to enjoy me. Relax and enjoy us." he said. I almost creamed, turned on by his rawness.

My body was worn out. Ty screwed me so good I lost count of the times I came. Instead of asking him to leave after, I asked him to stay. We took a bath together, and I learned more about him. His grandmother had died when he was 17. She left him some insurance money, and instead of blowing it trying to show off he invested in some property, renovated it, and turned it into a lucrative business. Ty wasn't a chef, but he hired the best he could find, and his restaurant was now one of the hottest in Atlanta. He had even made Atlanta's Hottest 30 under 30 for single men.

We were having a great time, but my mind still was clouded with thoughts of the accident and what Ty was holding back.

I also couldn't help but think if Andre were looking down on me from heaven, what would he say? Would he feel like I was betraying him? Did he love me so much that he wanted me to be happy even if it were with someone else? I wanted answers that I would never have but they still pegged me.

Ty took my attention off Andre when he slid inside of me in the bathtub. I scooted closer to him, put my arms around his neck and moaned in pleasure. I bit into his shoulder, and he bit into my neck. "Damn Katrina, I wanna stay inside you so bad." he begged. Next stop was pure bliss.

The next morning, Ty wasn't downstairs cooking breakfast. This time, he didn't overextend his welcome. I walked downstairs to a floral arrangement and a card that read,

"Have a nice day Katrina. Maybe, I'll see you soon.

T.Y."

It was simple, yet classy, and the perfect way to end something that never should have started.

I showered and got ready to get Sky. I was going to spend some quality time with her instead of trying to mask my pain with my late-night sneaky link. I was so caught up I hadn't gotten the chance to really appreciate raising an infant and the reward that comes from it. I caught a cab back to my car, then went to scoop my baby. When I picked her up, we went shopping again. We went to Atlantic Station, and I spent a couple grand on a 6-month-old, I think. I still didn't officially know how old she was. I knew she was too young to know or even care what was happening, but it made me feel good to spoil her. Andre and I did agree that we would spoil our child if ever blessed with one.

From time to time, I thought about what would happen if anyone ever found out Sky was stolen. Was there anything I could do? Did I have any rights to her? Would I go to jail? I put on a brave front, but I was worried. There was nothing I could do in the meantime except enjoy the time we did have together.

Chapter 10 Foolish

It took some time and a lot of appointments, but I finally found the perfect daycare for Sky. I even planned out the perfect routine. I would drop her off in the mornings, and Christina would pick her up for me in the evenings after school. She'd bring her to my house and chill for a few hours till I got home from work or whatever business I needed to take care of. I had been in hibernation for a while and knew that the best thing for me to do was to go back to work and get busy. I hadn't made time to go see Bella, and as evil as it is to say, I was just waiting for a phone call from the hospital to tell me she didn't make it so I could move on with my life.

I tried to pick up my mood by playing music. I listened to Brandy's "Sitting up in my room," while I laid my clothes out for the week. I played around with different hair styles and even talked myself into doing my makeup. I was looking like myself again and I missed being in the office around the hustle and bustle. I was in marketing and things were constantly evolving in the industry, but I always managed to keep up. I had plenty of contracts and a team of assassins. You tell us your vision for your company, and we execute a way to get that vision across to an audience. You want to appeal to the youth, urban community, expand out of the country, get a Super Bowl ad, we can get it done for you. I really loved my job because it kept me on my toes. Andre always said I focused on my career too much but I couldn't be like my mom, living paycheck to paycheck, barely able to pay the bills on time. She put up with a crappy job just to have one. I knew early on my pride was too big for that. Plus, I never wanted Andre to feel like he owned me because he made all the money.

After I got everything ready for work, I sat on the corner of the bed looking out the window. I was dreading what I was about to do. The detective had been calling, leaving message after message saying that it was imperative that we spoke. I didn't want to talk to him about anything because the way he had been treating me the entire time made me feel like I was a suspect. Furthermore, if I stayed away from him the least likely he would be to find out I had a few secrets of my own. In the short time I had her, Sky made me feel whole again, and I wasn't willing to give her up. Andre's death blessed me with something I would never be able to conceive otherwise, but it was getting harder by the day not to harbor any ill feelings towards him. Every time my phone rang, it was a loose end he left behind that I needed to tie up. Now the detective was harassing me about God knows what.

I dialed his number, and the line didn't ring for a whole second before a deep voice on the other end answered.

"Well hello Mrs. Billups. Thank you for finally returning my call." he said.

I replied with just as much snide as he did. "I've been going through a lot and have other affairs at the top of my priority list, but I'm sure you knew that." Before we got too far off subject, Detective Stone reeled it in. "Mrs. Billups, I need to meet you as soon as possible. Today if you have time."

"What for?" I asked.

"There has been an interesting turn of events involving the accident that night. I need to ask you a few more questions." he said.

I didn't know what he needed to ask me, but I knew it was some bullshit. It had been weeks and he was still looking into the accident.

I agreed to meet him at a coffee shop in Old Fourth Ward. As I drove through the crowded city streets, I could only imagine how my day was about to shift. Lately, I would wake up thinking it was going to be one way and it would always turn out to be something completely different. "Simple Things," by Miguel played on the radio. I yearned for the simplicity he sang about, but my life was much more complicated than that. My husband died while fucking around on me, had a baby, and a side piece he was planning to leave me for. How much more complicated could it get?

When I pulled up at the coffee shop, it seemed like the clouds came out. The sky was dark and depressing. I parked and could see that Detective Stone was already there in a corner booth. I got nervous. When I went into the shop, he waved me over. I sat down, and the waitress came with two coffees.

 "I ordered you a coffee black. You'll need it." he said. I wasn't down for the small talk, so I asked him right away what the urgency to see me was about. I opened the top to my coffee and started to add sugar. Detective Stone added cream to his. We engaged in a 10 second stare down before he broke the ice.

"Mrs. Billups, there's no easy way to say this, but the accident involving your husband wasn't in fact an accident at all. Initially we thought that Bella suffered head trauma from the wreck, but she has blunt force trauma consistent with a weapon found at the scene with your husband's prints on it. After performing our investigation, we didn't find any skid marks which means your husband didn't attempt to use breaks. We found his fingerprints on Bella's face, neck, and the handle of the carseat. I'm still putting all the details together Mrs. Billups, but I want you to know this accident wasn't no accident after all."

I couldn't be sure if my face showed anything, but my entire insides went to stone. The back of my head started thumping and my teeth were clenched. For what seemed like 10 minutes I was frozen. I wanted God to come down right then, scoop me up, and fly me away. My mind started playing tricks telling me to confess, but my heart told me to ride it out. As hurt as I was, I knew something wasn't right. I jumped to Andre's defense. "Are you kidding me? My husband wouldn't do anything like that, and you must be out of your mind to think so! Let me get this straight, you say he beat Bella up and tried to kill her. Then to cover that up, he throws the car with himself, the kid, and Bella into a ditch? How does that make sense Detective?" The story was far-fetched at best. If the detective wanted to convince me, he would have to come up with a much better explanation. Andre may have been a lot of things, but he was not a killer. I knew him, and there was no way I was going to let the detective put that on his legacy.

"Mrs. Billups, crime usually doesn't make sense. Unfortunately for you, the evidence speaks for itself. You see I looked at the crime scene and something doesn't add up. It wasn't just an accident. Your husband was up to something and I believe that you know what it was. I didn't come to you because I think your husband did this, I know he did. At this point, I'm trying to see if you are an accomplice or not. Are you able to tell me why your husband would want to kill Bella and *the kid* as you referred to her as? Is there something that he was trying to cover up?" he asked.

Detective Stone was an amateur at best. I looked at him like he'd lost his mind. I knew my husband was up to something, but he was a cheater, not a killer. That wasn't how we operated. Andre and I had faced his cheating before. Why would he kill to cover it up now? It didn't make sense to me, and even though Andre wasn't honest about everything, I wasn't going to let anyone convince me that the man I had known for 16 years was a monster.

I tried wrapping up the conversation. "Look, if this is why you called me here, then you're wasting my time. My husband would never do what you're accusing him of, and he wouldn't have a reason to. Where's your motive since you came in here telling me my husband tried to kill Bella?" I was heated, but Detective Stone wasn't intimidated.

"Motive? I was hoping you could help me with that. That's why we're here. I didn't bring you here to drink $4-dollar coffee. I want you to help me figure this out. If you have something to hide, now is the time to come clean because I can't protect you after this conversation. I'm offering my help, but if you don't want it, I can't make you. You just seemed like a smart woman, but I guess you are one of those ride or die chicks even if it means you got to die or throw your whole life away." he said.

He was really trying to piss me off. It was working, but I wasn't going to show it. "What do you mean you can't protect me after this conversation? I don't have anything to hide and you threatening me isn't going to make me come clean about a secret I don't have." I went to stand up and he grabbed my hand. "Please sit down. I'm sorry I may have jumped the gun." he acknowledged.

I didn't want to sit back down but I knew if I didn't, he would just harass me even more. He smiled and revealed his teeth that were overdue for a bleaching. It was like he was playing good cop bad cop and he was horrible at it. He already accused me, then acted like he was on my side, and now he was trying to manipulate me. "I know this is a lot to take in, but I have a damn good reason to believe that there was more going on in that car than you or I both know about." he tried convincing me. I was determined to maintain a united front for my husband's sake. "Detective Stone I don't know what you think is happening here, but my husband didn't have anything to hide and neither do I." I got up to leave again.

"Remember, I can't protect you after this conversation," he repeated. He was so sure of himself, but I still didn't look back. I walked out of the restaurant fighting tears. When I got in the car, I started punching the steering wheel and screaming. I was fed up. My whole life was a lie. Andre wasn't even around to make sense of it all. I was so tired of acting like we had it together. I wished there was someone I could share the weight of my secret with. The only thing that stopped me is the fact that I knew I wasn't willing to give up Sky behind it. I was in too deep. I reached in the glove box for a piece of tissue. When I looked up, Detective Stone was at my window. I wanted to pull off, but if I backed out right away, I would have hit him with my mirror. I rolled the window down and through my tears I mustered out. "What the fuck do you want?"

Detective Stone was relentless. "Mrs. Billups, I'm not trying to make you mad. I just thought you would open up to me and want to help me get to the bottom of what's going on here. I figured you would want to know what Andre was up to as well, but I see that's not where your head is." he said.

 "Please back up." I asked nicely. I put the car in reverse and backed out. It wasn't until I turned onto the interstate that I no longer felt like I was being followed. I turned the radio up as Dionne Farris' "Hopeless" played.

When I pulled up at my house, I was hoping there were no more surprises for the night. My heart couldn't take it anymore. I went inside and Sky was sleeping. I didn't say more than hi and goodbye to Christina. I put her money on the table and figured she was smart enough to see her way out. I was still speechless from finding out what they had accused Andre of. I didn't have any more room in my life for stress. I had my job, which I was slacking on, taking care of baby Sky, all of Andre's affairs, and now an open case for attempted murder/suicide. I was overwhelmed.

I made a late-night call to my VP and asked for more time off. She agreed to give me an additional 2 weeks. I understood the company still needed to run but life was coming at me so fast. Every time I tried to focus on me, something else would come up about Andre. Between him and trying to keep Sky off the radar, there didn't seem like enough hours in the day. I poured myself a stiff drink and put on my "Waiting to Exhale" soundtrack. Toni Braxton sang and tried to convince me to "Let it Flow."

Chapter 11 Is it a crime?

Saturday Morning, I got a call from the police station. They told me I could pick up my husband's belongings. I didn't know or care what they wanted to return to me but figured it was my duty as his widow to tie up the loose end once again. I called Christina and asked if I could drop baby Sky off with her for the morning while I took care of a few things. I knew Christina wouldn't turn me down even though she had her own problems arising. Her mom had been diagnosed with cancer and was taking a turn for the worse. She was unable to work, cook, or financially provide anymore. Christina was worried about her mom and confided in me that she needed to make all the money that she could to help. I started paying Christina triple what I usually paid to help her out as much as I could.

I took a shower as I tried to process all the confusion Andre left behind. When I was done, I stood in the mirror and was starting to notice myself again. My skin had returned to its soft, radiant state, and my hair was full and bouncy again. You wouldn't know by looking at me that I had just lost my husband or that I was trying to raise an illegitimate child. I went over to the closet and Andre's side was just as he left it. Brook Brothers Suits, Ferragamo's, Stacey Adams, and a host of other designers he used to fit right into the shiesty Sports Agent lifestyle. I was in no rush to deal with getting rid of his things because that too would require my energy and I had little to none left. I grabbed a pair of jeans off the hanger and a white T out of my drawer. After I was dressed, I grabbed Sky and put her on a full body onesie. I dabbed a little powder around her neck and kissed her as I did 100 times a day. I walked out of the house with a carseat in hand, and all I could think about was Detective Stone. He really believed my husband was a killer, and the odds were not in my favor that I would change his mind. I couldn't come to him and try the honest approach because that wouldn't be beneficial to anyone involved. My only option was to keep up the ruse.

I left the house and headed west. I dropped Sky off with Christina and put on my game face to get ready to go into enemy territory. When I arrived at the station I sat in the truck for a minute. I was hoping Detective Stone didn't have more bad news for me. I just wanted to get Andre's bag and go.

When I walked in, Stone was standing there with that accusatory look on his face. I was starting to feel like he just wanted anyone to blame. It didn't matter who, he wanted someone to take the fall. I refused to lie on anybody's sword. I was guilty of a lot of things, but I had nothing to do with what he was accusing my husband of. I signed Andre's things out without saying a word. I didn't want to entice the detective to ask me anything. I walked toward the entrance and out of my peripheral vision I could see Detective Stone following me. I wore sneakers that day, and it was a good thing because when I got to the parking lot, I booked it. I ducked down between the cars and zig zagged my way through each row. I managed to make it to the truck without being spotted. I could see Detective Stone looking around. I cranked up and he spotted me. He tried to hurry over, but I backed out. You could hear my tires screech as I threw it in drive and peeled out of the parking lot. I wasn't in the mood to talk and had no intention of doing so.

I headed straight back home afterwards. When I closed the front door, I rested my back on it as if I had just been on a high-speed chase. I put Andre's clear bag on the table and stared at the contents. I opened it up and the evidence included Andre's wallet, keys, jacket, and an empty Fendi pouch. I looked through his wallet at pictures of us. I sat at the table, and it wasn't long before I realized that Andre's phone wasn't in the bag. *Where is his damn phone?* I wondered. I remembered that the hospital gave me a bag with some of Andre's things as well, but I never went through the bag. I didn't want to because I figured it was just his bloody clothes. I ran through the house looking for the bag that I had tossed in a corner somewhere to deal with later. I found the bag in the laundry room. I dumped the clothes out and sure enough Andre's phone tumbled to the floor. I grabbed it and turned it on. The battery was low, and the screen was shattered. Took me 4 attempts but I figured out his lock code. He often changed it, but I always could crack it when I wanted to. This time it was 2330, Andre's two favorite basketball player's numbers. I took a deep breath as I hit the envelope icon to open his text messages. At the top of the log was Bella. I swiped to open, and the phone went dead.

I was frantic, running through the house looking for a charger. I found Andre's in our bedroom on the nightstand. I plugged the phone up and waited 3 minutes for it to get enough juice to power on. I tried again to read the exchange between him and Bella.

Bella: "Thank you for coming to the appointment with me. You're gonna be such a good dad."

Andre: "Of course, I wouldn't have it any other way but it's important that we keep this between us for now. If my wife finds out I won't be alive to raise this baby."

Bella: "How long can we keep it a secret from her before she finds out?"

Andre: "Just give me time Bella. There's history here you wouldn't understand. Trust me on this."

Bella: "Well this is Katrina's problem now too. You might as well tell her before it's too late."

Andre: "I know Bella. I'll tell her soon. Don't push the issue please. I promise I'm going to support you and the baby. I'm doing as much as I can right now without Katrina finding out."

Bella: "I won't push the issue for now, but we are counting on you."

Andre: "I Know Bella. I got you both."

I scrolled up to read an older exchange.

Bella: "Why have you been acting distant?"

Andre: "There are some things going on at home. I gotta be here for my wife for a minute. Are you going to be ok for a couple days?"

Bella: "What about me? Do I not matter? Am I not just as important? Have you told her about me and the baby yet?"

Andre: "Bella I told you I'm going to tell her."

Bella: "I can't stay here much longer. If my boyfriend finds out about us, it's going to be worse than anything your wife could ever do to you. I thought you said we were together in this, why does it feel like you're changing your mind?"

Andre: "I'm not going to let him hurt you and I haven't changed my mind. I'm going to be a man and do my part, but I need time to explain all this shit to my family. I love you but that doesn't mean I don't love Katrina too."

Bella: "Well, we are your family now so please just tell her or I'll have to be the adult in this situation."

Andre: "Bella, I told you about threatening me. Don't try and make me an enemy. I want to be here for you. Let me do that for you and the baby."

Then their most recent exchange the night of the accident….

Bella: "I need you to come back now! He's threatening to hurt the baby!!!"

Andre: "I'm on the way!"

  I did all I could to give Andre the benefit of the doubt. From the text messages, it was clear that there was more to the story than I knew. The detective was right. I couldn't believe I had to admit it. How much longer could I hide what he was really doing? I couldn't put the phone down and put myself out of my own misery. I needed to know everything. I went through the messages further and didn't find anything useful. There were 3 voicemails, all from Bella the night of the accident asking Andre where he was and how long before he would be pulling up. It seemed like the two of them were up to something, and it cost Andre his life, and would probably claim Bella's soon. The more I learned the more muddled my thinking became.

I went through the pictures and there were several of Bella's baby bumps and pictures of sonograms. She even had a picture of him and the baby side by side. I continued to swipe until I couldn't anymore. I threw the phone down and screamed, "why Lord?" I never questioned God, but I wanted an explanation. I lived my life right. I prayed every day and all night. I was kind and generous. Why was I going through such turmoil?

I went back downstairs and poured a shot of Cîroc. I was hoping the smooth taste would be just as smooth at drowning out the feeling of betrayal. I knew if I had seen those messages on the phone the detective probably saw it too. I knew he had started to piece things together, and that was his reasoning behind thinking Andre was the culprit behind this whole thing. The same way I had pieced it together, I knew Detective Stone could. Bella's true identity as my husband's mistress would soon be revealed. I already knew what was up, but I thought everyone else including the cops had thought Bella was a family member of ours, and the baby belonged to Andre and me. It became apparent that everyone else knew more than I did, and they were trying to play me.

I figured the detective was going to try and smoke me out, apply pressure until I fold. Little did anyone know although I portrayed a suburban housewife, I knew more about the game than I led on. I had dealt with cops a time or two in my life. I was 18 when I had my first run in with the police. It was around Andre's senior year and he was struggling to make ends meet. I just started college and was living on campus. Andre lived off campus. I would go to his house so much it felt like I lived there too. When he started having trouble paying the bills, I felt like it was both of our responsibilities to find a way to make it work. Alicia had the connect on this credit card scam. I told her I was looking to make a little extra cash and she put me down. We would use stolen cards to buy merchandise and sell it for half the price. I was the plug at school. All the girls that wanted the drip and the latest labels would come to my room and shop in what I called "Katrina's Kloset," which was just a cute suitcase where I kept all the merchandise. Girls would come over after getting their refund checks and place orders. I had a 48-hour buyback guarantee. If I didn't have what you ordered in 48 hours, it was free. I had a whole set up going making at least $500 a week profit. I sold that shit like hot cakes. Being a marketing major had its benefits. It was all good until some of the other girls started to feel like I was a threat because I started taking their customers. I had better style, so it was only natural that girls gravitated towards my suitcase more than the others. A girl named Dina, Alicia's sister, was my biggest hater. I never suspected her because she was the one that put Alicia on. I thought she was cool but turns out she felt some type of way that Alicia and I both were bringing in more cash than her. Dina was perfectly fine living in her own little bubble until she started worrying about us. Dina sent an anonymous tip to get us both busted in the commission of a crime. That same day Andre and I had a late date, so I was late to meet Alicia at the mall to buy some things with the credit cards. When I got there, I had already peeped that the cop had snatched her up. Instead of running and making it clear that I was up to no good, I went to the concession stand and got a sprite. I glanced around as if I was looking for Alicia. I slid the credit cards inside my cup of sprite and tossed it in the trash can. I smiled when I noticed Alicia and started towards her. "Hey, what's going on?" I asked. Approaching with a confused demeanor as if I didn't know why my friend was in cuffs. Instead of answering my question the cop aggressively turned me around and cuffed me as well. I wasn't scared because I knew that my trail was clean. I had connections everywhere. The boutique that I shopped in, I knew the owner. She didn't give a damn about me using stolen credit cards, she just wanted her shop to make some money. She was so down she would turn the cameras off before we even went into her store. There was never a way to tell who used the cards at the time they were reported being used.

I had another store where the manager agreed that if I purchased him a pair of sneakers a week, I could buy what I wanted with whoever's credit card I cared to use. I was careful, so I was confident they didn't have anything on me. Alicia and I knew that there was only one rule to interrogation, *don't say nothing.* All my responses started and ended with; I want a lawyer. We were held for a few hours and released after they couldn't get anything out of us. Dina had held a grudge with Alicia for the longest after that. Alicia and I became even closer, and from that experience I learned when dealing with police rather you're innocent or guilty, don't say anything!

It seemed like I had been sitting at the kitchen table for hours while I stared out the window into our backyard. I thought about leaving town and changing our identity. Possibly running off to France or Germany. There was no extradition to the US, and I could try and make a new life there. I visited Paris twice and always considered it a place I could live. Picking up and leaving was easier said than done tho, and truthfully, I wasn't ready to trade in my life to live like a queen pin on the run. I couldn't think of any other options because I was in so deep, I couldn't tell the truth if I wanted to. I would go to jail for kidnapping and God knows what else. I was at the point of no return. I figured the only way to make sure I didn't get caught up was to make sure there was no one else around that could contradict my story.

Chapter 12 Love is Wicked

I pulled up at the hospital around 9:00 pm. The sky was dark, and it felt like God was frowning at me. I knew he wasn't pleased with his child, but I would seek forgiveness later. I had to do what needed to be done in order to protect myself. If something happened to me then what would happen to Sky? Who would look after her if not me? I went in through the main entrance, and it was like a ghost town. I crept past the information booth and over to the elevator. I pressed 7 and sealed my fate. Everything was moving in slow motion. The elevator beeped with each floor it passed. When the bell rang for the 7th floor the doors opened. I peeked out both ways before stepping off. There was little movement on the floor, so I turned left and headed towards room 707.

When I walked into Bella's room she was still out. The swelling on her head had gone down tremendously and she looked like she was sleeping. I sat in the chair next to her bed and just watched. I prayed to God because I knew I was wrong. I asked him if he cared for me, how could he allow my mind to even think something so evil. I felt impulsive, but not in a good way. The same spirit that was on me the night I tried to kill Andre was back. It was my own selfish feelings that wanted to get rid of Bella. She probably had people that would miss her, even though no one had come to see her since she had been there. Sky would never remember Bella, and I felt bad that I would be responsible for that. With all of that in mind, I still stayed put.

I sat in the chair until the clock said 10:30pm. I had been sitting with Bella for over an hour. When I planned it out in my head, I said that I was going to do it and exit as quickly as I came, but there I was procrastinating. I didn't have the heart, so I got up and left the room. I headed back toward the elevator wide eyed. I couldn't believe I had even thought to do such an awful thing. I pressed the down arrow and at the same time my phone rang. I looked at the caller I.D. and it was the detective. I looked back towards Bella's room and thought about it again. I let the call go to voicemail. The elevator arrived and the door was closing. I only had a split second to catch it and I didn't. I walked back over to Bella's room and peeked over to make sure she was still out. I grabbed the pillow out of the chair next to her bed. It felt like cinder blocks were tied to each of my ankles as I walked closer to her. I put the pillow down over Bella's head and tried to push down with just enough force that she would eventually stay asleep forever. I didn't want her to feel any more pain or cause any more pain. I prayed while I smothered her. I prayed that she died. I knew it was awful, but I had been driven to a dark place. Bella's chest stopped rising. I pushed down with more force to make sure she was done for good.

I sat the pillow back in the chair. Bella still looked like she was sleeping. I felt a sigh of relief that the only other person who knew the truth about what happened in that car was dead. I started towards the door then stopped after I realized I could still hear the heart monitor beeping. I looked at Bella again and she didn't look like she was breathing. I knew I would need to get closer to her and do a pulse test. I was scared because I knew it was only a matter of time before doctors would come rushing in. I put my fingers under her neck to check for a pulse. Before I could confirm, the heart monitor started beeping crazy loud and I panicked. I ran out of the room and right into a doctor that was rushing in. I shouted, "I don't know what happened, the machine started making noises." The doctor asked that I leave the room. I backed all the way out of the intensive care unit to the stairwell and booked it. My heart was racing, and in my mind, I had just committed murder. Maybe I was a psychopath. I didn't want to believe that my husband could do something as awful as murder but look what I had just done. To make matters worse I had done it twice. I blamed love for both. Love was the root of all pain, and pain would make you do things you never imagined.

When I made it to my car I was in a panic. I never felt so crazy in my life. I couldn't believe the lengths I was going to cover up Andre's mess, just like I had done when he was alive. After smothering Bella, I knew I had dug the hole much deeper.

On the way home, I grabbed a cheap bottle of wine from the gas station. I drank half of it before I even made it to the house, the other half in the driveway. I just knew the detective would be at my door soon enough to ask about Bella, so I better get a lawyer. I picked up the phone and called an old friend, Malik Pierson.

"Hey Malik, it's Katrina, how you been." I asked him.

"Hey Katrina, pleasant surprise I've been fine. I heard about your loss and I'm sorry about everything."

"I appreciate that Malik. I actually wanted to talk to you about a few things concerning my husband." I told him.

"Oh yea, like what Katrina?"

"I can't go into details Malik, but I need to cash in on that favor you owe me from college?" I said, referring to him promising to always have my back if I ever needed a lawyer.

He paused, and for a minute I thought he might renege on me. "Katrina, it's better if you give me a heads up so I can know what I'm protecting you from. You know I got you regardless, but can I get some details?" he asked.

"Malik, all I can say is my husband left a mess behind when he died. You know Andre. His indiscretions have caught up

160

with us and since he's no longer around, I'm left to do the dirty work."

"Say no more Katrina. Call me when it goes down and I'm there. Stay dangerous." Malik warned me.

"Thanks Malik. Talk to you soon."

I never forgot when Malik told me if I ever needed a lawyer, I could call him. I still never told anyone his secret and felt like it was something that had bonded us for life. We didn't talk much over the years, but I had been watching him come up. Every time he had a big case it was in the news, and he hadn't lost one yet, not that I knew of. The case he was most famous for was the Candler Rd shooting that happened in the Park on Candler Apartments. Rahim, a young black kid, was accused of attempted murder on a police officer. The story was so big because the victim and the shooter had completely different stories. The cop, a white rookie, claimed that Rahim walked up on him and started shooting for no reason at all. Rahim claimed the cop rolled up on him and a group of his friends, hopped out and started searching everyone. Rahim, who's Malik's nephew, started throwing the law at the cop, telling him he couldn't search the young men without probable cause. The cop couldn't take being shown up. He pulled his gun on them and demanded Rahim get on the ground, but he refused. The cop pointed the gun to his head, cocked it, and threatened to kill him if he had to ask again. Fearing for his life, Rahim tried to wrestle the gun away. The cop got shot in the chest during the struggle and that one shot penetrated the cop's bulletproof vest. Rahim gave the cop CPR while his friends called 911. They all gave the same story; the cop was the aggressor. Rahim was still locked up and charged with attempted murder. There was so much tension in the Decatur community when this happened. Residents didn't trust cops and cops felt like public enemy number 1. Malik was the only attorney in town bold enough to take the case. Everyone else felt there was no way to win it. Malik was able to find out the gun the cop was using wasn't his registered service weapon which showed ill intent. The gun also turned out to have the bodies of 2 young black men on it. The cop ended up being the one charged with murder and sentenced to 160 years in prison. It was the craziest case ever and even made national news. After the trial, every city in Georgia had a billboard with Malik's face on it. He represented hope for the pool of innocent black men that had been railroaded by the system.

Now that I knew Malik was down with me, I spent the rest of the night into the early morning pacing the floor, waiting on that phone call, or a knock at the door. I was going to need more than prayer to get me out of the quicksand I was in. I kept taking my phone out of my pocket and then putting it back. I wanted to call someone but didn't know who to call. I just walked back and forth between the living room and dining area. I hadn't called Christina to let her know why I didn't show up to get Sky earlier. I was hoping she would understand that the day had gotten away from me and I planned on compensating her well for the inconvenience.

My phone rang, and I looked at the caller I.D. to see that the number was unknown. I knew it had to be bad news but was anxiously awaiting my fate. I answered, "Hello."

"Hi Mrs. Billups, it's Nurse Nia. We need you down at the hospital ASAP."

"What's wrong?" I asked.

"It's Bella, the Doc said you were here earlier, and he needs to ask you some questions about what happened."

"Can't he ask me over the phone?" I was acting suspicious and treating Bella like a stranger instead of family as the story goes. I calmed down and tried not to let my guilty conscience cause me to tell on myself. "I'm sorry Nurse Nia,

I'm just worried. Is Bella ok? I want to know what's going on."

The line got quiet. "Mrs. Billups, I wanted to wait until you got here to tell you but since you insist, you should know that Bella is awake and she's asking to speak to you."

Chapter 13- Losin my Cool

I couldn't believe Bella was asking to speak to me. I expected the cops would be there to arrest me once I arrived at the hospital. On the way back, I kept telling myself to turn around and book a flight out of the country to run away with Sky, but I could only run so far before I'd run out of money and resources. I pulled up at the hospital for what I was hopeful would be the last time. I didn't see anything out of the ordinary, but typically when there was a setup everything looked normal. I went over to the information booth, and the woman who was on the phone arguing with someone gave me a visitor's badge without even looking up. I signed my name on the guest sheet before getting on the elevator.

When I made it to Bella's room there were several people crowded around. I could hear the Doctor saying, "It's a miracle. She might make a full recovery. She appears to be alert and remembers everything about the accident." I was shitting bricks as I came through the door. When I looked over at the bed it was empty. Bella was sitting in the chair at the window. The sun was high in the sky, and I imagined she missed watching the sunrise. I didn't want to go to jail on such a beautiful day, but it was too late to back out. I walked over to her not knowing what to expect. I was hoping she didn't remember that less than 10 hours ago I was trying to kill her. I wondered what she would say. Would she ask where the hell her baby was? Did she remember she had a baby? Would she confirm the detective's beliefs that my husband tried to kill her, then wrecked the car to cover the whole thing up? If so, I needed to know why. Andre had screwed other women during our relationship. What was different about this girl that made him think he needed to kill her? I stood behind Bella and couldn't tell if she could sense me or not. I didn't know whether to tap her on the shoulder or call her by name. I crept a little closer. "Bella." I called

164

out. She didn't even move. I walked over to stand in front of her and her eyes were clenched as she fought back the tears that were already rolling down her face. I reached out and touched her hand. "You wanted to see me?" I asked. I didn't want to rush her, but I needed her to say something.

Bella was scared, doing her best to keep her composure. She rubbed her hand over head which was still half shaved and started crying harder. I felt her pain, but there was nothing I could do in that moment to subside it, so I just squeezed her hand tighter and tighter until she squeezed mine back. Then, she finally looked up at me.

The sun hit her face just right, and it told the story I had only known to belong to one man, they changed colors. I almost collapsed as I held my stomach trying not to throw up. I was sick. Bella's eyes were just like Andre's too. I started to wonder if I had the story wrong the entire time. So, I asked her, "Bella, I need to know what's going on. Why are you crying? What happened the night of the accident, and how do you know Andre?" Looking into her eyes, seeing her all timid, I could tell she was younger than I thought. I asked everyone to leave the room to give me and my "cousin" time to talk. When the room was clear, Bella limped over to the window and tried to stand. She turned back to me.

"I'm Andre's daughter. My dad and I met recently, and he was trying to help me get out of some trouble. I hate that we have to meet like this." I hate we had to meet at all, but I couldn't go another second without knowing how she came about. "What kind of trouble Bella, and what was Andre going to do to help you? How old are you?" I asked. "I'm 16. Last year, I got caught up with this older guy Terrence. Soon after, I got pregnant. I didn't have anywhere to go so I had to move in with the guy. It was all good at first, then we started fighting a lot. He would keep me in the house for days away from everyone. He would put me down because I gained weight after the baby. I was at my lowest point, so I started

165

trying to find my biological dad. I inboxed Andre on social media and he came to my rescue immediately. My grandma told me he was a deadbeat, who left my mama when he found out she was pregnant. Andre said had he known about me, he would have been more than happy to be a dad because y'all couldn't have kids together." She stopped talking when she saw the contemptuous look on my face. She realized she shouldn't have said it, but it was already out. Andre had told her the one thing I asked him not to tell anyone. My complicated pregnancies were personal for me, but somehow my husband didn't respect my privacy. Bella went to finish her story.

"When my baby's dad would jump on me, Andre would come pick me up and put me in a nice hotel. He did his best to protect me, even up to the day he died. He had plans to tell you, but he said we had to tell you at the right time. He tried to tell you a while back, but y'all had just had a big fight, so it had to wait. I couldn't wait though, my situation was getting worse. Terrence would get mad and hit the baby if she cried. When I tried to defend her, he'd take it out on me. I didn't know what to do. I love my baby, but I couldn't protect her. I planned to give her up safely by leaving her at a firehouse. I told Andre about it, and he told me that he wouldn't let his granddaughter go into foster care. He wanted to take custody of her, but said he needed some time. My situation didn't permit me any time. Terrence was getting more and more aggressive." she told me.

"What happened the night of the accident?" I asked.

"The night of the accident, you and I were supposed to meet at the restaurant, but somehow my mom found out about the meeting. She tried to confront Andre, and that's when he ran out of there. He didn't want to introduce you that way. He left me there with Terrence and my mom. Terrence went berserk and started punching me while I had the baby in my arms, accusing me of trying to set him up and give his daughter away. He even punched my mom in the face and broke her jaw. When Andre did get back, it was too late. Everything was up. He and Terrence started fighting. Andre was beating his ass, but Terrence never could take an ass whooping fair. He ran to grab his gun. Andre tried to get the baby and I in the car so we could clear shit. When we pulled out of the parking lot, Terrence was right on our tail. He started shooting at the car, and I remember feeling like I had been hit in the head with something. I was leaking blood everywhere. I heard Andre say he was going to get me to the hospital, and I'd be alright. The last thing I remember is hearing a loud bang before everything went black." Bella exhaled. It was as if she had been waiting to tell that story since it happened. After hearing her side, so many things made sense. I remember the nurse saying Andre told her he was in an accident with his daughter before going unconscious. It also explained why he left to go back out that night and why he had been so sneaky lately. Bella was shaking in fear as she leaned in to whisper to me. "Last night, Terrence was here. I felt him. He tried to smother me, and I know he took my baby, but no one is telling me anything. I've got to get out of here. He's going to hurt her, I know it. Andre told me you'd have his back through this. Is that still true now that he's dead because I could really use your help?"

I believed Bella. The only problem was, it wasn't Terrence who tried to smother her, it was me. I felt horrible knowing that I had almost killed a part of Andre for my own selfish reasons. I couldn't dare tell her the truth, but I felt bad about it. I let Bella roll with the story she believed. I didn't know what to tell her about the baby and didn't feel it was the time to mention her just yet. I told Bella for the time being, we would act as if we were cousins while I figured the whole thing out. She looked at me the same way Andre used to. I could tell she didn't believe me, and she probably felt that I would abandon her like everyone else had done. The truth was, my husband, her mother, and her child's father

Terrence, had all let her down. I didn't want to let her down too. I couldn't just take her baby and not give her any closure, no lifeline, no nothing. It had to be terrifying to be out on her own at such a young age.

We both gazed out the window overlooking the trees. She apologized for bringing Andre into her drama and getting him killed. I didn't know how to respond to that. Bella's feeding time was coming so I got up to leave without saying a word. "Please come back." she said, grabbing my arm. I gave her my word that I would, then I left the room.

Outside of the door, the doctor was there talking to one of the neurologists. I interrupted to ask them when they felt Bella would be well enough to come home. I couldn't tell them where home for her would be, but I still needed to know when she would be released. The doctor told me that her body had done most of its healing while she was in a coma, and if they could prove there wasn't any real nerve damage, she would be good. He said they were going to run some tests and do a lot of physical therapy to help her get better at walking again. Best case scenario, she would be able to come home in a few weeks and do outpatient therapy. I only needed about 2 weeks to work out my affairs. I told the doctor that I didn't want anyone bothering Bella and to let her rest. I knew the less pressure she was under the better.

When I got outside to my car, I was still in shock at what had just been revealed to me. Poor Bella. She was a young mom who didn't have a mom to teach her anything about being a nurturer. Speaking of her mom, I hadn't asked the most important question yet, who was her mother?

I needed someone to talk to. It was hard talking to anyone because I was only able to give them limited details. I didn't want anyone to know enough to incriminate myself, and to be totally honest, I was embarrassed. Embarrassed that the facade that I had worked so hard to keep up crumbled right before me in the worst way. My friends knew Andre wasn't a saint, but I never told anyone the extent of betrayal that I had suffered. I was a woman that to the world had it all together, but that was not the case. How could I tell anyone that I had been letting my husband play me for a fool, or that I'm not really this confident woman but instead insecure. I contemplated calling Malik, feeling that as a man he would be less judgmental, but I didn't want to tell someone who may be my future lawyer what was really going on. I could only think of one other person to call, Alicia. Alicia and I didn't see each other much since college but we were always there for each other when it counted. She knew firsthand some of the bullshit I used to go through in my relationship with Andre. She would always say, *"Sis, I hope it's worth it in the end"* and I'd always say, *"we shall see."* Alicia's husband wasn't perfect either, so I knew she would be someone I could confide in. I knew things about her that she wouldn't want to get out and she knew things about me. She was my closest female friend, and I was hoping she was willing to share the burden of my guilty conscience and help me figure out what to do about it.

I called her number, and it went straight to voicemail. I left a message, "Sis it's Katrina. Call me ASAP, I need to talk to you." As an afterthought I added, "please." I ended the call and was stuck sitting there in the car. I didn't want to go home, and my mind was nonstop racing. I left the parking lot hoping my next move would just come to me. I kept driving until my tank was empty. I pulled over at a gas station to get some gas, and my phone rang. It was Alicia. I quickly answered,

"Hello…"

"Hey girl what's up? I got your message, are you ok?" Alicia asked.

"Honestly sis I'm not. Can you meet me for lunch?"

"Sure when?"

"As soon as you can." I begged.

"Ok, let's meet at the Bistro spot in Atlantic station that we like. How's 1 o'clock?"Alicia asked.

"1 o'clock is perfect. See you then LiLi."

"Ok Trina."

I was so happy, I almost left my card in the pump. I hadn't seen my girl in a while and knew she'd be the pick-me-up I needed. 1 o'clock was just enough time for me to stop by the house to freshen up. When I pulled into my driveway, I could see the detective posted up on his car like he had been waiting for me all morning. My heart sank, and I cursed Andre for not letting me get the driveway that would allow for a full U-turn. I put the car in park and hopped out. I walked into my home and didn't speak to him at all. A few minutes later, he rang the doorbell. I answered the door and per usual he was being the annoying asshole he got paid to be. "It's rude to leave someone outside your house waiting for you," he said.

"I didn't ask you to stalk me outside of my home. That was your decision." I snapped back at him. The detective had a grin on his face as if he knew something I didn't. I was sick of him always acting like he had one up on me. "If you have something to say, say it or get the hell off my porch!" I stood there hand on hip waiting for him to leave. He backed down off the steps, never taking his eyes off me.

"I'm headed to the hospital Mrs. Billups. Since you don't want to talk, we'll see what Bella has to say since she is awake now."

He turned around and started walking toward his car. I slammed the door and went inside to put on a cup of coffee. I took a 5-minute shower and threw on some comfortable headed to jail gear. Before I left, I put a shot of caramel and whiskey in my coffee and put it in a to-go cup. I looked around, and the mess was starting to add up around my place. I thought about calling Christina to see if she wanted to make some extra money by adding being a maid to the list of jobs I hired her for. Sky had been at Christina's house going on 2 days, and she hadn't once hassled me about it. I tried not to feel guilty about neglecting Sky. Everything I was doing was to make sure she would be ok in the long run. That's the lie I told myself

I headed to the city towards the Bistro spot and couldn't wait to see Alicia. When I got there the place was empty unlike when we used to frequent it. I was happy that there weren't many people there. Alicia showed up 15 minutes late, and if you knew her that was right on time.

"Haaayyyy Boooo!" Alicia was her normal cheerful self. I stood up to embrace her and lord did I need that hug. We sat down and got into it. Alicia had been going through her own personal issues with her husband, and things seemed like they were getting worse before they were going to get better. When she asked how I'd been since the funeral, a dam had broken, and my tears started to fall. Alicia panicked, believing she said something wrong.

"I'm sorry Katrina. I know things haven't been ok and it's going to be hard for a while. Andre was your soulmate. Pain doesn't go away overnight after someone dies." She had no idea. I was sad that Andre was gone but that wasn't why I broke down. I was torn up because he left so much drama behind that needed to be sorted out. To right his wrongs, I had turned into a completely different person, and I knew eventually God would hold me accountable. I was out there doing the devil's work and didn't have any direction while doing it. I didn't plan on telling Alicia everything, but lord my heart was heavy, and somebody needed to know.

I told Alicia details from start to finish, dating all the way back to when Andre first started cheating on me which seemed to date back further than I had known about. I left out things like me trying to kill him, and my failed attempt at smothering Bella for the sake of confusion. Alicia didn't speak for about 5 minutes.

"I'm sorry that you've been going through this alone. Girl, we're sisters, and I should have been there for you. We both have been going through trials alone, and we always share our good news, but we have to be able to share the good, the bad, and the ugly. We have to pray for each other at all times." Alicia put her hands together and asked me to join her. I opened my heart as my sister said a prayer for me.

"Dear God, this prayer is for my sister. Please heal her. Keep her safe and covered for all her days, especially in her times of need. God, give me the strength to be strong enough for my sister when she needs me and her the same. Please protect our bond. In Jesus name, Amen"

Alicia was emotional. I could tell she was thinking about her personal battles as well. When the waiter approached, I waved him away. Once we were able to get our composure, I thanked her for everything. I knew I had made the right call in asking her to come meet me. I had no question that of all my friends, she would ride for me. She asked what my next move was, and I truly didn't know. I knew I had to go back to the hospital to see about Bella and make sure she was ok, but after that, I wasn't sure what to do. I was hoping Alicia could help me figure it out. I asked for her honest opinion on what I should do, and she gave it to me straight.

"Katrina, it's an ugly cake no matter how you slice it, however if Andre were here you know what he would do. He may have been unfaithful, but he was a decent man, and we both know that. Andre would not let his baby girl sit up in a hospital by herself with nowhere to go when she's released. Like it or not, that little girl and her baby are your family now. If you are going to honor your husband, then do it all the way. The only other choice is to turn your back and take the baby, but what kind of woman or wife would do something like that? Imagine what that girl is going through in that hospital with no support from her baby daddy and no family to support her. Katrina, I hate to say this, but you might have to be the one to fix this. For better or for worse Katrina." Alicia drove her point home.

"Till death do us part." I added.

I wanted to leave it there, but Alicia was right. If it were me, God forbid I wouldn't cheat on my husband, but if it were me, I would expect Andre to honor my legacy. That would be the right thing to do. I could feel my hair falling out at the thought of trying to raise a teenager and a newborn, but If I didn't step up, who would? I didn't have a solid plan, but I did make a promise to Bella that I intended to keep.

I told Alicia I was going back to the hospital, and she offered to ride with me. I was thrilled because I needed all the emotional support I could get. Alicia left her car parked in the parking garage and rode with me. We listened to 90's r&b music while we reminisced about old times back at college like when we would sneak in the window because we had missed curfew. I wish I could relive those days. Although not perfect, life was much more manageable back then. Now most mornings I didn't even want to wake up. I didn't want to die, but I wished I could be someone else and start over. If I could've started over, I might've ignored Andre that day in the gym.

When I got off the exit for the hospital, I could feel my stomach sink. I thought about telling Alicia that the detective

173

might be there, but there was no need in complicating things any further. If the detective was there, it would be best if she had a natural reaction anyway. I pulled in and we both hopped out. Meeting at the trunk of the car, we looked over at each other, and almost at the same time said our friendship proverb, "It's all good."

As the elevator stopped on each floor more people got off while others piled on. I was having second thoughts about showing up with Alicia. My intuition started going off and telling me that maybe I had made a mistake in bringing her. I didn't have the nerve to tell her now that she was there with me to just wait in the lobby.

I asked Alicia to wait by the door for a moment, so I could at least give Bella a heads up. To my surprise, when I walked in, I was the one that needed a heads up. Detective Stone was standing over Bella grilling her. He was trying to get her to admit that she knew more about the accident. He accused Andre of trying to hurt her and the baby and wanted Bella to admit it. She was crying and kept repeating, "I told you I don't know anything." I could see by the detective's demeanor that he was wearing his bad cop hat and trying to scare her. I went into protection mode and snapped at him.

"What the hell do you think you're doing? Do you know she's a minor? You have no right questioning her!" I told him. I pulled my phone out ready to call Malik.

"Whoa whoa, let's not take this personal." He said. He even had the nerve to place his hand on my shoulder as if I would be cordial about it. A doctor walked in and asked, "Is everything OK?" In unison the detective and I shouted, "close the door!" I put my finger in the detective's chest and backed him up. It was my turn to have the upper hand. "Listen Detective Stone, I've been really nice to you, more than I particularly care to be, but if you think I'm going to let you mess with my family, you haven't seen me take shit personal yet. So, let me leave it here. If you have questions, you need to address them to me."

Detective Stone wanted to rebuttal so badly, but what could he say? Instead, he tucked his tail as he should have and left the room. I walked over and hugged Bella who was still crying. I asked if she was ok. She could barely get her words out as she sobbed. I knew it wasn't a good time to tell her I had brought another uninvited guest with me. Before I could walk out of the room and tell Alicia there was a change in plans, she tapped on the door and peeked her head in. I turned around to introduce them, but before I could Bella called out to her, "Auntie *Lili?*!?!"

Chapter 14 Family Reunion

I'm sure my facial expression said everything I needed to say, but I still asked, "What the hell you mean *Auntie LiLi*?" They didn't hear me because the two of them were too busy having a reunion. Alicia ran over to Bella and hugged her. "What's going on? Why the hell are you in the hospital?" she asked. "Katrina, is this the girl you've been talking about, my niece?" Alicia questioned me.

"YES!" I said matter of fact, "And if you're Auntie *Lili* who the hell is her momma?" Alicia's eyes popped out of her head and she clearly made a connection I knew nothing about.

"Oh my God Katrina." she said, backing up to sit down.

"What do you mean oh my God? What do you know that I don't?" I asked. Alicia stared over at Bella then back at me. "A name Alicia. Who is her mom?" I insisted.

"Katrina, it's a long story." she said. But I wasn't going to let a long story get in the way of me getting the answers I needed. I gave her 30 seconds to sort it out in her mind that she wasn't leaving until she broke down to me exactly how she was involved. "So, are you going to start telling this long story or are we going to sit here all day?" I asked. All eyes were on Alicia.

"I have 2 other siblings on my dad's side. They're from Atlanta." Alicia started to explain. "I didn't meet them until I was 14 because they grew up with their mom. When she started having some problems with them, she sent them to Florida to live with us. One day we were one big happy family then these 2 girls showed up with faces just like my dad's. My mom was pissed but it wasn't the first time my father had to be reminded about a kid he left on tour. My dad was in the military so sometimes he'd go away for a while.

176

My mom finally had enough and left him. She sent my sisters to go live with our grandma. I didn't see them again until we were damn near grown, and I didn't find out about Bella until years later. My sister doesn't even call Bella her daughter." Alicia dragged on.

She said a whole lot without giving me the main key I needed, which was a name, and I wondered if she was purposely avoiding it.

"What is Bella's mom's name Alicia?" I asked, exposing the irritation in my tone.

"Her name is Britney." She finally confessed.

"Britney what?" I was so mad the name didn't ring a bell initially.

"Carmichael. Her and I have the same last name." Alicia informed me. In my rolodex of memories, I suddenly had a flashback of me getting put off my friend's porch after her mom told me she had been sent away to Jacksonville.

"What is your other sister's name?" I asked, but I knew it wasn't a coincidence. Alicia confirmed my fears when she told me her name was Bre. I thought when Britney and Bre got sent away, it would be the last I'd ever hear about them. I was embarrassed that it happened so close to me and I didn't even suspect it. I was pissed, but my heart also went out to my friend who was a kid at the time left pregnant and abandoned. I couldn't believe her mom would just send her away like that. Her story was almost identical to Bella's. I felt for her but not for too long. I couldn't believe my best friend would sleep with my man. Alicia claimed to not know, but even if she didn't, she was too damn close to the situation, and I didn't like it. I wanted to ditch Alicia and Bella. Alicia pulled me out of the room and tried to convince me otherwise.

"Look Katrina, we can't let this unfold in front of my niece like this. The plan still stands. Are you going to do what we talked about?" she asked. She was worried about the wrong thing. She should've been worried about us being friends after what I had just found out. Her niece had never been her primary concern before, and if she were, why didn't anyone check for her when she was laid out in a coma? Due to a conflict of interest, I no longer trusted Alicia, and the last thing I needed was someone around me that I couldn't trust. That was how I got in too deep in the first place, sleeping with the enemy. To know that the seed of deceit started from someone I used to call my best friend was like a fresh blow to the gut, even if it were nearly 16 years ago. So much more made sense to me in that moment that I was oblivious to as a child. Like Britney trying to flirt with Andre in the beginning, then acting like she couldn't stand him. Anytime he got near her she treated him so mean. They always acted like they had some type of beef and I couldn't understand why. It must have all been a front. She was never the same with me after he and I started dating, but I thought it was because she didn't want to lose me. Her suddenly leaving school without even saying goodbye. It was like pieces to a puzzle coming together.

"Katrina, say something please." Alicia pleaded.

"I don't know what to say Lili. It feels like I'm living in the twilight zone. I know there's no way you could have known about Andre and Britney, but you gotta understand my concern about the connection between all of you." I told her.

"Katrina, whether you like it or not, we are more connected on this than we thought but that shouldn't change anything. I am still the same person you knew, but coincidences happen. If you can accept that, then nothing has changed about this friendship and it's still all good." She reached her hand out as a truce. I couldn't stay mad at her as much as I wanted to. I didn't have anyone else, and I couldn't stand to lose another friend. I reached out to grab her and we embraced. Alicia asked me again, "So are we sticking to the plan of you trying to pick up where Andre left off?"

 "Yea girl, picking up where Andre left off." I said. We headed back into the room and Bella had lied back down on the bed and was looking out the window. I wondered what she could be thinking.

"What were y'all talking about out there?" Bella asked.

"Just trying to see how we are going to get you out of here." Alicia replied hastily.

"Is that so Auntie?" Bella questioned her.

"Yes, it is baby." Alicia told her. I put my two cents in, "Bella I told you I would get you out of here and that's what I'm going to do."

Bella's facial expression was bleak. Wasn't much life left behind her eyes. She was too young not to have hope. Most people don't realize hope isn't all it's cracked up to be until they're well into their 30s, but Bella was learning early in life. I could only pray the situation didn't taint her too much. Bella looked at her Aunt, but she spoke to me. "Katrina, are you really coming back for me, because last time someone said that they disappeared, and I didn't see them for a while." From the looks of it she was clearly taking a shot at Alicia. "Bella, you know I have too much going on in my life to try and take you in." Alicia said in her defense. "Auntie, how is it that the only family I have always got too much going on for me. I didn't ask to be here and the least y'all could do is be there for me when I need y'all. I almost died in that accident, and well before that when Terrance was beating my ass every day. You turned your back on me a long time ago." Bella scolded her. It was the first time I saw some fire in her. She didn't seem so timid when standing up for herself. Alicia sneered. "You see Bella, that's part of the problem right there. You think you're grown, but you don't want to be accountable like a grown up. Since you call yourself keeping it real, tell why you really can't stay with me or come around my family. Tell Katrina, who clearly doesn't know you like I do, what it really is. I was going to spare you, but since you want to put it out there, let's really put it out there." Alicia turned to me, and I wanted to stop her from going in, but on the other hand it needed to unfold. "Katrina, I tried to take this little girl in after my grandma died, and it almost ruined my credit. She came up to Atlanta and things were going good for a while then one day she just started to change. She was dressing different, talking different, and treated me like I was in her way. I thought it may be innocent like her coming of age or having a bad influence around her. Turns out, this heffa stole my identity, filled out an application, and got a job bartending! She stopped going to school and it took me months to find out. I confronted her about it, and she didn't even try to deny it. I told her she needed to quit the job. She told me she wasn't, so I put her out. I had to get a lawyer involved and got a $5,000 tab to have all the mess she made cleaned up. She's lucky I didn't send her ass to jail. It's not even what she did Katrina because kids these days are foul, my own included, but when I addressed the situation, and this teenage girl sized me up about it, there was no way she was going to continue to live in my shit." Alicia looked over at Bella to drive her point home. "Bella ain't innocent and she damn sure ain't naive. I tried to protect her ass from harm, and she came to my home plotting on me so she's a dub, kid or not." Alicia stormed out of the room.

"That's not how it happened." Bella looked over and said.

From a distance you wouldn't have been able to tell who the adult in the situation was because Auntie LiLi was being very immature about the whole thing. I wished I could bring Andre back from the dead so he could deal with his own shit because everyone involved was a nutcase.

I had to fight back my own visible emotions. My face always said what I was thinking. Bella was only 16 and had seen things adults twice her age hadn't yet. No one deserved the hand she was dealt. She was still lying in bed. I put my hand on her forehead and rubbed through what little was left of her hair after it had been shaved for her surgery. She flinched at my touch and I could tell she had been violated one too many times. It hurt my heart to see a child suffering like that. The sun was starting to go down and darkness approached. I asked Bella if she would be ok while I took her Auntie back to her car. She said she would be fine but confided in me that she was scared. I promised her I'd come back and sleep at the hospital with her that night. I waited until she dozed off and left the room quietly. I went to the lobby and Alicia was there sitting in a chair reading a magazine. We made eye contact, and she knew it was time to go without me saying anything.

We rode back towards the bistro spot in silence. When we pulled up, like a bad date I didn't even put the car in park. I pulled up beside her ride and waited for her to get out. We would have to find out what would come of our friendship with time, but things damn sure would never be the same.

After dropping Alicia off, I pulled my phone out to make the call I had been avoiding.

"Hello." she answered.

"Hey Christina, it's Katrina." I said, trying not to sound tense.

"Hey Katrina, I was just putting Sky to bed, are you on the way back?" she asked.

"Well, I had a few more things to take care of this evening. Would it be a bother if I came in the morning?" I asked her.

"No, it's fine. She's about to go to sleep anyway and I don't have any plans. She will be out of formula soon so you might want to drop some off if you won't be here first thing in the morning." Christina warned me.

"No, I'll be there first thing in the morning. Thank you. I'll take care of you when I see you ok." I wanted to remind Christina I knew I was in debt to her.

"Ok Katrina, it's no problem at all." she said.

On the way back, I stopped by the grocery store to get Bella some soups and other things to eat outside of hospital food. I also grabbed her some comfy pajamas and drawers since the only ones she had were hospital issued. As I checked out with the little things I had, it hit me that Bella hadn't had anyone for the past few weeks including me look out for her. This child was in the hospital alone and no one cared to find her. I tried to kill her, and her own family didn't care. I kept telling myself that my sin should be excused since I didn't know who she was beforehand, but I knew that God would make me answer for my horrible mistake on judgment day. I only hoped it wouldn't keep me out of heaven. When I got everything that I felt Bella would need I headed back to the hospital.

It seemed like the 100th time that I had pulled up at that place. I wasn't gone more than 2 hours but was hoping I didn't stress Bella out too much in thinking I wouldn't come back. It was her eyes that got to me. Her father's eyes used to pierce my soul and hers were no different. I loved Andre so much that I wanted to take care of any living part of him including his offspring that didn't belong to me. When I got on Bella's floor it was quiet. More quiet than usual for that time of evening. I looked in the room to see if she was awake. I dropped the bags on the floor when I saw that the room was empty.

182

Chapter 15 Beautiful Lies

I remained calm at first. I checked a couple of rooms thinking maybe she had been moved. When I didn't see her on the entire floor I started to panic. I asked the nurses, and all of them acted as if she was never there. When I got rowdy, the security guard removed me from the unit. Nurse Nia came running over to reason with him, "Wait wait, she's with me let her go. This is a wife in mourning. Cut her some slack please."

The security guard warned Nurse Nia if I acted a fool again, he would not only remove me, but he'd call the cops. I didn't give a damn about the cops being called. I wanted to know where they had taken Bella.

Nurse Nia was able to get me to calm down and had me follow her into a dimly lit room while she tried to explain what was going on.

"Katrina, after you left Bella confided in me that she thinks someone is trying to kill her. She begged me to stash her somewhere private. I moved Bella to a secluded area, and I told all the nurses on the floor not to say anything to anyone, but she's ok." Nurse Nia told me. I asked to be taken to her immediately.

We went over to a different ward that had a security guard at every entrance. When I walked in, Bella was standing on her own. I asked her if she was ok, and she told me she had a bad feeling about her baby. I figured it was time to tell the truth about Sky.

"Bella, please sit down. I want to tell you something, and I need you to know I did it for you and Andre's own good." I lied. Bella sat down and had a look of fear on her face. She was obviously scared of the news to come. I didn't make her

183

wait long and just came on out with it. "Bella, your baby is with me. After the accident the doctors assumed she was mine, and I didn't know how to contact any of your family, so I just took care of her."

Bella started crying. "Is she ok? When can I see her?" I told her that Sky was fine. "Bella, I would never do anything to hurt you or your baby. I've grown to love her and even gave her a name. I call her Sky, but what did you name her?" I asked.

 Bella smiled for the first time I had seen when she spoke of her baby. "Her name is Drea. Andre chose it." I started to cry thinking of all the times Andre and I talked about having a daughter. I was happy and sad at the same time. "When can I see her? I need to see my baby." Bella insisted. I appreciated her not making a scene like most mothers would have but I honestly didn't think it was a good idea to bring the baby to the hospital again. After all was said and done, I was able to convince her that Sky was better off and more importantly safer with me for the time being. She was composed knowing her baby wasn't with her lunatic ex-boyfriend but still fearful that Terrence would come and do her harm. She told the story again of someone trying to smother her while she slept. I felt a little worse each time she brought it up. I assured Bella that I would stand guard that night, so she could get some sleep. It didn't take long for her to drift off.

While Bella slept, I thought about the next few days to come. I grabbed Andre's ring that now sat on my necklace and thought about him. The pain from losing him was still debilitating but my coping skills were improving daily. It was dark and quiet in Bella's room. Normally when it got too quiet the worst of my pain would resurface. Before that could happen, I pulled out my phone to play a game. Solitaire was one of my favorites, but before I could start a new deal, I received a text.

I got butterflies just from seeing his name. I responded to the "Hey love wyd…" with a simple, "chillin." In my attempt to sound cool, available, but not too available, interested, but not too interested, the only word I could think of was, "chillin." Ty replied back, "Let's chill together. I got a bottle of champagne on ice, why don't you join me tonight???"

The three question marks made me nervous. The pressure was on. I hesitated before responding, "When and where?" With lightning speed, he sent back, "My place." I looked over at Bella who was still out cold. I felt bad for even thinking about it, but I had needs. Ty's text had come right on time, and I knew even if only for a night, he could distract me. I promised Bella I would stay watch, and I was already going back on my word. I guess my husband and I were more alike than I thought. I knew Bella would be hurt if she woke up and I wasn't there, but I didn't care about her feelings more than I did my own at the time. I backed out of that room, closed the door, and headed to the elevator.

When I got to my car, I was all giddy. I looked in the rearview mirror to make sure I was decent. I wasn't, but I pulled out of my parking space and managed to text "Send me the address." When Ty did send the address, I put it in the GPS, turned the music up, and blocked out all feelings of guilt while DMX asked "How's it goin down?"

It seemed like I had been driving forever when I finally pulled up at his mini mansion. Ty was really having his way. Young man, no wife, no worries, a successful restaurant, what more could any bachelor ask for. I walked up to the door and before I could knock the door opened. Ty was standing there in a robe, holding 2 champagne glasses. His forwardness didn't turn me off at all. He grabbed my hand and led me to a bath that was already drawn. There was some soft Jazz playing, and I knew a Kenny G track when I heard it. He was my favorite Jazz musician. Ty started to take my clothes off, and I didn't resist. I climbed in his Jacuzzi style tub while he poured me a glass of Dom. I relaxed, and Ty sat on the edge of the tub and watched me. He didn't say a word and neither did I. I looked into his eyes and caught a glimpse of his intensity. I drank my first glass of champagne like water and motioned for another. Ty gave me the bottle and grabbed another for himself. We both sipped out the bottle and he didn't say anything to me until he requested I get out of the tub. I climbed out with water and soap still dripping from my body. He grabbed the towel but didn't hand it to me. He stood there and held it. He watched my body shiver as the water dripped on his marble floor. I knew what he was doing so I didn't ask for the towel. I stood there and shivered. I did my best to appear confident. I wanted Ty to see me for something different. The first time we had sex, I was a wreck, and he appealed to my vulnerability. I wanted this time to be something he could appreciate and gain from as well. I walked out of the bathroom into his bedroom and climbed on the bed. Ty followed behind and climbed up with me. Before I could seduce him, he pounced. It was so fast I couldn't think, and it was over before I could blink.

I laid there in Ty's bed with him while he snored. I looked over at the clock which said 12:00am. I thought if I hurried, I could beat Bella before she woke. I slid out of the covers and slipped right into my pants. I thought Ty would be so good I wouldn't want to leave but it wasn't like that. I realized afterwards that I didn't like Ty as much as I thought. It was purely physical because when he fell short so did my feelings. I didn't have any business messing with him in the first place. I crept out of his house the same way I crept in and didn't bother saying goodbye.

I got back to the hospital in the nick of time. Bella's nurse was going in to check her vitals. I sat next to Bella in the chair, and it appeared I had been in that same spot all night. When she woke up, she looked over and smiled at me. I smiled while holding back the tears as I looked into the same eyes of my late husband.

Chapter 16 Special Delivery

The next couple of weeks I played catch up. It was so hard to stay on track, but I knew that life wouldn't stop happening and bills wouldn't stop coming so I just got back out there. Christina moved in with me. Her Mom had to go to an assisted living facility for full time care and since Christina was underage, she would have had to leave the state to live with her Aunt. Christina was adamant that she did not want to leave her high school. I knew that feeling all too well. I agreed to let her live with me. I loved Christina so it really wasn't a question. I did let her know she would need to follow the same rules she did at her mother's home, curfew and all. It was a bonus that I had my live-in babysitter readily available, and she still made money any time she helped me with Sky. I took her to get her learner's permit and she was able to drive the Lexus to see her mom whenever she wanted to. Christina was a good kid and I really appreciated her. I knew she had questions about where baby Sky came from, but she never asked.

Bella was in rehab and was scheduled to be released soon. I didn't talk to her or Christina about the change in our living quarters but figured neither of them would have room to protest. Things were starting to look up, and I was determined to focus my energy on what I had left in life and not on what I had lost.

I also regained my momentum at work. It was like I never left. My relationships were still intact, and my team was still at the top of the totem pole. Just when I thought the dust was settling, Detective Stone decided to show up at my job and shake things up.

It was a Saturday morning, and everyone was in the office. He couldn't have picked a better day to humiliate me. I spotted him getting off the elevator and rushed over to stop him from walking all the way in the office. He had a stern look on his face and was visibly frustrated. When I got close enough to him, he slammed me against the wall. "You're under arrest for evidence tampering." he accused. I had no idea what he was talking about and couldn't believe he had come to my job to put on a show. He put the cuffs on extremely tight and tried to sweep me out of the office just as quickly as he had swept in. My secretary Ronda ran over. "What the hell is going on? Why are you arresting her?" she asked.

"Why don't you stay out of it ok." Detective Stone urged.

I asked Ronda to get my phone and call Malik for me. "No!" Detective Stone interrupted. "She's gonna get your phone so I can take it in for evidence." Ronda asked to see a warrant, but he couldn't produce one.

 "If you don't have a warrant, you're not getting anyone's phone." Ronda pushed back. "As a matter of fact, you're not supposed to be arresting her without a warrant," Ronda told him. She walked closer as if she had the keys to the cuffs to release me. If Ronda was using this as an opportunity to show up everyone in the office, it was damn sure working. At work, I was the lead, so people were used to me getting them out of trouble, not the other way around. I appreciated Ronda jumping in, and not assuming I would figure it out on my own. Truthfully, I needed an ally. Detective Stone was mad but tried not to show it. Ronda knew a thing or two about the law and he did not expect that.

"Look y'all can bail her out later, but right now she's going in for questioning." Detective Stone snapped. Ronda threw her hand on her hip and got hostile, "QUESTIONING?!? I thought you said she was under arrest. You came and put my boss in cuffs because you wanna ask her some questions. If you want us to sue APD, just say that. Now is she under arrest or going in for questioning, Officer whatever the hell your name is?" I interrupted Ronda before she could dig in his ass anymore. I asked her again to just get my phone and call Malik. I knew Malik would be able to handle it.

We got down to the police station, and I was put in a room that looked just like the ones you see on TV. Detective Stone left me alone for about 30 minutes, and the air was blasting. I knew the police did that to make you uncomfortable, so you'd give in easier. I was freezing but not cold enough to throw my whole life away about it. Finally, Stone came in and started the interrogation. "Katrina, I like you, but I told you before that if you didn't tell me the truth, I couldn't save you. That's the point we're at right now. I can't save you. Now tell me what happened with you and Bella."

He had a twisted expression on his face and leaned toward me in the chair as if he knew I had a story to tell. I sat up and asked, "Did you learn this ridiculous tactic in detective school, and does it typically work for you because it's just aggravating the shit out of me." I told him. "Like I said before, I don't know anything about what you're talking about." I tried being as convincing as I could. He wasn't amused, and I didn't want him to be. I knew one thing, the less I said the better. He asked me again, and this time made the question crystal clear.

"Bella is saying that you told her to switch her story about what happened the night of the accident. My question is, if you convinced her to change her story, what was the original story, and what do you and she have to hide?"

I couldn't believe that. There was no way Bella would flip and tell the detective anything. She was young and naive, but she stood to lose just as much as me if not more if the truth came out. On top of that, if the detective had anything on me, he would have evidence to back it up. Until I heard some type of recording of Bella ratting me out, I wasn't going to believe anything he said. I wasn't going to be played by allowing him to put the two of us against each other. I replied simply with, "That's a lie and I don't know why you would make that up."

He laughed, "Well look at you. You think you know how to play the game huh. That little credit card fraud trouble you had back in college ain't nothing compared to what I'm going to do to you. It's a difference between the minor and major league Katrina, and I'm telling you right now you're a minor league player battling in the majors. You will lose."

If the purpose of his metaphor was to instill fear in me, it wasn't working. I was in too deep to confess. The only way I would believe the detective had me dead to rights would be when I heard the jail cell doors close behind me. Until then, I was keeping to my story of not knowing anything. "This is a waste of time because I don't know what you are talking about. I'm a grieving wife and you have done nothing but made my life a living hell." I scolded him. The detective pulled out a file and slammed it on the table. "Katrina, here I have a statement from Bella and an unknown witness that you did in fact ask her to change her story." It was an amateur move that I had seen in movies time and time again. The empty file that supposedly contains all the evidence in the world.

Before I started to get excited and speak out of turn, the door opened and in walked Malik. Just like the big-time attorney he was, he came in with all the bells and whistles. "This Interview stops here!" he demanded. Detective Stone jumped up, "Who the hell are you?" he asked.

"The more important question detective, is why am I here?" Malik responded with a smirk that was vengeful and calculated. He attacked, "You know, you'd be lucky if I don't advise my client to sue the hell out of Fulton County for the bullshit you pulled back at her office. I talk to your lieutenant and find out that Mrs. Billups isn't even under arrest. You put her in cuffs at her place of business because you wanted to ask her some questions? You tried to defame my client, taint her reputation, and risk her professional relationships for questioning? What I'm about to do to this precinct is way above your pay grade so you need to digress while you still have a job. Katrina, let's go." Malik didn't even put his briefcase down. He said what he needed to say, and Detective Stone had cottonmouth. As I slid out of the cold metal chair, I laughed and couldn't pass up the opportunity to rub it in his face. "Damn Detective, that was easy, and here I thought I might be here a whole hour." I flipped my hair and walked out the door with Malik right behind me.

When we got outside, I hugged his neck and thanked him for everything. Instead of celebrating with me, Malik's expression was somber. He asked me to join him for a drink, so I knew something heavy was bothering him. We stopped at No CeilinGZ, a bar on Peter street. I ordered a double blueberry vodka and Malik ordered a glass of Bourbon. He didn't wait for the drinks to arrive to get right to it.

"Katrina, I've looked at your case, and from 24 hours ago to now, it has gone from something that can't be taken seriously to something we may need to worry about. It says here that Andre is suspected of attempted murder and reckless endangerment of a child. It doesn't seem they have any hard evidence yet, but still, these are some serious allegations. What the hell is going on that you're not telling me?" Malik sat back waiting on me to give him the spill. His body language showed that he was really concerned that the case was more consequential than I led on.

I didn't intentionally hide anything from Malik. The information was on a need-to-know basis and since he now needed to know, I told him everything. The only detail I left out was the smothering incident with Bella. I was never going to confess to that.

Malik looked exhausted. He hadn't been on the case for a whole day and already looked like he had enough. I knew he wouldn't leave me when I needed him, but I hated to put so much on him at once. He was the only lawyer in town I could trust to defend me and see to it that my privacy was protected.

After a few more drinks there was nothing left to tell. Malik had all the details that he needed, and I had given up all I was going to give. I ordered our last round and we cheered to putting the mess behind us. I was confident that I would be ok. Malik was always up for a challenge, and now that he had all the information he needed, I knew he could finagle me out of the situation. I sipped the last of the alcohol and Malik stepped away to take a phone call.

I glanced up at the news and it was a typical day in the A. The weatherman reported we'd be getting some nice sunshine through the cool breeze. The people in the bar were already dressed and prepared for a warm day. Tank tops, shorts, and skirts everywhere. When Malik came back, he looked like he needed a cigarette. He was skittish and kept looking over his shoulder like he was being followed. "What's up, why are you looking over your shoulder like that?" I asked him. Malik was high strung. "I can't work on your case anymore. Effective immediately, I can no longer be your attorney." he said. I knew Malik had some ties to the Police Department and figured Detective Stone had spoken to someone over his head, but typically Malik wasn't easily intimidated. He tried to get up and leave but I grabbed his arm.

"Tell me what the hell happened on that phone call Malik!" He snatched away from me and left the restaurant. Our bill was no more than $60 but I left $100 on the table and chased after him. I ran Malik down to his car. I grabbed him and forced him to face me. He was distressed with tears in his eyes. "What the hell is happening Malik?" He threw an envelope at me. I opened it, and there were pictures of Malik and a guy at a restaurant. It looked innocent but the guy looked familiar. I just couldn't put my finger on it. "Who is this Malik?"

"It's Colin Miller, number 1 on America's most wanted list." Malik confessed. "He's wanted for murder, and he's been my best friend since middle school. He and his family are the reason I went to law school. They helped me financially and I vowed one day I would clear Colin's name. The problem is, I was with him the night they accused him of murder. The only way to clear his name is to implicate myself. It's complicated and I've been looking for a loophole that ensures we both stay out of prison. In the meantime, my boy is on the run, and I help him out. No one can see these photos, or I'm done." Malik collapsed into his car, and I was speechless. Everyone had secrets, even those that appeared to have it all together. I remembered seeing Colin on the news and thinking there was more to his story. Malik was usually so poised, but he was unhinged. He had accomplished so much, and I didn't want to be the reason he lost it all. I asked him who made the call, but he insisted he didn't know. Malik said they called and told him to go get the envelope off his windshield. They threatened that if he didn't drop my case, the story would be front-page news by tomorrow. He had his mind made up and there was nothing that I could do to change it. I backed away from his car and allowed him to pull off. He left without a second thought, and I couldn't blame him.

Chapter 17 Use me

I took the next couple of days off. I stopped going to see Bella after the Detective told me what she had accused me of. I didn't believe him but figured it would be best if I stayed away from her for a while. Instead, I spent time with the baby and Christina. I took them to the Georgia Aquarium, we caught a play at the fox theater, and checked out a few new restaurants in the city. The 3 of us naturally meshed really well and in all honesty, I wasn't looking forward to Bella coming to our home and altering that dynamic. I couldn't even get adjusted to calling Sky by her birth name let alone letting her mom come back and pick up where she left off. Deep down, I wanted Sky all to myself. Anytime I thought negatively about Bella, I would think of my husband and what he promised her. I felt like it was my job to keep Andre's word. I just hoped she and all of us would get along.

After we were done having girl's day out, the girls and I went to the Lizzie A. assisted living facility to see Christina's mother. During this visit, I went in and thanked her for raising such a wonderful child. I didn't usually go in to speak, but that visit was different because Christina told me they were putting her mother on hospice. I wanted to assure her mom that when she transitioned, I would look after her daughter the best way I knew how. Christina's mom hadn't celebrated her 40th birthday yet. Due to black women's lack of access to good healthcare, she wasn't diagnosed correctly or in time. My heart went out to her because it could have easily been me. Christina was 16 so her mom had done most of the raising. I just needed to make sure she didn't forget any of her teachings.

 After we spoke, I left out to allow Christina private time with her mom. I took Sky, and we went and sat in the lobby so I could read magazines and people watch. My phone kept ringing and when I looked down it was Ty. He had been calling me so much over the past couple of days. I had been distancing myself because I thought that we both knew it was a temporary fling we had. Clearly Ty hadn't been on the same page as me. I didn't owe him anything, but since he was so damn insistent on not giving up, I didn't have a choice but to let him know how I really felt. Reluctantly, I finally picked up the phone. "Hello…" There was a moment of silence before he answered me. "Katrina why are you ignoring my calls? I know you've seen them. I'm not good for a text or callback? You send me to voicemail and don't pick up the phone. That's messed up!"

It was flattering that he cared, and him speaking his mind no matter how vulnerable it made him look, was cute. Even though I lusted for this man I had to let him go. "Ty, I'm sorry. It's a lot about me that you don't know. I have a lot going on right now. I don't have any time to have fun or to play with anybody's feelings. Honestly, I'm still mourning. I want to focus on allowing myself to heal and not using temporary fixes like our stolen moments of passion as pain killers." I explained.

Again, Ty was silent before speaking again. It's like he was thinking of the perfect thing to say. "Katrina, why didn't you just tell me that? I don't like being ignored. The truth hurts but the unknown is so much worse. I just want a proper goodbye." he said. I loosened up and laughed a bit. When I laughed, he giggled too. "Ok Ty, what do you want from me? What is the proper goodbye? Goodbye is goodbye, it all means I won't see you anymore." I assured him. He asked me to join him for dinner at his restaurant one last time, and I knew that was code for I want you. I wanted it too, but I said last time was the last time. He already had me going back on my word. I had to admit I was curious. I agreed for one last dinner. Truthfully my intentions weren't much different from Ty's. My first thoughts after I accepted the date was to shower, smell good, and have an energy drink. I wanted to be ready for whatever. I agreed to meet with him later that night.

After we wrapped up at the facility, I took the girls home and got ready for my date. I didn't know what the future held for me, so I wanted to enjoy every moment as if it were my last. I enjoyed Ty's company, and even though he came up short during our last rodeo, maybe having a goodbye round was what he needed to redeem himself. I put on some Sade, "The sweetest Taboo." I went into my closet and looked at my array of cocktail dresses. I thought about what Andre used to like. He loved when I wore shades of brown. He said it made me look naked. I put on a suede caramel colored dress and red lace heels. I put on some red lipstick to make it all pop. I tied my hair in a high bun, I grabbed a black clutch, and I was complete. I felt sexy and in charge. I had nothing to lose and was anxious to see what the night would bring.

I let Christina know I would be back in a few. On the way out the door I caught one last glimpse in the mirror and made a last-minute decision to take the bun down. I popped the rubber band and let my hair fall. I was pleased with my decision and was so glad I kept the mirror by the door for those last-minute changes. It was just like me to be indecisive about my look.

I pulled up at Ty's restaurant, and it was a busy night. I knew I wouldn't have to wait for a table, but I still didn't feel like being bothered by a lot of people. Ty met me at the door and led me towards the back. I asked where we were going, and he put his finger over my lips. I followed his lead. We went up some steps that led to an area with 3 private rooms. Each was labeled, "Insomnia," "Atlanta Confidential," and "Da City." Ty walked me inside of Atlanta Confidential and the decor was immaculate. Ty said the rooms were reserved for those that needed privacy. They even had their own entrance and exit nearby so you didn't have to be seen by the crowd if you didn't want to. The vibe was sexy, and if Ty's intentions were to get me in the mood it was working. Something about the room felt familiar but I couldn't put my finger on it.

Ty and I talked like old friends while we sipped red wine. It was refreshing to be around him. It helped that he was easy on the eyes. He asked me to tell him face to face why I felt the need to cut him off. It was harder than I thought it would be, but I was ready to face the music. I told him that I couldn't be with him anymore in any way. I confessed that I used him to take my mind off what was really hurting me, and I apologized if he caught feelings. He seemed to take it well. He excused himself from the table. I sat alone in the private room waiting for him to return. When he came back, he had a gift box. I took a deep breath while trying to process why he was making it so hard to say goodbye. He opened the box, and it had a charm bracelet in it. The charms are what made it special. There was an anchor, a life jacket, a cross, xoxo, it was truly thought out, and the diamonds looked real. I smiled at him and asked "Is this a real charm…" I could barely finish before he said, "Come on now, you know you deserve nothing less."

Ty and I had a special moment but him buying diamonds was a bit much. I didn't understand why he was being so nice to me knowing we couldn't be more than new strangers. I accepted his gift and let him put it on my wrist. I didn't embellish in the moment too much because I was starting to feel too mushy. Changing the pace, I asked him flat out, "Are we going to your place after this?" Ty smiled, "We don't have to. I know you need your space so I'm going to honor that. If it's meant I'll see you around Katrina." He tried to sound confident, but I knew he was playing with me. He knew damn well I wanted him and bad, but he wanted me worse. He was trying to make me beg, but I wasn't going to beg him for anything. He stood there staring at me, waiting for me to say what I felt, which was I don't want to leave, but instead I said, "You know what you're right. I should go." I got up to leave and when I got to the door he was on my heels. He grabbed me and pinned me on the door with both wrists. "Why are you so damn stubborn Katrina? You know you don't want to leave." I could feel the breath from his lips as he pronounced every word. He started to kiss me. I melted, and my body naturally reacted. I went limp and instead of pinning me he was now holding me up by my wrist because I couldn't stand. He started at my neck, and right there in the private room he reminded me why I had a soft spot for him in the first place. Ty must have been having an off day last time, but he was back on. He looked me dead in the eyes with every stroke and it was so intense. I bit my lip trying not to moan too loud in his restaurant. He told me the room was soundproof which is why it was private. I was still scared. Ty assured me that no one could see in the room and the cameras were turned off because he turned them off on purpose. He said he was the only one with access to them so there was absolutely nothing to worry about. After his reassurance, I let go. Like a woman in heat, I ripped his shirt open and started to nibble on his bottom lip. I rubbed my sharp nails across his abs. Slowly I went down, not taking my eyes off him. Now Ty was the one who couldn't stand. I wanted to give it all up to him that night. I was sleeping with a man who was about to go away forever because I knew for sure I was never speaking to him again.

We finished up at the restaurant and he had me follow him back to his place. We had rounds 2, 3, and 4 before passing out. I woke up in the middle of the night and laid there staring at the ceiling. My mind had started running and I couldn't go back to sleep. I crept out of his bed and went outside on the balcony. I grabbed the bottle of wine that was on the floor on the way out. I stood there naked letting the late-night breeze cool me off. I looked back through the French doors at him sleeping like a baby. That's when it hit me. I walked back inside looking for my phone so I could call Malik. It was late, and I was worried he wouldn't pick up. I called back-to-back, and finally he picked up. He answered in a raspy tone. I whispered into the phone, "Malik, wake up, it's important." Agitated, he responded, "What

Katrina! It's the middle of the night, this better be an emergency." It was an emergency, but I wouldn't be able to convince him so soon. I asked him to send me a copy of the pictures he got in the envelope the other day. He snapped at me, "Why would I do that Katrina? I don't want those pictures getting out any more than they already have." Pleading I begged. "Malik this is important, I won't let the pictures get out but please send me a copy." Malik hung up the phone in my face and I wasn't sure if he was going to send them or not. I kept a close eye on Ty because I didn't want to wake him up.

A couple minutes later, Malik finally sent the pictures. I pulled the one up of Malik and Colin hanging out with two women in a Restaurant. I looked closely at the picture on the wall, and it was the same picture on the wall in the private room that Ty and I were just inside of at his restaurant. I looked at the other picture of Malik in the parking lot with Colin, and it was Ty's restaurant parking lot. Ty told me he was the only one with access to the cameras, but why would he want to blackmail Malik. I texted Malik back and asked how long before he got the pictures had they been taken. Malik said it had been two days prior. I called him again. This time he was more open to listen to me. "Malik, I don't want to get you involved again but I think I might know who set you up." I could tell Malik was sitting up to make sure he had heard me correctly. "Wait, you know who set me up? Who was it and how do you know them?" Malik wanted all his questions answered right then and there, but I didn't have time to start from the beginning. "Malik, it's a long story, but I think I'm connected to him. I'm with him now."

Malik went from concerned to downright frantic. "Where the hell are you K? Are you in danger? Should I come get you? Katrina, what are you not telling me?"

I couldn't panic because Ty was sleeping just a few feet away.

"Malik, I didn't know this shit was relevant until just now ok. I was fucking this guy and…... never mind it's a long story. Just write this down, hurry up." I rushed him. I could hear him scrambling for a pen. "Ok Katrina, I'm ready."

"4721 Tracy Lane. Atlanta, GA. Ty…. damn I don't know his last name. Anyway, if anything happens to me that's where I'm at. I'll tell you more details later. Bye." I hung up the phone and walked back inside. I looked over, and Ty wasn't in bed sleeping anymore. My heart dropped. I wondered if he had heard my entire conversation. I tried getting my nerves together because if he didn't know something was wrong already, he would be able to tell by the way I was acting.

I grabbed my things from near the bed. I slipped into my clothes, grabbed my purse, and went to leave the house. I bumped into a column in the hallway and dropped my keys on his marble floor. It was so damn loud. I trembled in fear thinking he would be coming out in a second to stop me. I made it to the front door to open it. Ty's car wasn't in the driveway where he left it. I looked back and listened carefully for any movement. I crept over the threshold of the door like a cat, one tip toe at a time. I contemplated making a run for it but decided it would be better if I crept slowly so I could listen for any other footsteps. I made it to my car, and it wasn't until I locked the door that I started to feel a little safe. I cranked the car up and backed out of neverland because I never wanted to see it again. When I got to the end of the driveway, I turned left into the darkness. I couldn't accelerate my engine before I felt him breathing on my neck. I knew it was too good to be true. In the movies they always get caught and it seemed so in real life too.

"Where are you going so soon Katrina?" Ty asked.

"Home." I said, panic-stricken. "Is that ok? Can I go home? We're finished here right?" I asked. Ty chuckled. "Oh no we're just getting started baby. Now take me to her." I didn't know who the hell he was talking about or why he was in my car with a gun pointed at my head. He demanded again, "Take me to her." I turned around to face my fate. "To who? I don't know who the hell her is!" Ty looked at me as if I was bullshitting him, but I truly was lost. Fed up he shouted, "Take me to my fucking kid! I'm tired of playing these games with you. You're going to die tonight playing with me. Take me to my baby Katrina before I spill your blood on this nice leather." Ty made it as clear as possible, but everything was foggy for me. I mean he could only be talking about one kid, but why would he call Sky his kid? Was it possible I had been sleeping with the baby daddy to my late husband's daughter's kid? I didn't want no parts of it. Ty had the gun pointed at my head, but there was no way I was taking him to that baby. In my mind, I was her mom, and no mother would ever put her child in danger. I told him I wasn't budging until he told me what the hell was going on. Ty made me pull back into the driveway and walked me into the house with the gun in my back. We sat in his living room and he asked, "What do you want to know?" That was a ridiculous question because I wanted to know every little detail if he had it. The truth, because he had been lying to me the whole time. He finally sat the gun down and started to reveal. "Bella was my girl. She and I dated on and off for a couple of years. I didn't know she was just 15. I met her at a bar so figured she was of age. When I got her pregnant, that's when she started being evil. Then, she linked up with Andre who she claimed was her dad and that nigga tried to kidnap my daughter."

It was hard to believe that Andre would intervene in someone else's relationship without being asked. Ty wasn't the most trustworthy source, so I wasn't quick to believe anything he had to say. I called Ty out on his lies. "Why didn't you tell me this in the first place? Why should I believe you now?"

"I didn't lie to you Katrina. I didn't know that you had anything to do with this. I still don't know what's going on. All I do know is you have my daughter. Why or how you got her is no longer my concern. Where she is now is what I need to know." Ty said.

"Who told you I have your daughter Ty? How do you know she is with me?" I asked.

"Let's just say it was an anonymous tip. This whole time you've been playing me, Bella too. You took my baby, and I don't know if you're crazy, dumb, or both, but I want her back so I can get on with my life."

I snapped at him, "I didn't take your baby. I took care of her because you were nowhere to be found when she needed you." Ty got upset and picked the gun back up. He pointed it at me sideways and shouted, "You took my motherfucking kid! You can't do that. She's not your blood. You played me Katrina and now you want to sit up here acting like you're the victim, like you ever gave a damn about anybody besides yourself?"

Once again, I was a dollar short and a day behind because I didn't know what the hell he was talking about. Why did he keep saying I kidnapped her when he wasn't at the hospital to get her? No one knew he existed. I brought up the conversation I had with Bella. "Ty you didn't even want your child. Bella told me about you being abusive toward her and the baby. Now you want to act like daddy of the year. This is all a front." I accused him. Ty didn't waiver.

"I don't know what she has told you, but she's a manipulative liar. She had your husband believing that I was the bad guy when all along it was her. Bella don't know shit about loyalty, and she will fuck over any and everyone if it means putting herself in a better predicament. I never thought she would betray me, but she did and now I'm here to collect. All I want is my kid. Andre tried to protect Bella and it ended badly for him." Ty said.

Ty was blaming everyone else but himself for his problems. It was hard to believe that Bella was the bad guy when she was in the hospital because Ty had put a bullet in her head. I didn't have time to piece it all together before he cocked the pistol back and demanded again that I take him to the baby. I didn't know what to do, but I wasn't taking him to my home to see the baby. I told him the baby was with Bella at rehab. Ty got upset that Bella was out of the coma and hadn't contacted him. She didn't owe him anything after all he had done to her. A grown man taking advantage of a teenager. I was disgusted that I gave him the time of day.

We transitioned to his car, and I drove while he sat in the backseat with the gun to my neck. We rode in silence the entire way. I wanted to ask more questions, but I didn't want to upset Ty more than he already was. I was thinking of what move to make once we arrived at our destination, but I couldn't come up with anything.

Chapter 18 Love and War

We pulled up at the rehab facility, and it felt like I had a 50lb weight at each foot. I kept chanting under my breath, "God please help me." Ty walked in with his arm around me like we were a couple in love. Little did anyone know, he was trying to keep the gun hidden. When we walked into Bella's room, she was asleep. Ty looked at me and he knew it was a set up. He closed the door and walked over to Bella. He poked her with the gun. "Wake up sleeping beauty." Ty said in an ominous tone. Bella woke up and looked like she had seen a ghost. I hate I had to bring her into it, but I was out of options. Bella sat up on the bed. "Terrence, what are you doing here?" she asked. "Oh, Terrence is your real name? You lied about your name too?" I interrupted.

"I didn't lie. My name is Terrence Young, but I go by Ty, and Katrina we're not here for you and me to get better acquainted, are we?"

Bella shifted her attention to me. Before she could ask, Ty spilled the beans. "Bella, you didn't know that your nanny was screwing me real good while she was supposed to be looking after our baby or was that a part of your plan too?" The room was filled with faces of confusion. Each of us had a different understanding about what was unfolding. Bella gained her composure, and while staring down the barrel of the gun tried to reason with Ty. "Terrence, I know that I haven't been the best girlfriend to you, but please don't take this out on our baby. It was me that lied, not her. She's only a baby. This isn't her fault." Ty didn't seem to care about Bella pleading for mercy. He pointed the gun wildly and asked again, "Where the hell is my baby Bella? I will kill you, right here right now, and I'll walk out like nothing ever happened."

I didn't know how Ty thought he could pull that off, but I didn't want to test him. I thought about trying to wrestle the gun away, but the way Ty had picked me up when we were getting busy, I knew he could overpower me. I decided to let it all play out. Bella looked at me waiting for me to take the reins and say something. It occurred to me I was the only one who knew where the baby was. If I gave her up though, Ty could still kill us both after. He wouldn't make it far, but Bella and I would be dead. I tried thinking of another lie to tell that would buy more time, but I couldn't think of one. Ty had enough and forced me over to the corner. I knew my time was up, so I started to pray. I closed my eyes and waited for the loud bang and the darkness, but it never came. I peeked my eyes open, and Ty was standing there frozen. He was shaking as he tried to pull the trigger. Tears fell from his eyes, and he cursed himself. "Fuckkk!" He looked me in the eyes with the cold stare of death. "Don't torture me, if you're going to kill me just do it." I urged him. Ty pushed the gun against my skin. "Shut up Katrina!" he demanded. I was just waiting on the curtains to close. Bella still sat in her bed. She had made strides, but she was still very weak and incapable of fighting. Ty tried to be tough, but I caught a glimpse of his weakness, it was me. I could tell that no matter what he said he had felt something for me, otherwise why was it so hard for him to just pull the trigger. I saw my chance, so I took it. "Ty, was anything we shared real, or was it you acting the whole time?" My eyes were soft trying to convince him.

"Even if what I felt for you was real, none of that matters now Katrina. I'm in too deep. I'll have to live with that." he said.

I pushed the issue. "If it didn't matter, tell me it was nothing, and I'll leave it alone. Tell me that what we did was just you acting the whole time. The way I made you feel. Was that all you just playing the part? Say it was and I'll let it go." I told him. Ty was on a mission, but while on that mission he fell for me. I liked him too, but I didn't take him seriously enough

205

to lose sight of what was important. My main priority the entire time was Bella and Sky's safety. If I had to play Ty to ensure that, I had no quarrels doing so. Ty couldn't admit to me that we were nothing, but he kept the gun on me. He stared from behind the barrel trying to look tough, but I could tell he wasn't a killer. Bella looked on, most likely wondering what connection I made with her man that was causing him to hesitate on killing us both. "Ty, why can't we just talk about this. Why ruin everyone's life over something that can be worked out. I know where the baby is, and you know me. You know that I'm a good person. Whatever I've done was with good intentions. I too was betrayed. My husband didn't tell me any of this. I had to find out about him and Bella and Drea after he was dead." Ty thought about what I had said and started to lower the gun. I could see that just like me, he had lost himself all in the name of love. Call me crazy, but I felt bad for him. Ty sat down and started rubbing the gun against his head. He cried, and Bella sat there speechless. It was like she had never seen that side of him, and it confused her. I started walking toward Ty and I wanted to get the gun, but I knew if I failed on my first attempt he would snap right back into reality. Instead, I hugged him. I held him tight, and I wanted him to know that I understood his pain. We both were in pain, and we processed that pain the best way we knew how. I finally let him go, and he looked up at me. His eyes said that he was sorry, but the words never left his lips.

Before we were able to completely de-escalate the situation, Malik burst into the room with Detective Stone. They startled Ty and by reflex he picked up the gun and aimed it at the detective. Without blinking, Detective Stone shot 6 times hitting Ty with 4 bullets. Ty hit the floor and I went down with him.

I was in shock. My ears were ringing, and I couldn't make out the words Malik was saying. Ty was gasping for air and blood was coming out of his mouth. It tore me up to see him that way. Earlier he wanted to kill me, but we were having a breakthrough. He was out of his mind, and it had driven him to a point of no return. I had been there more than once, so my conscience wouldn't allow me to shun him. I sat up and put Ty's head in my lap. "Breathe!" I coached him. Detective Stone kicked the gun away. Malik pulled me up off the floor away from Ty. His head dropped out of my lap and hit the floor hard like a basketball. The entire time Bella didn't say a word. Doctors rushed through the doors and tried to help. Malik asked me what happened. I didn't want to say anything while the Detective was in the room with us. I looked over at Bella, and with one finger over my mouth I motioned for her to not say a word. Malik caught my signal and pulled me out of the room. "Katrina what the hell is going on? You better start talking and thinking about protecting yourself instead of everyone else." Malik demanded. I told him that the pictures being used to blackmail him were taken in Ty's restaurant. I explained how Ty was connected to the case and who Bella really was. Malik was horrified. He told me that he was back on my case and this time he promised not to leave my side until it was all over. Malik said he didn't feel right not keeping his word to me after I kept his secret from all those years ago. I was thankful that Malik was coming back around and grateful to God that Bella and I had survived the ordeal.

When the doctors cleared the room with Ty, Detective Stone came over to ask me some questions. He was much more humble this time around, and he started off with an apology. He told me that he would need to get a statement from Bella and I when we were ready. Malik told him that he would bring me down to the station in the morning. I agreed to let him interview Bella if I was in the room because truthfully, I had questions for her too.

Chapter 19 If Only You Knew

Ty survived his injuries and was released from the hospital within a week. He was sent straight to jail where he was held on no bond and sat to await trial. The same week that Ty was released from the hospital, Bella was finishing up her rehab. Her and I were much closer since Ty was no longer in the picture to shake things up. We were able to settle on a story that would protect the both of us. In the end, she just wanted to feel safe again and make sure her baby would be ok. I wanted the same, so it was easy for us to agree that the part about Andre being her real father, and me kidnapping the baby from the hospital should be left out. Instead, the story was just as it had been all along. Sky was Andre's daughter, and Bella and Andre were cousins. Ty was a jealous ex-boyfriend that was mad because Andre tried to help Bella get away from him. The night of the accident, Ty snapped and got violent. We didn't lie, we just omitted some of the truth. Ty was charged with second degree murder, child endangerment, attempted assault on an officer, and so much more. It was clear he wouldn't be getting out anytime soon and no one would believe anything he had to say anyway.

Bella agreed that it was best that I raise Sky because I could give her the life she deserved. I didn't feel right just taking the baby, so I assured Bella that just as much as Sky was family, so was she. I told her that I had a room for her at my home, and she wouldn't ever have to feel like she didn't have a place to go for as long as I was around.

I was in close contact with the detective who kept me informed every step of the way. Ty's trial was coming up soon and they needed Bella and I both to be witnesses. I couldn't wait for it all to be over. It was like a nightmare that lasted too long. Malik told me the case against Ty was pretty cut and dry and he'd be lucky if he got less than 40 years, which was a best-case scenario for him.

When the trial started, I was a nervous wreck. All the evidence showed Ty was responsible for killing my husband, but something inside of me wouldn't settle. I lied on the stand, and it was harder than I imagined it would be. Not because I promised to tell the truth, but because I had to look Ty in the eyes while I accused him of being a lunatic when in reality, I wasn't much different. I tried convincing myself over and over that I wasn't as awful of a person as I felt. I had been sleeping with the man accused of killing my husband and I had to live with that. For the past several months, I had been thinking Andre was this awful person when all along he was just who I had known him to be, imperfect but not a monster.

The outcome for Ty's trial was just as Malik predicted. He was sentenced to life in prison with no possibility of parole. I was worried the whole time that he might try and petition the court for a paternity test, but he never mentioned it. When the judge announced his sentencing, Ty cut his eyes at me and mouthed, "Take care of my baby." He glared at me until the guards took him away.

Not immediately, but with time the girls and I got close. We weren't the "Brady Bunch," but we made the living arrangement work to the best of our ability. Christina and Bella didn't do much talking, but they didn't have much in common either. Christina was more of a schoolgirl, and Bella's life was more of a bad hand that she was trying to win with. A lot of the uneasiness between them also came because Bella was jealous that Christina had more of a connection with Sky than she did. The few times Bella tried picking Sky up she wailed uncontrollably. Bella didn't have patience like Christina, so she couldn't be bothered. It showed in her relationship or lack thereof with her child.

As much as I could, I tried bringing us together by having game nights, movie nights, and whatever else I could conjure up. One Friday, we were all watching Terry McMillan's, "Waiting to Exhale." I gave the girls life lessons on relationships and how to avoid the no-good men out there. While I was trying to play the part, my phone kept vibrating. I ignored it at first because I didn't want any distractions, but after the fifth call I looked at the caller I.D to see that it was the same number that had been calling for the past few days. The number wasn't familiar, but the person had been texting trying to get me to meet with them. I declined the request, but lately the texts were getting more and more revealing. They sent me personal information about myself and Andre that no one else outside of him and I could've known. Against my better judgment, I finally responded to the text message and asked who they were. The person on the other end refused to reveal their identity and insisted that I would have to meet them in person to find out. After we wrapped up movie night, I agreed to meet in the mall parking lot as they had requested. I knew it was crazy to be going to meet someone I didn't know, but it felt like it may be another loose end to the never-ending saga, and I wanted to get it over with. I told the girls I needed to make a late-night run and I'd be back soon. I packed my weapon in my purse for security and headed to meet the stranger.

I pulled in behind the building and flashed my headlights twice just as the text had instructed. I didn't see anyone at first, so I waited. I was a nervous wreck, looking around constantly, keeping the truck in drive so I could pull off with lightning speed if need be. After about 20 minutes, I could see headlights approaching. The sky was dark, and the lights blinded my rearview vision. I could see the car stop behind me, and the driver side door opened. The driver started walking fast toward my truck. I panicked and sped off. I could only see a shadow, but I was scared. I turned onto the main street and the car pulled out behind me. The person was right on my bumper. I made a quick right, but I couldn't shake them. I looked at my tank and I was on E. I wasn't going to be able to run forever. I reached in my purse and pulled out my .22. I made sure it was loaded, and I pulled over in the first lit parking lot I came across. I hopped out of my truck and pointed the gun at the car in plain view with every intention of blasting their ass if it was a set up. I waited for the driver to get out. The door opened, and 2 arms stuck out of the window. A familiar voice shouted, "Don't shoot!" I lowered my weapon, but I couldn't understand why she was there.

"What the hell are you doing?" I shouted at her. "Are you trying to get shot?"

"I'm sorry Mrs. Billups, but I have very important information for you. I didn't want to tell you over the phone. I needed to meet you in person to make sure you understand what's going on." she said.

"What are you talking about? What important information? What's so important that you're willing to lose your life over it? You're sending me all these strange texts. How do you know these things?" I asked.

"Your husband told them to me. He told me to tell you when the time was right, and I promised him as his dying wish that I would see to it that I did that for him." she said.

"Wait a minute, you talked to my husband before he died? Why didn't you tell me?" I asked.

"I'm here to tell you now if you're willing to listen." she said.

I walked over to my truck to put the gun up and met her halfway to listen to her story. She pulled out a cigarette, and I never would have known that she smoked. "So, tell me what is so urgent that you have me out here in this parking lot this

211

late at night. You could've at least waited until morning." I told her.

"Actually, I couldn't. Morning could be the difference between life and death for you." she warned.

"Life and death? What the hell is that supposed to mean?" I asked.

With her lungs full of smoke, Nurse Nia dropped a bomb on me. "Look, when your husband came in that night, he was critical. I believe that he knew he was going to die. He wanted someone to know the truth about what happened in that car, and I was the one he trusted with that information. I was in the corner of the room watching the doctors do their best to save him. Your husband locked eyes with me. He pulled me close to him and asked me to record something. He told me he needed someone to get a message to his wife. He told me to tell you he meant what he said. Your husband recorded his dying testimony on my cell phone, and I think this is something that you would want to hear." I was in shock. I couldn't believe Nurse Nia had been holding back information. She pulled her phone out and pressed play. I heard Andre's voice, and a cold chill went all over my body. For someone who I imagined was in agonizing pain, he sounded incredibly calm.

"Katrina baby, if you're listening to this it means I won't get a chance to tell you the truth face to face. I hate that we were fighting last I saw you, but that doesn't change that I always have and always will love you more than anything in this world. I took you to that fancy restaurant that night because I had someone I wanted you to meet. I had been procrastinating for so long and after we left the counseling session that day, a spirit just came over me and said do it. The someone I wanted you to meet was my daughter Bella and our granddaughter Drea. I found out about them a little while ago. I didn't know what to think at first. She's telling

212

me all these things and who her mom is. I had no idea that her mom was ever pregnant by me. I was young when I made that mistake, and it was something I never thought would come to light. I feel horrible even having to tell you this, but I slept with your best friend Britney. She and I were at a party drinking and one thing led to another. I was young and my hormones got the best of me. It only happened once Katrina. I wish I could take it back, but I can't. I swear I never knew about this child. I wanted to tell you as soon as I found out about her, but I was so scared of losing you. I had done so much already, and I felt like this would be too much for you to handle. The day you overheard me talking on the phone, I was talking to Bella, but I was too scared to tell you then. She was in some trouble and told me she was in an abusive relationship with this guy. She needed my help. She said he had been abusive towards the baby, and she was in fear for her life. I tried to step in and help her, but it was all a set up. Bella started talking about giving the baby up for adoption. I thought about us, and how bad we wanted a child. I figured this would be an opportunity for us to make that happen and for me to make things right with Bella for leaving her all those years ago. I convinced Bella to allow me to legally adopt Drea. The week that we were going to get everything together, Bella changed her mind, and said she wanted $20,000 for the baby. I was infuriated, but I had already grown attached to Drea, and I really wanted to make her a part of our family. I started to see that Bella was toxic, and it would be in Drea's best interest to be with us anyhow. I agreed, and I gave her the money. I called her after our counseling session and told her it was enough of the games. I was ready for her to hand the baby over. I got a lawyer involved to make sure that what we were doing would be considered a legal adoption. He got us some paperwork drawn up and I was going to have her sign them that night. Bella picked the restaurant that we should meet at, which just so happened to be a spot a friend of mine owned. I never knew her picking that place was all a part of her plan to cross everyone out. She was supposed to help me explain everything to you and turn the baby over, but instead everything went left. When I went to get her out of the back, Ty, the guy you met at the restaurant was there saying that he paid $20,000 for the baby too. I didn't even know Ty was involved, but he's Drea's father. He and I got into a fight because he thought I was plotting against him, and I felt like he and Bella were both in on it together. The next thing I knew Britney showed up, and I didn't want you to find out about the situation like that, so I rushed out of the restaurant. When we were headed home, Bella texted me to come back. She said that Ty snapped and was threatening to kill her and the baby. Although she betrayed me, I couldn't leave my daughter out there like that. I dropped you off and rushed back because I thought she and the baby were in danger. When I got there, Ty was choking Bella demanding his money back. I got in between them and was able to get her and the baby out of the restaurant. When I got her to the car, I told her I was taking her to the police for extortion if she didn't give me the baby or my money. She started flipping out in the back seat, then she threw Drea out of the car while I was driving. I tried to stop her, but it was too late. When I swerved, my gun flew from under the seat. She grabbed it and tried to shoot me. I was trying to wrestle the gun from her, and it went off, but she was still fighting. I fought back, and lost control of the car. We spun out, and I don't really remember what happened after that. I woke up on the stretcher, and now I'm here. I don't know where Bella or the baby is. Katrina, I'm recording this to let you know I love you, and I know I was wrong for not telling you the truth up front, but this is everything. I don't know what's going to come of this, but I need you to do something for me. I need you to make sure the baby stays with you. Whatever happens, you can't let Bella get to her. Not Bella or Britney. I've seen this girl do things you wouldn't think a 16-year-old is capable of. There is so much more I need to tell you, but please do whatever it takes to see to it that Drea is ok. Even if I have to go away for a minute, I need you to take care of that."

Andre started struggling to breathe. "Hang in there man." I heard someone say. "There's internal bleeding. We have to get you to surgery right now." A doctor spoke up. There was chaos in the room, and the recording stopped after that. Nurse Nia added, "He wanted you to get to the hospital as soon as possible to save the baby, but he didn't give me your number before they rushed him out. That's why you didn't know about it until the detective called. He just kept saying, tell Katrina I did this for us, and I was going to say something. I made up the story about Bella being his cousin and the baby belonging to him because I felt like he was telling the truth. At the time Bella couldn't speak, so she couldn't dispute anything. Your husband wanted me to do whatever I could to protect that baby. Mrs. Billups, I've been a nurse for 20 years. I know when a person is lying to me, and I ain't never seen a man lie on his deathbed."

For a moment, Nurse Nia was drowned out by the sleeping dogs waking up. Could I have been played? The whole time I had been thinking that Bella was a victim, but could she have been the mastermind behind it all? She was only 16, but that didn't mean she couldn't out-think me and two grown men. I appreciated the nurse for keeping her promise to my husband, but I resented her for waiting so long to tell the truth.

"One last thing." she added. "Your husband asked me to write these down and give them to you. He said he never forgot." Nurse Nia handed me a sheet of paper with dates on it, five dates. I looked them over, and my eyes filled with tears. The nurse asked what they meant, and I could barely speak. I took a deep breath and got choked up trying to get it out. I knew the nurse was telling the truth because no one could have known the dates and she had every single one.

"What is it Mrs. Billups?"

I balled the paper up and held it close to my heart. "It's the dates I lost my babies. I didn't think he knew about them all." I felt so guilty I was inconsolable. Andre had every single date for every single miscarriage and had even picked out names for all of our children. He was sharing that pain with me, and I didn't even know. Nurse Nia started to cry along with me. We embraced, and she did her best to convince me I wasn't a bad wife. I started to think back at how quickly I was to believe all the lies that were told to me after my husband died. I knew Andre, yet I let a bunch of strangers who I didn't know sway what I felt about him. After listening to Andre tell his side of the story, he made the most sense.

I got my bearings in order, and I was clear on what my next move needed to be. Bella seemed like such a sweet girl, and to find out that she was the reason behind the accident sent me into a rage. I thanked Nurse Nia and asked her to keep the information between the two of us. As I walked away to leave, she warned, "Be careful Mrs. Billups, your husband said Bella is dangerous." I waved at her and gave a head nod. The way I felt, it was Bella that would need to be careful. I knew I needed to be calm and calculated if I was going to outsmart her. I wasn't dealing with your typical 16-year-old. I took my .22 back out and put it in my pocket.

I got on the expressway to head home. Puddles in my lap as I thought about Andre. He was my everything, even with his flaws. I missed him, and I would avenge his death, whatever that took. My first order of business was Bella. I got off at my exit and gripped the steering wheel like it was my last dollar. I was sick of letting people play my husband. Bella's young ass was going to pay for starting this. If it wasn't for her, none of it would have happened. I would still have my husband, and who knows where she would be, but things could go back to the tolerable dysfunction that we once had. When I pulled up the house was dark. I figured the girls had gone to sleep, and contemplated waiting till morning to address the elephant in the room. I had a flashback of what

Nurse Nia said about Bella being dangerous and knew waiting another night would be like rolling dice with my life. I put the truck in park, and I was prepared for anything.

I was quiet as a mouse when I walked inside. There was a queer feeling, and my gut said something was up. I looked around for any signs of movement. I didn't see anything. I cut the light on and there they were. Christina was laying on the floor, hands tied behind her back, and Sky was in her bassinet. I didn't see Bella immediately, but I knew she was the culprit. Christina cut her eyes over towards the kitchen, and I figured that's where Bella was hiding. I crept around to the other side. I could see Bella crouched down behind the cabinet with a knife in her hand. I lunged at her, and we began to struggle over the knife. She swung wildly and managed to cut me on the forearm. My adrenaline was rushing so much I didn't feel it, I only saw blood. I grabbed a frying pan out of the dish rack and swung it at her. It caught her on the shoulder, and she screamed in pain. She ran into the dining room. She put the knife to Sky's neck and threatened to slit her throat if I didn't back off. I stopped in my tracks. I put my hands up, "Please Bella, Sky has nothing to do with this." I begged her.

"Stop calling her that! Her name is Drea not Sky!" Bella shouted.

"I'm sorry. I didn't mean to call her that. I know her name is Drea. Can we please not involve Drea in this. What do you want from me? I'll give you whatever you want. Just don't hurt her please." She pressed the knife down harder on the baby's skin. Sky started to cry. I moved closer to her pleading, "Bella please."

"You guys really will do anything for this damn baby. I don't get it. Why not just have your own? Oh, I forgot you can't. My daddy lost his life for her and now you are about to throw yours away too." Bella said, menacing. She was a

217

psychopath, and I was starting to see everything that my husband was talking about. That innocent girl's act at the hospital was all a facade. I tried to reason with her, "Bella, what you're doing right now is going to end bad. What's your endgame? What do you think happens after you kill the baby?" I asked. "I kill the baby, and I go on with my life, that's what happens. What do you think will happen?" she asked. I didn't say anything, but I had already devised a plan. I was just waiting for my partner to do her part. Bella pointed the knife in my direction and asked me to drop the pan and get down on my knees. That wasn't happening. She threatened to cut the baby again. "Now!" I shouted. Christina kicked Bella in the back of her leg, and she fell to the ground. The knife flew out of her hand and landed in the bassinet. I ran over to see if Sky had been cut. Luckily, the knife landed next to her foot and didn't touch her. Sky was such a blessed baby. I picked the knife up and told Bella to stay down. I helped Christina up and cut the tape off her wrist. She removed the tape from her mouth and started kicking and shouting at Bella. I stopped her and asked her to call the police.

When Christina left the room, Bella sat up. I couldn't believe that she was playing everyone all along. I wanted to kick her ass like a grown woman, but I figured it was best to let the cops deal with her. Bella looked up at me and said, "You think I don't know huh?" I didn't know what she was talking about, and frankly I was sick of dealing with her mind games. I didn't entertain her and figured if there was something she wanted to get out she'd say it. She teased, "Katrinaaaaa, can you hear me talking to you? Don't you want to know what I know, or should we wait on the cops to get here?"

Fed up I demanded, "Just say it already, what the hell do you know?" She was happy to be getting under my skin and even happier to spill the beans. "I know you tried to kill me." she revealed. My eyes got wide and if she had any doubt my facial expression confirmed it all.

"Terrence didn't know what hospital I was in because I was listed under my father's last name. Besides, Terrence wouldn't have had a reason to kill me. All he wanted was his baby. There is only one person I could think of that would want me dead, and that person is you Katrina. What do you think the hospital would say if I told them I remember what happened that night? I'm sure they have cameras that they could roll back." Bella sat up trying to hide the pain she was in from Christina putting it to her ribs. I called Christina back in the room and told her to take the baby and my car and go somewhere safe. I told her not to talk to anyone until I called her. I gave her my debit card, I.D, and keys.

After Christina left, it was time for me to get rid of Bella. I sent a text to Nurse Nia to ask for a favor. When she told me she would take care of it, I knew that I didn't have anything else to worry about. I texted one other person, and my plan was in motion.

I told Bella we were taking a ride, and for the first time that night, I sensed that she was scared. She was right where I wanted her to be. I put her in the trunk, and I drove her out to a piece of land one of my clients owned that had been vacant for months. I popped the trunk, and with a gun pointed at her face I demanded that she get out. For all she knew, we were in the middle of nowhere, and no one was coming to save her.

"Why Bella, why did you hurt the only man that really tried to help you?" I asked.

"He should have never left me in the first place. Had he been around from the beginning, I never would have ended up in this situation. He left my mom, and he didn't care what happened to me. What kind of man abandons his only child?" she asked. She waited for an answer that I couldn't give her.

"Bella, this could have gone another way. You didn't have to do it like this. I know you were scared, with the baby and all, but you could have been genuine with us, and we would have helped you." I still was hoping somehow that she would come to her senses.

Bella laughed at me. "You still don't get it do you Katrina? I was never scared. I planned this whole thing out. It appears I'm the only one with good sense in this situation, so let me break it down for you. Terrence, or as you so affectionately call him Ty was just a pawn in my game. It's not a coincidence that I got pregnant by my father's associate. I've been planning this for a while now. I found out on Facebook Terrence's restaurant was Andre's favorite spot to go to. I applied for the bartender job there. I told them I was over 21 on the application and thanks to Auntie LiLi's identity I was able to pull it off. Once I was in, Terrence was puddy in the palm of my hands. He had a thing for my eyes. You know how that is right? It's why you fell in love with my father. Anyway, Terrence was just collateral damage to me. I needed someone who was close enough to Andre to give me the information I needed without suspecting anything. When Andre would come into the restaurant, I would casually ask Terrence about him. He told me everything I needed to know, and that's how I found my way in. Terrence didn't find out he was being played until it was too late. That night at the restaurant, when we were supposed to meet, my father and Terrence had a huge blow up because I schemed them both out of $20,000. Imagine that, two friends getting played right under each other's noses. They both wanted Drea, and I just wanted the money. Once I had my cut, I left them two to figure out who gets the baby. May the best man win, and I guess it wasn't Andre or Terrence." Bella smiled, exposing her devilish grin. She wanted me to go back and forth with her, so I did.

"Bella, you're too young for this game. In the end you never get to pick your consequences." I said to her.

"Katrina, you know what? I think I need some more money. I got my $20,000 from Andre, and my $20,000 from Terrence, but you haven't paid your toll. I'm taxing you the same since you're so interested in taking my child away from me." Bella threatened.

Bella didn't have an ounce of regret on her face. She had no alliances, so she didn't have an emotional aspect to affect her judgment. She had been planning her get back for years, and it was clear she was going to up the ante as much as she could. "Are you proud of yourself? All the lives that you've ruined." I asked.

"I don't feel bad for doing what I did. Andre deserved what he got, him and the baby. I only wished she got run over by a car when I threw her out, and I wish I didn't miss when I shot him. As for Terrence, who cares what happens to him." she said.

I couldn't believe how cold she was. She was so young but didn't have an ounce of empathy in her. I shed a single tear because it was finally over. I got the closure I needed, and I wouldn't have to ever deal with Bella again. I lowered the gun, and Detective Stone came from behind the tree and put her in cuffs. "You set me up?" Bella shouted. She had finally been outsmarted. I gave Detective Stone the copy of the audio recording from Andre, and he had his own evidence hearing Bella say out of her own mouth that it was her that threw the baby out of the car, and her who caused the accident. I texted Christina to make sure she and the baby were ok. It was such a relief to tell her it was finally over.

CHAPTER 20-Window Seat

As time went on, we struggled getting back to normal. Even though we didn't have to worry about Bella or Ty for a while, it was still going to take some time before we would feel safe again. The prosecutor offered Bella a plea. She turned it down, so she was facing 20 years taking it to trial.

Malik worked with the prosecutor in the case. Bella's defense was based solely on trying to create reasonable doubt. Her defense attorney painted a picture that Bella was this young girl taken advantage of by the adults in her life. He made it seem like my husband was this awful man that had abandoned her, and everyone else was out to get her. The defense attorney put me on the stand. He asked about my husband's relationship with Bella, and I stated what I rehearsed. I was sure to make eye contact with the jury just as Malik had taught me. Of course, they brought up Sky and accused me of kidnapping. Luckily, the paperwork that Andre had drawn up was in fact legal. I had to forge some signatures, but Malik helped us get the process completed and the records were sealed. The judge wouldn't let the defense go on about it. They threw another wrench in the case when they asked me about the night I tried to kill Bella. The prosecutor objected asking, "Where are these facetious allegations coming from?" I looked out in the courtroom for her face. I spotted Nurse Nia who gave me a head nod. The Judge hit the gravel, "sustained." I confidently told the Defense attorney, "I don't know what you're talking about. I would never try to hurt Bella." I was dramatic but poised. The judge asked, "Do you all have evidence for this claim?" Bella's defense attorney looked back at his team who shrugged their shoulders. "No, your honor, I apologize. The hospital is normally under 24-hour surveillance, but the footage from the night in question mysteriously isn't there anymore. No further questions."

The Judge, Your Honor Lateesha Myles threatened Bella's lawyer that if he threw out another accusation with no proof to back it up, he would be held in contempt. I exited the stand and walked out of the courtroom. I was met in the hallway by Nurse Nia and a handsome man. "Hey Nia, Thank You for everything. I really appreciate it." I told her.

"Don't thank me, thank this guy. Meet my boyfriend Jose, the head of security at the hospital. This is who helped me out with that footage." Nurse Nia said. Jose reached for my hand. "No thanks needed ma'am, just helping out my girl here." I shook his hand and hugged Nurse Nia before heading outside to wait on Malik to come out with the verdict if they were able to reach one.

A little while later, Malik came out smiling. Bella was found guilty on all counts. First degree murder, attempted murder, assault with a deadly weapon, child neglect, and about 10 more charges. Just like that, she had thrown her life away playing in the Lion's Den. She was sentenced to a juvenile facility and would be transported to a women's prison when she turned 18 to finish out 20-year sentence. I asked about Ty's murder charge, since the truth was, he didn't murder my husband after all. Malik told me the D.A agreed to reopen his murder case, but all the other charges would still stand.

Malik and I went out for drinks to celebrate after our big win. We had rid our lives of murderers and crazy people, and now it was time for family therapy. I was so happy to be able to focus on Christina and Sky without looking over my shoulder or feeling like someone was after me.

At Kiki's Kaleidoscope, a bar that specializes in exotic drinks, hookah and live performances, Malik and I were throwing them back. Malik had something to celebrate as well. He didn't have to worry about his personal life getting out there to the public. I pulled out my checkbook and tried paying Malik for everything he had done. He refused to accept the check. I was finally able to force it in his pocket, but he pulled it out and ripped it up. He made so much money from his other clients he was able to do a few pro bono cases a year. I told Malik about the quick sale I had done on my home. I didn't get nearly what Andre and I had invested into it, but it was the last chapter for me. I loved that house, but the memories from the past few months were too dark. When Malik and I finished up, I was excited to go home and share with Christina that everything went great.

We moved into a condo in Buckhead, and although it wasn't my style, I had to admit that being in the middle of the city was a great distraction. Everything was at my doorstep. There was a locally owned coffee shop just a few feet away, a grocery store within walking distance, and a lounge up the block that I'd go to when I was in the mood for a drink. We were living life like a trio of city girls, and it was just what we all needed.

We celebrated Sky's birthday shortly after the trial. I still didn't know her official birthday, but I had given her one anyway. I chose April 19th which I thought was a good day.

Christina was getting ready to graduate, and had gotten herself a full scholarship to college, an HBCU at that. I was so proud that we were able to honor one of her mom's final wishes. I told her she could have the Lexus as a graduation gift, and I would pay the insurance if she kept her G.P.A at a 3.0 or higher. I had become so selfless since becoming a mother figure. I wished that Andre would have gotten to experience this side of me. I still thought about him every minute of the day, but I didn't have to fight back the tears. Each day it became easier to forgive Andre for making the mistake all those years ago that would haunt us forever, and it became easier to forgive myself for how I went about the whole thing.

I decided to plan the girls and I a little weekend getaway before Christina went away. I wanted to go out of the country, but I couldn't secure a passport for Sky without her paperwork. I tried to get a copy of her birth certificate, but the clerk at Vital records had been giving me the run around. Instead, we booked a flight to San Diego. The sky was beautiful, and the beaches were amazing. We stayed near La Jolla Cove and went to the beach every day. Sky just giggled her heart out the entire time, and I couldn't imagine life without her. Each and every day she reminded me more and more of Andre. She was gonna be tall like him and was just as valiant. While at the beach, her and I built sandcastles while Christina showed off her beach body. She was 18, and just a little boy crazy. Guys were approaching her on the beach, and she was loving every minute of it. I let her live because I knew she could handle herself.

The feeling was surreal. The sun on my skin, and water at the tip of my toes, I felt content. Christina had never left Georgia before and was so amazed by San Diego she suggested we stay there to start over. She really enjoyed seeing a different side of the world, and I enjoyed being able to share that opportunity with her. I loved San Diego as well, but I only had one home. I was a Georgia girl.

After our vacation was over, it was back to life and back to work for me. Although everyone knew the stunt the detective pulled was a scare tactic, it didn't stop them from wondering what kind of life I had been living to have the police come to my job and arrest me. The law says you're innocent until proven guilty, but in life once you're stained it's forever. I threw myself into some work projects. After what I had gone through, I wasn't going to let the stress of what other people thought bother me.

I was in my office wrapping up some last-minute paperwork for a deal I was closing when Ronda came in. She had been my guardian angel because while I was busy with my personal life, she made sure that all my deadlines were met. My clients had no clue about the events that were taking place behind the scenes. Ronda sat an envelope on my desk. She said someone dropped it off for me insisting it was very important. I tossed it to the side so I could finish up my paperwork and get home. I told Christina that I would cook us a fancy pasta dish, and if I were going to keep that promise, I'd need to get home by 7:00pm. Ronda sat down in the chair across from me and grabbed my hands to stop me from writing. "Are you ok?" she asked. Fighting to keep it together, I confessed to her, "I'm at about 50%." I had to face each day as it came. Some days were good, others not so much. "Katrina, if you need more time off it's fine. I can take care of this stuff. Your clients are good and whatever needs to be done, I can take care of it until you are ready to come back. You're no good to us if your head isn't in the game sis." Ronda was right and maybe I wasn't all the way in, but if I didn't come to work, I would be stuck at home letting the four walls close in on me, and that could be fatal. Ronda thought I came back because they needed me, but the truth was I needed them. I needed people around me, and I needed to do my job. It was the one thing I was still somewhat in control of. I thanked Ronda for her concern and assured her that with time I would be ok. I asked Ronda to give me a moment and went over to the bathroom. I had been feeling sick since we got back from vacation. My doctor said it was food poisoning, and me stressing was not helping. I was starting to think it may be something else because 2 weeks had passed, and I still felt lightheaded. I had been throwing up after every meal and was losing my appetite. One minute I had energy and the next I'd be looking for a couch. I walked back in the office to Ronda's twisted up mug. "Katrina, are you sure you don't need more time?" She asked me the same question one too many times, so I got assertive. "Ronda, I'm sure, OK." I knew she didn't like the tone I had taken with her, but I did want her to back off. She didn't push the issue anymore, and instead she stood up to leave. Before closing the door, she added, "The guy who dropped that letter off said that he needed you to respond to it sooner than later." I looked over at the envelope that addressed me but didn't have a sender's name or return address.

I was ready to wrap up, so I started packing my things to leave. I put my coat on and turned around to a ghost or at least that's what it felt like seeing her. "Well hello Katrina. Long time no see." We eyed each other up and down, and it was obvious that neither of us was pleased to see the other. "What the hell are you doing here, and what do you want?" I asked, making it clear I wasn't interested in the small talk. She sat her purse down as if I would allow her to get comfortable in my office. "Why I gotta want something?" she asked, smirking. Since she wanted to play dumb, I cut right to the chase. "Because you are trifling, and a trifling hoe always wants something. First it was my man, now what do you want, my life?" I asked. Her demeanor was cocky as she looked me up and down. "I already had your man, and I damn sure don't want your life, but you do owe me." Britney said, leaning into my desk. "Being that my daughter is in jail, thanks to you, I'm here for pain and suffering." She held her hand out as if I had something to give her on the spot. I couldn't hold back my laughter. "Britney, I'm not giving you shit. If you want what Andre left for me, his real family, you're going to have to take it, outta my ass." It was taking everything in me not to whoop her ass right there in my office. "I don't have to take it from you Katrina. You're going to willingly give it to me." she said. I walked around the desk, so she was in arms reach. "Oh yea, and why the hell would I do that?" I asked. I had physically outgrown Britney over the years and I could tell she was uneasy. "Well Katrina if you don't give me what I want, I'll just take you to court." she threatened.

"Take me to court and ask for what? Rights to my husband's property and money? You think you're owed that? Britney, you're even dumber than I remember. You better get your ass out of my office while you still can walk!" I started backing her out chest to chest. She turned to leave, but I knew she wasn't done. She had a Joker's grin on her face, and from what I remember of my ex-friend, that meant she had a wild card. She stopped in the doorway. She turned around and said, "I never said I'd take you to court for his money and property. I'll take you to court for the only thing you love more than that." She held up a picture of baby Sky. "You can keep this copy for yourself." she said, tossing the picture at me. I picked the picture up and stared at it. It was Britney holding Sky who looked just a few days old. There was a date in the corner, so I was getting closer to knowing her official birthday. Britney throwing that picture in my face sent me into protective mode. I had been more of a mother to Sky than her or Bella. I was going to show her what messing with my baby girl would get her.

I called out to Ronda to see if she was still in the office. No one answered me. "Who is Ronda supposed to be, your security guard?" Britney asked. I couldn't take anymore of her snide comments. I squared up, and the look on her face said she didn't believe I would deck her until I did. I punched her right in the mouth. She tried fighting back, but with the anger I felt inside, she didn't stand a chance. After I thought she had enough to know that rolling up on me at my place of business was a mistake, I let up. I demanded one last time, "Get out of my office Britney!" She scrambled to grab her things and jetted.

I waited 5 minutes before leaving to allow her some time to get ahead. I picked the picture up and on the back of it was an amount, $30,000. It ran in the family. Britney was trying to extort me too, but she had lost her mind. I wasn't paying her $30,000. I did love Sky more than anything, but I wasn't going out like that. I placed the picture in the same frame as Andre and me. I had to consider if Britney was more involved in this plot than I knew about. After all, Andre said she showed up at the Restaurant that night out of nowhere.

It had been a tumultuous night. When I got to the parking garage, I was startled by Ronda sitting in her car smoking a blunt. She quickly put it out, but it was clear what she was doing. I knocked on the window and Ronda shook her head, not wanting to open it because she still hadn't blown out her last puff. Before she passed out from holding her breath, I knocked again and demanded, "Open the door!" Ronda opened the door and started copping pleas. "Katrina I am so sorry. I thought you would have been gone by now. I'm usually the only one here this late. I only do this when I know the coast is clear. I'm sorry, it'll never happen again." I waved my hand to let her know she could save it. "Are you gonna tell anyone?" she asked. I thought she would've known me better than to ask me that. I gestured for her to share the love. Ronda smiled at me and passed the weed over. "Ronda, I don't care about you smoking weed. Half the fools we work with smoke weed. The higher the position they're in, the harder the drug they're on. I'm just gonna say this, when you do that here rather you think you're the last person or not is dangerous. The wrong person comes in late to pick up some paperwork and boom you're busted. We all got blemishes, some of us are good make-up artists." I passed the weed back to her.

"Katrina, if I ask you a personal question, you promise not to get mad?" Ronda asked, keeping her eyes intently on the small rip that was preventing the blunt from pulling correctly. Weed made everyone inquisitive, so I played along. "Yea girl, I Promise, ask away." I told her.

"I just saw a girl rushing out of the door all lumped up, and you come out here and your clothes all stretched out. Did you and her have a fight?" Ronda gave the blunt a hard pull to confirm she fixed it. "Yea, now that's the OG I know." Ronda said, pleased with her repair. I kept it real with her because I felt like I could. "Yea we fought, and clearly you see who won." I said. We both laughed. "What was y'all fighting for?" she asked. "She's someone who used to mess with my husband, and she's coming now to expose their history. She came into my office and got out of pocket, so I put her back in one." I revealed. Ronda passed the weed back to me.

"I can feel that. I ain't letting nobody disrespect my man in my face either. If I gotta put my hands on you for you to get the point, then so be it." Ronda and I had worked together for 3 years and that was our first time having a personal conversation. It was normally all business with us. Ronda was 25 and on the right track to be a senior exec by the time she was 30. She rubbed elbows with all the right people and had a personality that would take her places. She was cute and down to earth and that was a winning combo. Her and I finished the blunt, and she asked if I wanted to go hang out. I couldn't believe she was so bold. It was her gift and curse. "Ronda, I'm really tired and I just wanna go home and get some rest." She wouldn't take no for an answer. "Katrina, you can sleep when you die. Life's too short and you'll never say, you know what, I didn't get enough rest. So tonight, let's go turn up one time for the one time. I got a hoe bag in the back with some spare outfits, and you bout my size you can fit one."

I had to smile at the pitch. We were in marketing and Ronda was using that skill. I was convinced hanging out with her would probably be epic. Before I could get the yes out, she was grabbing the hoe bag and asking me to choose between a cheetah print dress or a black leather skirt. I chose the skirt. I tucked my white work blouse in and opened the top 3 buttons to show off some cleavage. It ended up being a cute combination and was perfect for the occasion.

Ronda and I landed at some spot she suggested called The Roxy. I told Ronda I wanted to go somewhere lowkey, and this spot was a mix of low key and flashy, a nice blend. The guys there were the 30 and up crowd, and unlike most spots they weren't hanging on the wall, they were mingling.

Before Ronda and I could find a table, two gentlemen approached us and asked that we join them at their table. Ronda dragged me over, and we sat in their VIP section where they had a few other friends and bottles of Cîroc on ice. "What are you drinking ladies?" one of them asked. "I'll take Cîroc and sprite please." Ronda replied. "I'll have cranberry with mine." I requested. As he passed us our drinks, he asked our names. He introduced himself as Darren. He was handsome but not my flavor. He and Ronda seemed to get along better anyway. Darren's cousin Miller walked over to introduce himself. He reached for my hand and pulled me up. "We'll be back cuz." He said to Darren. I asked where we were going and he said, "Somewhere much better than this." When we got outside of the club, he showed me that he had two tickets to see Maxwell and his live band. He asked, "You down?" I didn't know if Miller was his real name, and I could barely see him behind his thick beard and glasses. Living on the edge had given me a thirst for danger. I asked that Miller give me a few minutes to tell Ronda what was up, so she didn't worry about me. I came back out of the club a short while later, and he and I headed towards the city. We pulled up at Variety playhouse, an intimate live music venue. He and I grooved to so many classic hits. "Sumthin', Sumthin'," "Till the cops come knocking," "Fortunate" and many more. I really enjoyed the concert and my company. Afterwards he asked if I wanted to grab a bite to eat from Vortex, the spot known for its famous burgers. He and I waited 30 minutes for a table and didn't let the waiter leave to put the drink orders in before we said in unison, "I'm ready to order. JINX!" The waitress laughed. "That's so cute. How long have you guys been together?" she asked. Neither of us answered. The waitress, realizing she had just made it awkward, asked, "So what can I get for you two?" I ordered first then Miller. He also requested 2 shots of Rum.

"So, what do you do for a living?" I asked.

Proudly he said, "I take care of people's problems?"

"What are you a doctor or something?" I was curious.

"Or something." he said.

I didn't like his short answers, and figured it meant he was in between jobs. I didn't overthink it. I pulled my phone out to text Christina that I would be home late. "Are you texting your boyfriend?" he asked. "Maybe." I said. "Well, that would be disappointing because you're here with me." He replied, rubbing his hand through his beard. I leaned in close and asked, "Do you really care who I'm texting or are you more concerned about us right here right now?" He leaned over and kissed me which confirmed we were on the same page. We talked a bit more before the drinks and food came.

After eating, we took a stroll up Moreland avenue. We grabbed some ice cream from Zestos. We stood on the corner talking, taking in the much-needed cool breeze. I was able to get a better look at him. He was handsome. Deep Cocoa complexion, smooth skin, full eyebrows, and Lips. After my last experience with Ty, I didn't want to move too fast with anyone. I was enjoying the evening, but I was going to leave it at that. I asked Miller to take me back to my car so I could head home. He was reluctant but grabbed my hand and led me back to the car.

We took the long ride back to my office to get my car out of the parking garage. We said our goodbyes, and Miller gave me a kiss goodnight. When he asked for my number, I declined and told him I'd see him around. When he left, I went back into the office because I needed to use the ladies room. I put the code in the door and used my phone's flashlight as my guide. I went into my office to put my purse down and tripped over something. I turned the light on and dropped everything in my hands after seeing that my office had been trashed.

The things on my desk were thrown about everywhere, and the walls were spray painted. The only thing left unharmed was the picture of Britney and Sky pinned to the wall. I knew who had done it, but I didn't know how. I was going to hunt Britney down and beat her so bad she would wish she never. I went to the bathroom and got myself together. I sprinkled some water on my face and tied my hair up in a ponytail. I called a girl I knew that owned a cleaning service and offered to pay her double her rate if she could send someone down that could get my office together in 2 hours. She asked for pictures and after I sent the damage, she sent back the tab, $300. I sent her $600 and it was all set. She sent 2 girls and one guy. They got busy. They had all the right cleaning aids to get the spray paint off the wall and by 3:00 am they were done. They did so good I tipped even though I had already paid double.

I called Ronda when I got home and told her I was safe. I didn't tell her what happened at the office, but I told her I was going to take her advice and take a few days off. I told her that I had locked my office up and I wanted her to keep a close eye that no one went in there for a few days. I didn't want the loud smell of the cleaning products to set off any alarms. Ronda gave me her word that she would look out. I was so tired I didn't even take a shower. I fell into the bed face first. I kicked my pumps off and I couldn't tell you my last thought.

Chapter 21-God's Plan

The next few days, I spent most of my time at the house with the baby. Christina was busy hanging out as much as she could before she had to go away to college. Most days I stayed in pajamas. I wouldn't unwrap my hair. Brushing my teeth and taking a shower was as far as I'd go with my hygiene. I didn't want to leave the house because I felt like I was being watched. I had every intention of handling the situation with Britney, but I didn't know where to start. I couldn't go to the police, and I damn sure didn't want to drag Malik back into it. Because my mind was so loaded, I had to do some work, or I would go crazy.

I grabbed some paperwork to prepare to go over some numbers, then I saw the envelope that Ronda had given me. I remembered she said it was urgent, but it didn't matter much anymore because it had been several days since I had it. I ripped the envelope open then the doorbell rang. I slammed the envelope down, agitated that someone would be popping up at my house. I didn't even ask who it was before flinging the door open. I was ready to take all my frustrations out on whatever bold soul had the audacity to invade my layer. I never expected that person to be someone I hadn't seen in years.

My mom didn't say anything. She walked in without being invited and hugged me. I couldn't say the last time I remember my mom hugging me. I didn't protest, and I hugged her back. I asked her to join me in my living room. Sky was laying on a blanket on the couch. My Mom's knees buckled as she cooed and drooled over the baby. "Katrina, she is the most beautiful thing I've ever seen."

"Thanks Ma. What are you doing here?" I asked her.

She asked me to come sit down next to her. "Katrina, I've been looking for you for years baby. I'm so sorry for the kind of mother that I've been, and I have a new perspective on life. I'm saved now, and I want to mend our relationship. It's the only thing I haven't been able to accept and move on from. Now I'm still a work in progress so I don't know where we will end up, but we have to start somewhere."

I was speechless. I didn't know if I wanted her there or not. Was it bad timing or perfect? "Ma, I don't know what to say. So much has happened." She cut in. "I can see that. I have a beautiful grandbaby that I didn't know about. Looking just like her father. Where is Andre?" I put my head down. "You see Ma, that's what I mean. A lot has happened that you don't know about. Andre passed away a few months ago."

"What?!?!! Katrina what do you mean passed away? Baby you've been dealing with all of this on your own. I'm so sorry?" I assured her I was ok. It was nice of her to care, but I didn't want her sympathy. She didn't like Andre, and she treated him so mean it was hard for me to accept her condolences. As if she were reading my mind she said, "I know it's hard to believe I care because I didn't like Andre but that was a very different time for me. Today, I want to support you no matter what decisions you make." I took what she said with a grain of salt. I offered tea and she accepted. I went into the kitchen and made 2 cups and brought out some homemade strawberry cheesecake. Ma and I talked about some of the things she missed in my life, like my wedding, my many miscarriages, my turmoil, and my shame. She didn't blink funny. She listened closely and was present. It was what I had needed from her years ago, but better late than never.

Sky started to get fidgety and agitated. Ma picked her up before she started fussing. Sky took to her like she had known her all her life. She didn't fuss and laid right in Ma's chest. I asked her to stay for a while and watch a movie with me. She was more than happy to. I put on Spike Lee's "Crooklyn," one of our favorites. I watched my mom while she fed Sky some of her cheesecake. It was weird seeing her nurturing side. I never would have thought she had the ability to be, but she was great with Sky. I told Ma that I was going to put Sky down because I was getting tired. She told me to go get some rest and let her put Sky to sleep. I suggested that she stay the night and the three of us and Christina could go to breakfast in the morning. I got some extra blankets for the guest room and told Ma to make herself at home. I showed her Sky's bedroom, then I went to lay down.

I woke up at 3:30am. I felt an eerie sense of calm and I wondered if my mom had bought that energy with her. I went to Sky's room to check on her. She was sleeping on her back snoring and had kicked the cover off. I covered her back up and went to peek in on Christina. She was sleeping as well. I headed back across the family room to my bedroom. I hit my foot on the table and tried to muffle my scream. It felt like my toe was broken. Frustrated, I knocked a pile of papers off the table. After pouting for a few minutes, I picked the things up off the floor, and I came across the envelope Ronda had given me again. I finally pulled out its contents. There was a DVD disc not labeled, but there was a letter that came with it, and it read...

"Mrs. Billups,

No good deed goes unpunished. I helped you out, and now it's your turn to return the favor. You have 1 week to meet me with $50,000 cash. Do not contact the police, and do not try and find out who I am. Remember, I am always watching you."

~Anonymous

I put the DVD in the disc player and hit play. There was a title screen that read, "The Coverup." When it started to play,

236

I was the main character. I could see me walking in the hallway of the hospital, then the scene switched, and it showed me in the room with Bella. I could see myself pacing the floor, then finally grabbing the pillow out of the chair next to her bed to smother her.

I knew immediately who it was that had sent the letter, Nurse Nia's boyfriend Jose. The only question was, did Nurse Nia know anything about it, and was she in on the blackmail. This guy wanted $50,000 like I could pull it out of my ass. I had to make sure that tape didn't get out, but if I did pay him, how could I be sure that he wouldn't try and come back for more money in a few years. My deadline was approaching, and I needed to decide quickly. I played the video again to make sure I wasn't dreaming. I knew that if that video got out, I would likely go to prison for most of the rest of my life. I got up to take the video out and the light came on. I looked over, and my mom was standing there, eyes fixated on the TV. "Katrina, what was that you were watching?" she asked. I wanted to tell my mom to mind her business, but I didn't want to be so rude to her. "Ma it was just a video. Nothing you need to worry about." I hit the power button on the DVD player to turn it off.

"Well, if it's nothing I need to worry about, do you mind playing it again? I thought I saw someone I knew." she said. She was overstepping her boundaries. I was not the 15-year-old kid she could intimidate. I put the DVD back in the envelope and took it in the room with me. My mom followed me in my room insisting that I let her see the disc. I told her I couldn't do that.

"Katrina, I don't need to see the DVD. I was just hoping you'd prove to me that I didn't see what I thought I saw, which is you trying to smother somebody. Tell me what's going on?" my mom imposed on me.

I stopped her, "Look Ma, I appreciate you being here but please don't overstep. I have more than a few things going on right now and there's no way you could understand the things I've done in my past that I regret now." I was pleading with her to let it go. "Ok Katrina, no matter what you have or haven't done, I have your back. I understand when you do things that make sense one moment, and the next seem completely irrational. I also know from experience when you're going through something, the worst thing to do is shut everybody out. I am your mother, and you can trust me with anything."

 I grabbed the letter that came with the DVD. I handed it to my mom and went to put the DVD back in the player. I hit play, and let my mom watch me commit attempted murder. I watched her closely to see what her facial expression would say. Would she be appalled so much that she'd turn me in? Would she go back to not talking to me? After the clip was over, she walked over and hugged me. "This too shall pass. I got your back no matter what. Just like that day in the principal's office. It's you and I against everybody else. Go get some sleep baby. We're going to have a big breakfast in the morning, and we'll deal with it then." She took over like a matriarch would and didn't give me an opportunity to give any push back.

The next morning when I woke up, I smelled the aroma of heaven coming from the kitchen. My mom must've woken up and gone shopping. I walked in and she had fish, grits, eggs, biscuits, and pancakes. I hadn't had her home cooking in over 15 years. She never really cooked. When Christina woke up, naturally she had a confused look on her face. I introduced Christina to my mom, and she quickly relaxed and became more friendly. I said I was going to get Sky ready, and my mom insisted she would do it.

By the time we came back downstairs, my mom had Sky ready, and the plates were made. Christina took her plate to the room. "You just gon let her go in her room and eat away from the family?" my mom asked. I had to explain to her it was a different time, and we didn't even eat at tables anymore. I told my mom to follow me into the living room and pulled the coffee table closer so we both could eat on it. We laughed at how she wouldn't let me step foot in the living room to eat back in the day, and there we were about to throw down in my living room. Jokingly I said, "I can do what I want in my own house. Just like you used to tell me." Ma laughed before bringing the video back up. "So, Katrina, what do we do if they tell the cops about the video?" Mouth full I said, "Ma I honestly don't know. The past few months of my life have been so crazy, maybe I belong in jail."

"Don't say that Katrina. There's power in the tongue." she warned.

"Well Ma, what do I do?"

"You could leave the country if the heat comes." She didn't even smirk when she said it. I couldn't blame her because I damn sure had thought about it. I confessed to her that I didn't have a birth certificate for Sky, and it was a long story. I found out then that she worked at vital records. She was a clerk.

"Katrina, I can get you a birth certificate for Sky if that's the problem. Just give me her full name." she said.

"As a matter of fact ma, I want you to get me a copy of someone else's birth certificate too." I requested.

"Who Katrina?"

"Bella Carmichael. That's all I know about her Ma. Can you help?"

"Ok, that name is pretty unique. I'll find her. Anything else?"

"What about a social security card Ma? Can you get me a copy of Sky's?"

"I know someone over at one of their offices. I'll see what I can do." she said.

I pulled out my phone and told Ma I was going to send her a text copy of what I needed so she wouldn't forget anything. She stopped me from typing. "Katrina, this phone stuff is new to me, but I don't think we want to go creating any more trails that lead back to you. They already got your ass on tape, let's not text. Matter of fact we never had this conversation or any in the future about this, you feel me?" Ma asked.

"I thought you were saved. You can't say ass Ma."

"Girl, I am saved. I ain't no damn Saint though. There's a difference." she told me.

After breakfast was over, my mom had to head to work. She told me she'd get right on top of the things I needed and call me later. I asked Christina what she had planned that day and she said she was staying home and wanted to have some girlfriends come over. I told her that was fine, but I needed her to watch Sky for a while.

I went and met up with Malik to confess yet another sin to him. Malik took a deep breath and put the DVD in his office disc player. He watched his good friend do the unthinkable, and he was visibly disturbed. "Katrina, what the hell were you thinking? This isn't a game. That's attempted murder on film for the world to see if it gets out. That's what you did with your legacy? I don't know how the hell we get out of this. What are they asking you for?"

240

"$50,000 that I don't have to spare right now. Everybody and their mama is trying to extort me. I'm even more worried that if I pay now, eventually they'll come back and want more. I can't trust they haven't made a dozen copies of this. Malik, I know I messed up, but I don't know what the hell to do. I was out of my mind that day." I tried to explain to him. I was hoping he could see my heart. Malik laughed at me. "What's so funny?" I asked.

"You better tell somebody you were out of your mind because that's the only chance we stand in beating this." he said. "Really Malik! Insanity? Nah, I'm not playing crazy for these folks. I did something crazy, but I'm not gon be beating on my head and rubbing my stomach on the stand to win this. I'm crazy, not crazy crazy."

"Look Katrina, I'll think about how we get out of this. I need 48 hours. Let me make some phone calls. Tomorrow morning let's meet and discuss our options." he said.

Later that night, Malik called and said that we needed to meet ASAP. I sent Christina a text asking her to keep an ear out for Sky. I went to meet Malik at his Condominium. He met me downstairs. He asked, "Before we get upstairs, I need you to keep an open mind and know that your longtime friend always wants what's best for you." I was hesitant because he was giving a disclaimer speech. When we got upstairs, I could see that someone was there already. When we got in the living room he turned around and Malik said, "Katrina meet Miller, Miller meet…" Miller cut Malik off. "Man, I know shorty. I saw her when I was out the other night. Is this a joke?" He asked Malik. I was confused why the guy I met the other night while out with Ronda was standing in Malik's condo. Malik was also confused. "Wait, you two know each other? How and why do you know a hitman Katrina?"

"Don't tell my business like that." Miller warned Malik.

"Trust me, she's not one to talk. You don't have to worry about her telling anyone. She's actually the client I told you about." Malik spearheaded the convo.

"Why are you telling him about me Malik?" Now it was me being defensive.

Miller looked a little different than he did the other night. As a matter of fact, after getting a better look at him it was Colin Miller, number 2 on America's most wanted list.

"Malik, is this Colin?' I asked, revealing that I knew who this guy was.

"Well Katrina, I can't go around calling this nigga Colin Miller, now can I? I call him by his last name as an alias. Let's sit down so I can break down why we all are here." Miller and I sat down and for a moment caught eye contact. He smiled at me and eased my fear a bit. I thought about him and I being together the other night. I remember he mentioned he solved problems for people. I never would have thought he was a hitman. Malik sat on his desk. He turned to me, "Katrina, I've looked at this from all angles and considered all solutions. The truth is, there isn't but one."

"And what is that Malik?" I asked.

Miller chimed in, "We gotta kill this mothafucka that's blackmailing you. That's it, that's all. I don't like to discuss details. I just need a yes, a deposit, and it's as good as done."

They both sat there waiting for my answer. "Katrina, I'm telling you as your lawyer this is truly our only option." It couldn't have been Malik's first time soliciting Miller's Services because he was unmoved.

"Malik, do you hear yourself? You're talking about killing someone like it's a walk in the park. You're sitting here with a hitman like he's a regular dude. What the hell is wrong with you?" It wasn't until I said it out loud that I realized how ridiculous I did sound judging anyone. I still thought Malik was out of his mind for even asking me. I grabbed my purse and stood to leave. Malik scolded me, "Don't call me to represent you in Sky's adoption case either because that's what's going to end up happening to her." I stopped in my tracks. I turned to Malik, "You dirty bastard. You leave her out of this!"

"It's the truth Katrina. What do you think is going to happen to the baby you've been trying so hard to protect? The truth is you messed up, and you've been messing up ever since you started this mess. There is no turning back now. Once you open the gates to hell you can't control the demons that get loose. So, we're either gonna kill the last one or let his ass roam free and ruin you. Your choice!"

I thought long and hard about what he was saying. Even though he was scolding me, I knew he knew his shit. If Malik was telling me murder was the only option, then it was my only option. I was turning into the devil. Malik interrupted my thoughts. "Katrina, you don't have time to hesitate. I need an answer because we need to do this sooner than later. The more time this guy has, the more tapes he'll make, the more people he'll tell. If we're doing this, it goes down tonight." Malik looked over at Miller who was impassive. Finally, I mustered out, "Ok."

There was no way I was going to prison, and I damn sure wasn't letting Sky get caught up in the system. I turned to Miller and said, "It's a go." Miller didn't say anything. He nodded his head and got up. He walked over and dapped Malik up. "You got that for me?" he asked.

"It's on the way." Malik said smiling. Miller went to leave.

"The money Katrina. That'll be $10,000." Malik said, holding his hand out. I turned my face up, but before I could get a word out, Malik sarcastically said, "$10,000 now or your life later." He didn't need to say anything anymore. I wrote him the check and he did the wire transfer to Miller.

Three hours later my phone rang. It was 2:00am and I knew it had to be bad news. Good news waits till morning, bad news can't. My phone ringing at 2:00am meant someone couldn't wait 5 more hours till sunup to tell me the deal. Although I was awakened out of my sleep, I was wide awake when I answered.

"Hello."

"Hello Katrina, it's Miller. I need you to wake the hell up right now and come meet me."

"What?! Come meet you for what? It's 2:00am." I reminded him.

"Katrina it's 2:00am and I don't want sex. So, you know it must be something serious. Get your ass out of bed and come meet me on Conley road in the abandoned apartments near Moreland, now!"

He slammed the phone down. My heart was beating fast, and I couldn't make it stop. I didn't want to go, but I didn't want to face the consequences of not going. I threw on some jeans, a t-shirt, and classics.

When I got down to the apartments it looked like a scene out of a horror movie. I was scared out of my mind. Miller popped out and led me to the unit he had Jose in. When I got there, he was tied up and had been beaten badly.

"He told me he had something you should know. I figured we might end up having to kill more than one person today." Miller said, looking at Jose.

"What is it that you need to tell me? Nothing's going to save you, so I don't know why you're trying. You threatened my livelihood and now you're gonna pay for it." I told Jose. He was struggling to get in a position where he could speak clearly.

"What if I told you she had it planned from the very beginning. Listen to the tape again. If you listen carefully, it's me recording him. You can hear me tell your husband, *hang in there man.* I was rooting for him." Jose tried explaining. I hit him. "You're lying!"

"You don't have to believe me, but it's the truth." He pleaded.

"You expect me to believe that they let a security guard in the room with my husband while he was about to die?" I asked.

"Katrina, you're not following me. This started way before your husband was pronounced dead. When he first came in, I helped the doctors get him in the room. He asked me to record something for him just in case he went to jail. The doctor made it clear to him that his injuries were severe but nothing he couldn't recover from. I recorded him because he thought he wouldn't get a chance to speak to you in time before shit hit the fan, but he never was under the impression he was going to die. I went and told Nia about it because I thought it was bizarre but when she found out who he was, she started plotting. She claimed to know you from the maternity ward. She spoke about your husband having money because he was a big sports agent, and she had a plan to get us paid. I just went along with it because I wanted a quick come up, but I feel awful now that all this shit went down.

Nia ain't one to play with and she just been playing puppet master this whole time." Jose admitted.

"Wait, what are you trying to tell me? If his injuries weren't that serious, how did he die? Why did he leave a recording for me?" I asked.

"Nia Killed him! She was the anesthesiologist in the room, and she made him a deadly combination. He had a pre-existing heart condition and he told her about that. The dosage she gave him sent the man into cardiac arrest and he never stood a chance. She's been doing this a long time, so she knows how to get away with murder. Andre left the recording for you because he thought he might go to jail, not die. How would I know about his heart condition if Nia didn't tell me that?" Jose argued. He had a point. Not many people knew about Andre's heart problem. He had only recently told me about it when we were in our counseling session. "Nia wanted to kill your husband so she could corner you with the baby, then, she planned to double back once you got attached and threaten to reveal the secret and the recording Andre left. When you came to the hospital that night and tried to kill that girl, it just became another avenue to blackmail you." Jose explained.

I kept a straight face, but I considered everything he said. I even thought about letting him live. I didn't want to leave a big trail of bodies, but I didn't want a lot of witnesses either. Miller cleared his throat and asked, "So my love, what have we decided this evening?" He asked like it was a dinner choice. Jose pleaded with me. "Please, I'm sorry, but I'm not the one who deserves this. I was caught up with Nia. I would never do anything like this again! I'll make sure that tape doesn't get out." Miller punched Jose in the stomach. He could sense my reluctance. "Stick to the plan Katrina." Miller warned. I proceeded and gave him the signal. Jose shouted, "What does that mean? Please don't kill me." Miller grabbed the knife and walked over slowly towards him. I could tell he enjoyed the stalk. Jose was crying, and he was a long way from the tough guy security guard he portrayed at the hospital. I left the room because I didn't want to see Jose be killed. I wasn't even sure if I made the right decision, but I knew karma would sort it out in due time. I couldn't believe I had to add Nurse Nia to the list of people that tried to play me. She would eventually get dealt with too, but I had some other loose ends to tie up first.

Chapter 22 Last Night

I hated social media. As a marketing specialist, I felt it was dumb to use it for any other purpose than making money yet there I was searching for LaBresha Carmichael, and she was nowhere to be found. I found Britney but no Bre. Again, I was forced to reach out to Malik so he could hire me a P.I. Malik had someone on speed dial. I ended up catching a $1,200 tab and was guaranteed I'd have a full file on Bre by the end of the week.

As promised, Malik reached out on Saturday with the file. She was living in Savannah, GA and had 2 children that she was raising. She worked at a diner on Tybee Island and lived a very simple, yet what appeared to be a fulfilling life. There was a number to reach her, but I knew calling wouldn't cut it. I needed to speak to her face to face.

I left that next morning headed to the island. The weather was perfect, 82 degrees. I rode the entire way with the window down, listening to 70's RnB. It was a perfect beach day. I spent the morning there watching the crowds grow larger as the day got later. At 4:00pm I walked over to the diner that Bre worked at. I sat at the counter where she stood flirting with some guy. She still had her same mischievous smile, and I could tell by her body language and the ring on the man's finger that she was the same ol' Bre.

It took her 10 minutes to notice that I was staring at her. She was rattled at first, then tried to play it off with a smile. She came around the counter and greeted me with a hug which confused me.

"Hey Katrina, long time no see. What brings you to the island?" she asked.

"Business and Personal. I need to speak to you privately." I told her. I got up to leave a tip on the counter for my coffee and waited on Bre to lead the way to somewhere we could chop it up.

She took me out back to the smoke area for the employees. Bre looked at her co-worker who caught the hint quickly and put his cigarette out to give us a minute to talk. When the coast was clear, I told Bre straight up, I knew about Britney, Andre, and the pregnancy. I drove the conversation so she wouldn't think to ask me any questions about how I found out. I asked Bre to start from the top with how Andre and Britney hooked up. Bre sat down and got comfortable on a milk crate that looked like it had been through the ringer.

"Katrina, the day we met it was because you involved yourself in a beef that wasn't yours. You were right about that part, but the beef wasn't mine either." Bre went back to that day in 1999 where our world first collided. "The girls that jumped me that day were jumping me because one of them was Andre's girl. The party I told you about where we played truth or dare, Andre had a dare to kiss Britney. They both made good on it. Word got out to Andre's girl at the time and rumor had it that she and her girls wanted to jump Britney. They couldn't find her, so you know how that goes, they got the closest thing to her. That's the only reason I was in it. After that truth or dare game, Britney started liking Andre for real. It was just a kiss, but she had a Jones. She kept it under wraps until Andre started liking you, her best friend. Britney took that personally. She felt like Andre was only talking to you to get back at her. She was so paranoid when you started dating him, she thought you were in on it. She came up with this grand plan to talk to guys he knew to make him jealous. She started dating guys on the football team, trying to get his attention. None of it worked. Her messing with all those guys didn't do anything but ultimately get us put out of my mama's house. You know she thinks because we're twins, we share a brain. And you thought I was the bad one." Bre said somberly.

"Wait, y'all are twins? I never knew that. Why are y'all in different grades and why do you purposely not tell people?" I asked her.

"I got kept back in elementary school and kids used to tease me. When Britney had a growth spurt, we just started telling people she was older and that's why we were in separate grades." Bre explained.

"Ok back to Andre. If he and Britney didn't hook up, how did she get pregnant?" I asked.

"That came later. We went to Jacksonville to live with my father. He was in the military, so we ended up settling down permanently with my grandma. Bre and I would go to the FSU campus to party with the older crowd and she ran into Andre by chance. There was so much liquor between the 3 of us, it's foggy. I remember Britney told Andre you were talking to Chris from high school, and he was pissed. He drowned himself in 1942 that night. They hooked up once, and obviously it was a mistake because Andre transferred schools right after and never talked to her again. She would send him letters. She hinted around being pregnant but never told him the truth. In her mind it was a secret she had over him and she would use it when the time was right." Bre said, puffing her cigarette like a pro.

"What happened to Bella after she was born?" I asked.

"After Bella was born, my grandma took us in hiding. I wasn't the one who had a baby, but she even made me stay in the house. Britney couldn't leave or be seen by anyone until she healed. My grandma would say, *I don't want anyone to be able to smell you done had a baby.* The only people that knew were my mom, my dad, and my grandma. We were all so careful to make sure the secret stayed in the circle. Britney was not even allowed to refer to Bella as her daughter. Everyone thought we were cousins. That went on for years until my grandma passed away and Bella needed a place to go. Britney started feeling guilty and reached out to help but she did more harm than good. She told Bella everything including that she was her real mom and who her dad was. Ever since then, Bella started acting out. Britney put her out and she went to go and live with our other sister Alicia. Shit has just been a downward spiral since then. Part of the reason I moved here was because I wanted to get away from everyone. I wanted to step up to try and mentor Bella but what do I know. My life ain't all peaches and cream. Besides, I haven't seen her in at least 5 years. Britney and I don't talk like that because she crossed me on something personal, but that's all I know Katrina." Bre finished confessing.

I asked her if she could get me a cup of water. Bre headed inside while I digested everything I had been told. I had to think of a way to proposition her to get her on my side. I knew Britney would be coming to collect any day now and I needed a lifeline. When Bre came back outside with my drink I got right to it.

"Bre, what if I could help you find Bella? I would need you to help me do something but if you help me, I can help you." I told her.

"Help you with what exactly. I do want to see Bella but not if it means getting in an entanglement with my family over it. I don't wanna sound cold, but I have my own problems." Bre whined. She was right where I wanted her to be. She cared a little but not too much. My plan might work after all.

"Bre, this is going to sound crazy but I'm asking you to keep an open mind. I know where your niece is. I can take you to her right now but there's a contingency." I kept my game face on, but I was shaky. "What do you mean by contingency?" she asked.

"If you're interested in seeing Bella, I can take you to her, but I need your help with something. In all honesty you're my only hope. Bre, so much has happened over the past year, I couldn't bring you up to speed in just one day. Bella had a baby. Her name is Sky. Bella couldn't raise Sky, so she found Andre and I and asked that we help by legally adopting her. Some bad things happened, and Bella got herself in some trouble. I just want to see to it that I am still able to raise Sky as Bella, Andre and I agreed. Bella's gonna be out of the picture for a while and someone needs to be there for this baby. She's been with me for the past few months, but Britney showed up trying to extort me the other day. I think she is going to try and fight me in court for Sky. She doesn't even want to take care of the baby. She just wants to hurt me. I already legally adopted Sky, but I don't even want Britney to have visitation because I don't trust her. If it comes down to it Bre, I need you to vouch on my behalf that I am 100% capable and the better person to raise this child. Besides Britney, you would be next of kin and your opinion would matter tremendously." Bre stood there stunned.

"You don't have the time to raise an infant Bre, and Britney is unstable. I can give that baby all the love, time, and financial support she needs to thrive in this world. All I'm saying is let me continue to raise her as I have been. I'll take you to who it is you still have a chance at forming a relationship with because let's be honest, Bella needs you, Sky is straight. I'm asking that you give me what I want, and I will do the same for you." I stuck my hand out hoping Bre would agree to shake on my terms. I wasn't as convincing as I thought.

"Katrina, are you serious? You're telling me you know where my niece is, and she has a baby that you've been raising?

What type of mess is that? I haven't seen Bella in years and now all of this."

I should've used more finesse, but I didn't have any time for that. Bre's manager came out and waved her over. "Listen, I gotta go. Come back tomorrow and we will talk." I agreed and got up to leave before any more of my desperation started to show.

I was able to snag an oceanfront view room on the island that night. I grabbed a pack of Heineken from the store earlier and was having a sip on the balcony when my phone rang. I almost forgot about him, but the call reminded me I had more personal business to address. I picked up, "Hello Miller. How have you been?" I asked him.

"I've been good Trina. How about you?" he asked.

"Just peachy. To what do I owe the pleasure?" I was short but not rude.

"I'm down here in Tybee Island and I could've sworn I saw you at Island Hotel. Wanted to know if you wanted to go out and grab a drink or something?" he asked.

My first thought was to turn him down, but something told me that was a bad idea. Besides, it couldn't be a coincidence that Miller was on the island. I agreed to meet with him at a bar up the street.

When I got to the spot, Miller was already there. He stood for me when I greeted him at the table. We embraced, and I sat down across from him. He had already started drinking. I joined him and ordered a Bob Marley. I broke the ice by asking the reason he was on the island in the first place. Miller claimed he had "an assignment" so I knew he was down there on a murder for hire. After seeing what he was capable of I didn't want to ever end up on that man's bad side. After a couple more rounds, I brought up Malik.

"What's the deal with the two of you? Malik is my friend from way back, and I can't help but feel like I'm involving him in something that may come back to haunt us all. Isn't Malik supposed to help you clear your name of murder? How can he do that if you keep dropping bodies everywhere you go?" I took a sip of my drink and allowed him time to answer.

Miller threw back the shot he ordered. "Malik and I go way back too, since we were kids. I'm the reason he started going to law school. He had this grand idea that one day we'd be able to get Philly cops to reopen my case. I told Malik, that ain't happening, but my boy never gave up on me. In the meantime, I had to find a way to make money off the books. Since worldwide news accused me of being a murderer, this just fit. People see me and if they believe what they've heard then they already think I'm the boogeyman. It's easy for me to make money in this field. I started as a debt collector, breaking legs, tying up wives, but eventually that got old. Too many witnesses in that business. I started doing murder contracts because me and the people I go into business with we both got a lot to lose. I do my part, and I don't have to worry about them looking for me." Miller explained.

I was surprised he told me so much. Miller and I took one last departing shot. He walked me to my room and that was it, or so I thought.

I woke up tied to the bed and my mouth had been gagged. I started pulling at the ropes trying to get loose. I heard the toilet flush, and Miller came walking out of the bathroom. I started cursing, but it didn't make a difference because he couldn't understand what I was saying with my mouth gagged. Miller put his finger over his mouth warning me if I screamed, he would slit my throat. I nodded my head to let him know I understood. When he removed the gag, I asked why he had me tied up.

"Remember that assignment I told you I was on? It's you Katrina. This is business, not personal." Miller said.

It was easy for him to claim it was business, but it felt very personal to me that he was about to murder me, and I didn't even know why.

"If you're going to kill me, at least tell me who put a contract on my head." I asked. Not like I could do anything but haunt their ass in the afterlife. Miller repented with his eyes, but his mind was made up. I knew he was about his money so I told him I would double what they were paying plus an additional $5,000 if he gave me a name. Miller paced back and forth thinking about the proposition.

"I knew I liked you Katrina. You got yourself a deal." he said, cutting me loose. He pulled a picture out of his back pocket and passed it to me. It was of 2 little girls sitting in the bleachers in gym class. We both still had the same face. It was Britney and me. "This is the only picture the person had of you. I told her I needed a week to get it done so you have a few more days to tie this up because once a contract is open it can only be closed by a kill." Miller said. He didn't have to say anything else. I got his point, and I knew who put the ticket on my head. "Katrina, I hope you know this stays between me and you. The less people know the better, besides I don't want Malik to know I almost killed one of his dear friends." Miller explained.

"Must be some career you have Miller, lying to everyone, no loyalty to anybody." I was pissed at him. I would have preferred he took me out straight up instead of luring me to the bar. Miller told me I would need to wire the money before he left my room. I made a few calls and was able to get the money transferred to his account immediately.

The next morning, I packed my things up and got ready to head back to Atlanta. I stopped by Bre's job again to see what she had decided. She was busy bussing down tables, but when she saw me, she made her way over. She sat me down in a back booth and talked about how hard it was for her to sleep last night. She was struggling with the decision. On one hand she felt as an aunt she should have done more. On the other hand, she feared bringing more harm than healing. I tried to encourage her. "Bre, Bella doesn't have anyone. You don't have to be perfect to make a positive impact on her life. I'm sure she would appreciate knowing someone loves her without any ulterior motive."

Bre tapped her nails on the wooden table. "I'm just worried how she's gonna receive me. Everyone in my family has offended this girl at one point or another. Why would she think I'm any different? After what Britney did to her, I doubt she'd give any of us a chance." Bre sounded like she had given up before even starting.

"Bre you won't know if you don't try. At least you can say at one point you tried." I told her.

She exhaled heavily. "Here's what I am willing to do. If you promise to truly look out for Bella's baby and no matter what, never give up on her, then you have a deal. Also, I want to be able to see the baby a couple times a year. I don't want her to be estranged from me like Bella was. If you agree to that, then I'll make sure Britney leaves you alone."

"You got a deal Bre. What do I need to do?" I asked.

"Do you remember when I mentioned Britney crossed me on a personal deal we had? Well, she stole insurance money from me. When my grandma passed, I had the check sent to her address. Britney cashed it. I didn't involve the law because at the time I had my own legal issues, but you tell her before she collects from you, I'll be coming to collect from her, all $30,000. There's your leverage Katrina, now take care of what you need to, and I'll see you soon." Before Bre got up to leave, she asked me why Andre didn't come down to speak to her since it was his grandchild. It hit me that I hadn't told her he passed.

"Andre is dead Bre." I gave her a minute to gather herself and we departed ways.

It took me longer than I expected to get back to the city. The traffic was bad, and the misty rain made it almost impossible to see. I sat there thinking of Andre as Billie Eilish sang "Ocean Eyes" to me. The song describes exactly how he made me feel when I looked into his eyes; consumed, devoured, overpowered, and I loved every minute of it. I looked over to the passenger side and there he was.

"Katrina baby, I miss you, I need you, please don't ever leave me." he asked. I knew I had to be dreaming but I wanted to touch him before it was too late. Just as I went to grab his hand, there was a loud siren and the person behind me laid on the horn. I dozed off in traffic. Andre hated it when I drove tired. Maybe it was his way of waking me up.

When I finally made it home, I was beat. I spent a little time with Sky, caught up with Christina, and went to sleep right after.

The next morning, I woke up ready to tackle the day. My next order of business was to find Britney and make sure she kept her mouth shut. I planned to use what Bre had told me and if that didn't work there was always that open contract that needed closing. Britney could leave town, or earth. I would give her the privilege of the final decision. I called her phone, and I could tell by the tone in her voice she was shocked to be hearing from me. She probably thought I would be dead already. I asked her to meet me downtown at Kiki's Kaleidoscope so we could talk. I was anxious to show her up. I dressed to the nines for our lunch date, ready to deliver a eulogy for the story that started all those years ago.

"Outside table for two." I told the hostess. She grabbed two menus and seated us quickly. The spot wasn't crowded that day, so Britney and I had the entire section to ourselves. I got right to it. "Britney, I'm gonna be honest. It's taking everything in me not to leap across this table and whoop your ass for that stunt you pulled back at my office. Don't think for one second that this meeting can't go left, and I resume my regularly scheduled program and put my foot up your ass. I'm going to try once to reason with you, but if you get out of pocket or speak my daughter's name in a disrespectful manner, I'm on your head. Now that I've made myself clear, I brought you here to tell you I'm not giving you shit. What I will give you is an opportunity to get the fuck on with your life without any further repercussions for the pain you've caused." I stopped there so I could give it time to marinate. I'm sure Britney wasn't expecting the meeting to go that way. Her facial expression said it all. I continued. "Britney you got some nerve trying to extort money for a baby that you don't even want. On top of that, you got your own debts to clear before you try collecting on this one. That little insurance fiasco you pulled on Bre, well she's thinking about following through and reporting your ass to the cops. Before she is able to do that though, you have someone else looking for you." I said.

"Oh yea, and who is that?" she asked, cockily but I knew she was getting more and more nervous with each reveal. "I'm just gonna say the cops are the least of your trouble when I have a bounty on your head double the price of the one you put on mine. Let's see who finds Britney Carmichael first!" I slammed the photo of the two of us in the bleachers on the table. "Checkmate bestie!"

 Britney was shocked, wondering how I knew about her dirty laundry. I threatened Britney that if she ever contacted me again, I would expose her. I excused myself from the table so she would be left with her thoughts. I went outside and made a call to Christina to check in on her and Sky.

When I got back inside the restaurant, Britney was pissed off. I figured she had come to grips that there was no way for her to win.

"So, Britney, what have you decided?" I asked her.

"I've decided that you and Bre aren't even worth the headache of dealing with all this mess." she said.

"I'll take that as you got my point. If I see you again, you know what's up. Now stay away from me and MY family." I warned her.

I got up to leave and felt like I left 30 lbs. of bullshit back in the booth. When I got in my car, I was so happy I squealed. I turned the music up and bopped to some Nivea, "Okay," right there in the parking lot. I opened the visor mirror and caught a glimpse of a familiar me that I hadn't seen in years. I had the glow. My face was rounder, lips fuller, and my hair had grown at least 2 inches in the past month. I didn't notice before, but the way the sun hit my face that day it showed clear as day. I pulled my phone out and scheduled a doctor's visit. I told the doctor it was an emergency and I wanted her to see me right away. She said that I could come in the next morning.

When I met with my doctor, I told her straight up, "I think I'm pregnant." Dr. Semaj looked at me like I had lost my mind. She and I had discussed my infertility issues on several occasions, and she made one thing clear, I couldn't get pregnant anymore or it would kill me. She didn't think a test was necessary, but I insisted. I knew what my body was telling me.

When the results came back it was just as I suspected, I was pregnant. As bad as I wanted a child it came at a time I was not expecting it. Even though it wouldn't be Andre's baby it would be just as special to me. I was 6 months and was carrying very small. Based on the math, I had gotten pregnant rather quickly by Ty. Possibly the night we were in Andre and I's bed. Dr. Semaj had a ton of health concerns and test she wanted to run. The Doctor told me to come back next week so we could make sure my bun was baking properly.

I left the doctor's office feeling uneasy about everything. I pulled out my phone and called my mom. It would be the first time I confided in her about something like this. My mom picked up the phone in a bubbly tone. Not like a woman who had just found out the awful things she knew about me, but like a mom who was happy to hear from her daughter.

"Hey ma, I have news and I don't know how to take it, but I need to share it with someone before I have a panic attack." I told her.

"Katrina what's wrong baby. Spill the beans." My mom asked.

"Ma, I'm pregnant! 6 months pregnant. I'm scared, I know I'm gonna be a single mama, and I need some support right now." I was as direct as I could be. It was exactly how I was feeling.

"Katrina, it sounds like I'm gonna be a grandmother of 2. I don't care who won't be around. I'll be there." she said.

Before we ended the call, I thanked my mom for her support. I looked up at the clouds as if I were talking to Andre and asked him to help me figure this all out. Even though it wouldn't be his baby, I still prayed to him like he was my parenting partner. I went from a woman who couldn't have kids to possibly ending up with 2. The universe was confusing the hell out of me.

I couldn't sit in my feelings about being pregnant too long because I needed to start working on a way to facilitate the meet up between Bre and Bella that I had promised. Bre was excited about getting to know the little girl she remembered from all those years ago. I hoped for her sake she would get a better experience out of it than Andre and I had.

Chapter 23 Your Eyes

Once I had Bella's visitation days down, I offered Bre to come up from Savannah so we could arrange the visit. When she made it to Atlanta, I put her up in a 5-star hotel room. I scheduled the visit for Saturday which was 3 days away.

I worried my ass off the entire time. I was so ready to get the visit over with. I hoped that Bre kept to our agreement no matter what, but just in case I had some insurance.

I picked Bre up on Saturday morning, and just as I expected she was not prison ready. From her cleavage showing, to the tight ass jeans she had on, and the bag that wasn't see-thru, we had more than a few adjustments to make. Because I was prepared for her not to know any better, I had an extra outfit and a clear purse for Bre to carry her things in. Once she was able to change clothes, we were ready to head to the youth prison.

It was my first time visiting a youth prison, and to my surprise it was rather nice. It wasn't the Marriott, but for it to be somewhere dangerous criminals lived, it looked to be very sterile. Bre and I got ready to go through the metal detectors. I went through first, then her. I could feel my palms sweaty as our bags went through the conveyor belt. The guard stopped it and looked at Bre's bag intently. "Bag Check." she yelled. When the bag came out, a male guard grabbed it to get a closer look. There wasn't much to be seen in the clear bag. Bre was wide eyed looking over at me as if I had tried smuggling drugs in. The guard waved his wand over the bag. "She's good chief." The security guard passed Bre her bag and let us go.

"We've been having problems with this thing all day. Sorry about that ma'am." The young handsome guard apologized to Bre while flirting with her.

Her and I followed the rest of the group to the back where the inmates awaited their visits. When Bre and I came around the corner, I saw Bella already sitting at a table. I hoped she didn't see my face and make a scene or run away. I slowed my pace and allowed Bre to get out front.

Bre stopped in her tracks when she saw her. Bella stood up and tears started to fall down her face. I stepped from behind Bre who had also started crying. They ran to hug each other as if they had missed one another all those years. I figured it best I didn't interrupt the reunion. Bella still didn't notice me, so I slipped off to the back out of her view.

From what I could see, they looked like they were getting along. They had held hands from across the table and were affectionate with each other. I was nervous the reunion would go too well and Bre would break her alliance with me for Bella. I left the room out of fear I would be spotted.

I patrolled circles around the lobby. My heart was in my gut, ready to hear all the details of their conversation.

When we got back to the car, Bre was quiet. I could tell by her facial expression Bella had thrown a wrench in our plans.

"You wanna go get something to eat?" I asked her.

"I'm tired. I just wanna go back to the room please." she said dryly.

I hopped on the freeway to take her back. The suspense was killing me. There was no easy way to bring it up, but I asked Bre if we were still going to stick to our plan that we had discussed. Bre was irritated by my question. I decided to leave it alone until I figured out what it was her and Bella had talked about. When I pulled up at the hotel, I asked Bre to give me my jacket and clear bag back. She had an attitude about that too, but there was no way I would let her out of my car with it so attitude or not, she was going to have to run it. She left the items on the seat and got out of the car without even saying thank you.

When I got back home, my mom was there with the girls. I asked her to come to my bedroom with me so we could discuss what happened at the prison.

"So how did it go baby?" my mom asked, flopping down on my bed.

"Ma, I'm really not sure. Bre was silent on the ride back. I couldn't gauge her." I said.

"That means she's hiding something baby. You may not know what, but the fact that she wasn't honest with you is enough for you to know whatever pre-existing arrangement y'all had has been compromised. Please tell me we got some insurance on this situation?" my mom asked.

I loved that she said we, as if we were in it together. My mom had showed up just a few days ago and had already jumped headfirst into my mess with me. She was the only person I trusted whole heartedly, not because she had proven herself to be trustworthy, but because I knew what her flaws were and having my best interest at heart was always at the center of her discontentment with me. For that, I trusted my mom would align herself with whatever would be best for me.

"Katrina I finally got those documents you asked me for. The birth certificates, socials, and shot records!" Mom bragged.

"Dang Ma, you really are the truth." I complimented her.

She left the room and brought me back three envelopes. I held them in my hand for what seemed like 10 minutes. Finally, my mom said, "Katrina, now or never baby."

I opened the envelopes and pulled out all the contents. I unfolded Bella's birth certificate which showed she was born in Jacksonville, Florida and her birthday was in February. That confirmed Britney's story about them hooking up in Florida after he went away to college. I looked for the father's name and didn't find one. I looked at the mother's name and it showed Britney Carmichael. Seeing it on paper still set off a slight echo in my heart. I continued to scan over the certificate and discovered the birth type showed multiple and Bella was listed as baby #2. She was a twin! Speechless to say the least, I could hear myself breathing. Bella had a twin out there somewhere. It wouldn't be impossible because the gene is passed down from the mom. It felt like I was getting played again. Why would Bre keep that little detail to herself? I opened the second certificate. Name Bailey Carmichael, birth type multiple, baby #1. It hurt me to know that Andre would never know he had not 1 but 2 kids.

I read Sky's birth certificate next. Her full name was Drea Breelyn Young. I skimmed over the remainder of the information. Birthday, May 21. Father's name, Terrence Young. Mother's name, Bailey Carmichael.

There I was, listening to myself breathe again. My mom snapped her fingers. "Katrina, what is it? What does it say?" I pulled out the remainder of the information in the envelope. Just like mom said, there were socials and shot records for Sky. My mom sat there staring at me waiting for me to reveal the information I discovered. It was clear by my face that I was flustered, and I couldn't just tell her it was nothing. I really didn't know how to explain it though. I was disoriented. The paperwork was claiming that Sky was Bella's twin Bailey's kid, and if that were so, why would Bella have Bailey's kid, or was Bella really Bailey. I decided to quickly change the subject with some just as important and relevant news. I told her about the risk I had taken earlier to ensure we did have some insurance. I only didn't tell her before out of fear she would try and talk me out of it. I had risked my freedom, but I was hoping it would prove to be worth it.

I pulled out the jacket I had loaned Bre earlier. I picked at the seam until I was able to pull out the dime size mini recording device I had stashed in it. I held it up to show ma.

"I almost had a heart attack trying to get it in." I said.

"What is it?" she asked.

"It's a recorder ma. I had to know what Bre and Bella would talk about. I know I can't really trust her in this, so this is my insurance."

I pulled out the playback device I purchased with the recorder to playback what I was dying to hear. Ma went over to close the door. She knew what we were doing was top secret, and I appreciated her instinct. Before I hit the play button, I took a deep breath. I didn't know what to expect but something told me it would be the final piece of the puzzle.

The Conversation

"What are you doing here? Tell me what's going on. Why are you here?" Bre asked her niece.

"The plan fell through. That's all I can say."

"What do you mean all you can say? Tell me something. This doesn't make any sense." Bre sounded disconcerted.

"Why are you here with Katrina? She's the reason I'm here Auntie."

"Katrina brought me here to you. I didn't know how to find you otherwise and Katrina came to me. Bailey, why is Katrina calling you by your twin sister's name? Did you take care of it?" Bre asked.

"No, I couldn't. Something bad happened. I'm sorry Auntie. I know how much you wanted it to work but I messed up."

"Shh, lower your voice before you get us caught. Now tell me what happened. I'll clean this up like I always do." Bre told her.

"At first everything was going well, just like we planned it. I got close to Bella, and she didn't suspect a thing. I learned Bella's mannerisms, her schedule, I knew about all of her friends. I became her. I would show up randomly to see if I could fool the people she knew. I got so good at it even our mom couldn't tell the difference. When it was time, I convinced her to go to the lake. You know the one you told me about where the city is buried underneath. That's where I did it. By the time they pulled her body out, it was too late. The Doctor said I would have been a perfect match, but she was in the water too long. I messed up Auntie. I was too scared to come back home and tell you, so I just assumed her identity and went with plan B." she confessed.

"It's ok. We will find another way to get you a heart." Bre said.

"Do you think I'm a bad seed like the Doctor said when I was born?" Bailey asked

"No, I don't believe that. It's why I came to find you. Grandma believed that mess about you being a bad seed. That's why she gave you up, but I knew you were special, just like me. Give me some time to figure this out, and I promise I will work on getting you out of here as soon as I can." Bre assured.

"One last thing Bailey. Katrina said there's a baby involved, and your mom is back in the picture. What's that about?" Bre asked.

"The baby was my plan to try and get the money for the surgery since it didn't work out with Bella. My mom is just being her usual greedy self and trying to capitalize off the situation. I was able to get $20,000 from Andre and $20,000 from the baby's father. Do you think that's enough to get us moved up on the donors list?"

"It's enough for them to consider it."

"I have it. It's in a secret account in the baby's name." Bailey explained.

"Write down the account information for me. I'll also need to use some of it to secure you an attorney." Bre explained.

"Promise you'll come back Auntie."

"I will baby."

The recording picked up Bre's footsteps as she walked away. The last words before the metal door could be heard closing was. "I'll show you bitches who the bad seed is."

Epilogue

"Pusshhhhh!" Dr. Semaj yelled.

I was pushing as hard as I could without leaving my ass on the table. I screamed, and I cursed Ty for what was happening to my vagina. I hated him. The pain was unbearable, and I assumed it was because I was trying to pass a 9 lb. baby out of my cooch. My mom was there with me holding my left hand while I fought for dear life to get that baby out of me. Finally, I could hear a faint cry. It was the sound of new life. I looked at everyone's faces for confirmation that my baby was ok. Dr. Semaj was speechless.

"Mom, what's wrong?" I asked? She was too busy staring at the baby.

"Mom!? What's wrong? Give him here, I wanna see him." I demanded.

The doctor laid him on my chest, and he screamed and screamed. I was scared. Andre Jr. didn't scream like that when he was born.

"Is he OK?" I asked.

The doctor assured me he was fine and just needed to be cleaned up. I looked at my mom and asked that she go over with them to clean him up. She had a bit of a confused look on her face, but she didn't say anything. I closed my eyes and prayed. I didn't know Ty's family history and just wanted my baby to be healthy.

Seemed like forever when they returned with my baby who I still hadn't settled on a name for.

"His eyes are open Katrina, look." My mom passed him to me.

I looked down at my little man and I screamed. "God, thank You? Thank You God!" Those eyes looking back at me, there was no question who my baby's father was. The timing didn't add up, but it didn't matter. The eyes never lied, and my baby had my husband's eyes.

"Ma, you see this?" I asked her. I was hysterical.

"I see it baby. If these eyes could talk, they would tell a whole story. I'm so happy for you baby. What are you going to name him?"

I looked over at the doctor who was crying. She had been on the journey with Andre and I and knew we were witnessing nothing short of a miracle.

"I am going to name him Drew Billups. I think Andre would like that." I kissed my son. I now had a son, a daughter, and a bonus teenager. I was being blessed in the midst of my storm. I knew I had unfinished business, but for once I was gonna set it aside and be 100% present for my children. When the time was right, I would be prepared to put the final pins in everyone's coffin.

A message from the Author.

Thank you for your support. This book means a lot to me and will be the first of many projects to come. Get excited about reading again as we enter the era of KiaMeshia B. Books.

Thank you for giving me a chance.

www.ingramcontent.com/pod-product-compliance
Lightning Source LLC
Chambersburg PA
CBHW070450030726
47503CB00004B/975